THE CASE OF THE PURPLE CALF

BRIAN FLYNN was born in 1885 in Leyton, Essex. He won a scholarship to the City Of London School, and from there went into the civil service. In World War I he served as Special Constable on the Home Front, also teaching "Accountancy, Languages, Maths and Elocution to men, women, boys and girls" in the evenings, and acting in his spare time.

It was a seaside family holiday that inspired Brian Flynn to turn his hand to writing in the mid-twenties. Finding most mystery novels of the time "mediocre in the extreme", he decided to compose his own. Edith, the author's wife, encouraged its completion, and after a protracted period finding a publisher, it was eventually released in 1927 by John Hamilton in the UK and Macrae Smith in the U.S. as *The Billiard-Room Mystery*.

The author died in 1958. In all, he wrote and published 57 mysteries, the vast majority featuring the super-sleuth Antony Bathurst.

BRIAN FLYNN

THE CASE OF THE PURPLE CALF

With an introduction by
Steve Barge

DEAN STREET PRESS

Published by Dean Street Press 2020

Copyright © 1934 Brian Flynn

Introduction © 2020 Steve Barge

All Rights Reserved

The right of Brian Flynn to be identified as the Author of the Work has been asserted by his estate in accordance with the Copyright, Designs and Patents Act 1988.

First published in 1934 by John Long

Cover by DSP

ISBN 978 1 913527 49 5

www.deanstreetpress.co.uk

INTRODUCTION

"I believe that the primary function of the mystery story is to entertain; to stimulate the imagination and even, at times, to supply humour. But it pleases the connoisseur most when it presents – and reveals – genuine mystery. To reach its full height, it has to offer an intellectual problem for the reader to consider, measure and solve."

BRIAN Flynn began his writing career with *The Billiard Room Mystery* in 1927, primarily at the prompting of his wife Edith who had grown tired of hearing him say he could write a better mystery novel than the ones he had been reading. Four more books followed under his original publisher, John Hamilton, before he moved to John Long, who would go on to publish the remaining forty-eight of his Anthony Bathurst mysteries, along with his three Sebastian Stole titles, released under the pseudonym Charles Wogan. Some of the early books were released in the US, and there were also a small number of translations of his mysteries into Swedish and German. In the article from which the above quote is taken, Brian also claims that there were French and Danish translations but to date, I have not found a single piece of evidence for their existence. Tracking down all of his books written in the original English has been challenging enough!

Reprints of Brian's books were rare. Four titles were released as paperbacks as part of John Long's Four Square Thriller range in the late 1930s, four more re-appeared during the war from Cherry Tree Books and Mellifont Press, albeit abridged by at least a third, and two others that I am aware of, *Such Bright Disguises* (1941) and *Reverse The Charges* (1943), received a paperback release as part of John Long's Pocket Edition range in the early 1950s – these were also possibly abridged, but only by about 10%. These were the exceptions, rather than the rule, however, and it was not until 2019, when Dean Street Press released his first ten titles, that his work was generally available again.

The question still persists as to why his work disappeared from the awareness of all but the most ardent collectors. As you may expect, when a title was only released once, back in the early 1930s, finding copies of the original text is not a straightforward matter – not even Brian's estate has a copy of every title. We are particularly grateful to one particular collector for providing *The Edge Of Terror*, Brian's first serial killer tale, in order for this next set of ten books to be republished without an obvious gap!

By the time Brian Flynn's eleventh novel, *The Padded Door* (1932), was published, he was producing a steady output of Anthony Bathurst mysteries, averaging about two books a year. While this may seem to be a rapid output, it is actually fairly average for a crime writer of the time. Some writers vastly exceeded this – in the same period of time that it took Brian to have ten books published, John Street, under his pseudonyms John Rhode and Miles Burton published twenty-eight!

In this period, in 1934 to be precise, an additional book was published, *Tragedy At Trinket*. It is a schoolboy mystery, set at Trinket, "one of the two finest schools in England – in the world!" combining the tale of Trinket's attempts to redeem itself in the field of schoolboy cricket alongside the apparently accidental death by drowning of one of the masters. It was published by Thomas Nelson and Sons, rather than John Long, and was the only title published under his own name not to feature Bathurst. It is unlikely, however, that this was an attempt to break away from his sleuth, given that the hero of this tale is Maurice Otho Folliott, a schoolboy who just happens to be Bathurst's nephew and is desperate to emulate his uncle! It is an odd book, with a significant proportion of the tale dedicated to the tribulations of the cricket team, but Brian does an admirable job of weaving an actual death into a genre that was generally concerned with misunderstandings and schoolboy pranks.

Not being in the top tier of writers, at least in terms of public awareness, reviews of Brian's work seem to have been rare, but when they did occur, there were mostly positive. A reviewer in the Sunday Times enthused over *The Edge Of Terror* (1932), describing it as "an enjoyable thriller in Mr. Flynn's best manner" and Torquemada in the *Observer* says that *Fear and Trembling* (1936) "gripped my interest on a sleepless night and held it to the end". Even Dorothy L. Sayers, a fairly unforgiving reviewer at times, had positive things to say in the *Sunday Times* about *The Case For The Purple Calf* (1934) ("contains some ingenuities") and *The Horn* (1934) ("good old-fashioned melodrama ... not without movement") although she did take exception to Brian's writing style. Milward Kennedy was similarly disdainful, although Kennedy, a crime writer himself, criticising a style of writing might well be considered the pot calling the kettle black. He was impressed, however, with the originality of *Tread Softly* (1937).

It is quite possible that Brian's harshest critic, though, was himself. In *The Crime Book Magazine* he wrote about the current output of detective fiction: "I delight in the dazzling erudition that has come to grace and decorate the craft of the 'roman policier'. He then goes on to say: "At the same time, however, I feel my own comparative unworthiness for the fire and burden of the competition." Such a feeling may well be the reason why he never made significant inroads into the social side of crime-writing, such as the Detection Club or the Crime Writers' Association. Thankfully, he uses this sense of unworthiness as inspiration, concluding: "The stars, though, have always been the most desired of all goals, so I allow exultation and determination to take the place of that but temporary dismay."

Reviews, both external and internal, thankfully had no noticeable effect on Brian's writing. What is noticeable about his work is how he shifts from style to style from each book. While all the books from this period remain classic whodunits, the style shifts from courtroom drama to gothic darkness, from plotting serial killers to events that spiral out of control, with Anthony Bathurst the constant thread tying everything together.

We find some books narrated by a Watson-esque character, although a different character each time. Occasionally Bathurst himself will provide a chapter or two to explain things either that the narrator wasn't present for or just didn't understand. Bathurst doesn't always have a Watson character to tell his stories, however, so other books are in the third person – as some of Bathurst's adventures are not tied to a single location, this is often the case in these tales.

One element that does become more common throughout books eleven to twenty is the presence of Chief Detective Inspector Andrew MacMorran. While MacMorran gets a name check from as early as *The Mystery Of The Peacock's Eye* (1928), his actual appearances in the early books are few and far between, with others such as Inspector Baddeley (*The Billiard Room Mystery* (1927), *The Creeping Jenny Mystery* (1929)) providing the necessary police presence. As the series progresses, the author settled more and more on a regular showing from the police. It still isn't always the case – in some books, Bathurst is investigating undercover and hence by himself, and in a few others, various police Inspectors appear, notably the return of the aforementioned Baddeley in *The Fortescue Candle* (1936). As the series progresses from *The Padded Door* (1932), Inspector MacMorran becomes more and more of a fixture at Scotland Yard for Bathurst.

One particular trait of the Bathurst series is the continuity therein. While the series can be read out of order, there is a sense of what has gone before. While not to the extent of, say, E.R. Punshon's Bobby Owen books, or Christopher Bush's Ludovic Travers mysteries, there is a clear sense of what has gone before. Side characters from books reappear, either by name or in physical appearances – Bathurst is often engaged on a case by people he has helped previously. Bathurst's friendship with MacMorran develops over the books from a respectful partnership to the point where MacMorran can express his exasperation with Bathurst's annoying habits rather vocally. Other characters appear and develop too, for example Helen Repton, but she is, alas, a story for another day.

The other sign of continuity is Bathurst's habit of name-dropping previous cases, names that were given to them by Bathurst's "chronicler". *Fear and Trembling* mentions no less than five separate cases, with one, *The Sussex Cuckoo* (1935), getting two mentions. These may seem like little more than adverts for those titles, old-time product placement if you will – "you've handled this affair about as brainily as I handled 'The Fortescue Candle'", for example – but they do actually make sense in regard to what has gone before, given how long it took Bathurst to see the light in each particular case. Contrast this to the reference to Christie's *Murder On The Orient Express* in *Cards On The Table*, which not only gives away the ending but contradicts Poirot's actions at the dénouement.

> "For my own detective, Anthony Lotherington Bathurst, I have endeavoured to place him in the true Holmes tradition. It is not for me to say whether my efforts have failed or whether I have been successful."

Brian Flynn seemed determined to keep Bathurst's background devoid of detail – I set out in the last set of introductions the minimal facts that we are provided with: primarily that he went to public school and Oxford University, can play virtually every sport under the sun and had a bad first relationship and has seemingly sworn off women since. Of course, the detective's history is something not often bothered with by crime fiction writers, but this usually occurs with older sleuths who have lived life, so to speak. *Cold Evil* (1938), the twenty-first Bathurst mystery, finally pins down Bathurst's age, and we find that in *The Billiard Room Mystery*, his first outing, he was a fresh-faced Bright Young Thing of twenty-two. So how he can survive with his own rooms, at least two servants, and no noticeable source of income remains a mystery. One can also ask at what point in his life he travelled the world, as he has, at least, been to Bangkok at some point. It is, perhaps, best not to analyse Bathurst's past too carefully . . .

> "Judging from the correspondence my books have excited it seems I have managed to achieve some measure of success for my faithful readers comprise a circle in which high dignitaries of the Church rub shoulders with their brothers and sisters of the common touch."

For someone who wrote to entertain, such correspondence would have delighted Brian, and I wish he were around to see how many people enjoyed the first set of reprints of his work. His family are delighted with the reactions that people have passed on, and I hope that this set of books will delight just as much.

The Case of the Purple Calf (1934)

"This Great Kirby motor-car case. A particularly horrible and soul-shattering murder. Of that I don't harbour the slightest doubt. And the fact that the Commissioner of Police himself calls it a clear case of suicide won't alter the facts."

THE publication history of Brian Flynn outside of the UK is an odd one. The first four titles were published in the US – although not in order, with *The Murders Near Mapleton* (1929) being released before *The Mystery Of The Peacock's Eye* (1928). *The Creeping Jenny Mystery* (1929) and *Murder En Route* (1930) followed, albeit with the former being retitled *The Crime At The Crossways* – a title that certainly confused the cover artist, who depicted a villain skulking under a crossroads road sign, whereas those of you who have read that book will know that the Crossways is the name of the house where the murder occurs. The US publisher then skipped the next few titles until resuming with *The Spiked Lion* (1933) and *The Case Of The Purple Calf* (1934). Why the other books were not published is alas an unsolved mystery, as is the reasoning behind another change of title: *The Case Of The Purple Calf* became *The Ladder Of Death*. At least that eliminated the danger of a purple cow on the book jacket.

The Case Of The Purple Calf is a fascinating book, a great example of Flynn's desire to keep the reader guessing what is going on by presenting a crime, or in this case a series of crimes, with little apparent logic to tie the cases together – until Bathurst makes all the right connections. In this tale, there are the unexplained deaths of three women, apparently in car accidents. When Bathurst discovers the same travelling funfair had been operating in the vicinity of all three deaths, he chooses to investigate without, initially, any back-up from the police due to a complete lack of evidence, forensic or otherwise. But what does the Purple Calf night-club have to do with it?

This book marks Flynn's first foray into the criminal conspiracy, a theme he will return to a number of times in the course of his writing, most notably in the interesting-but-flawed *Conspiracy At Angel* (1947), the novel so savaged by Barzun and Taylor. However, in *The Case of the Purple Calf*, Flynn strongly maintains the whodunit element to the story. In some later novels, the question posed to the reader primarily concerns the nature and purpose of the criminal's plan. However, in *Calf* that question is paired with the mystery of the murderer's identity and motivations as well.

It also features a surprisingly rare setting for a classic mystery novel – the funfair. While there are occasional visits to village fêtes (John Dickson Carr's classic *Til Death Do Us Part* being one of the most memorable), and the travelling circus, such as in Clayton Rawson's *The Headless Lady* and Leo Bruce's *Case with Four Clowns*, the travelling funfair or carnival appears rarely, particularly in British detective fiction. Some US writers, such as Fredric Brown, used the setting on more than one occasion, in books such as *Madball* and *The Dead Ringer*. In British fiction, a fairground carousel appears in the dénouement of Edmund Crispin's *The Moving Toyshop* (an idea appropriated by Alfred Hitchcock in his film of Patricia Highsmith's novel *Strangers On A Train*), and there is a Hall of Mirrors in Carter Dickson's *The Skeleton In The Clock*. Perhaps the scarcity of funfairs in golden age crime fiction is simply due to writers' limited knowledge of the carnival life, and thus they may have found it hard to render with authenticity.

That, thankfully, didn't stop Brian Flynn from using it as the partial setting for this novel. One hopes that some of the goings on aren't representative of real fairground life, as I am sure you'll agree when you read the book, reprinted in its original form for the first time since 1934.

Steve Barge

Chapter I
DEATH OF A LADY

"I disagree with you, Bathurst," said Sir Austin Kemble. "I'm sorry, but I disagree with you *in toto*."

"Oh—quite," returned Anthony Bathurst, fashionably—grey eyes amused. "After all—it's as well to be thorough. Though few seem to appreciate the fact. I loathe tendencies and mere inclinations. I should hate you to disagree with me half-heartedly. It would be so perniciously anaemic."

Sir Austin shifted in his chair uneasily. "Prove to me," he commenced—

"Oh—help," interrupted Anthony—"he talks of proving. 'O roseate optimism. O pink-tipped Eos.' If I should die think only this of me—only more so."

"I'm sixty-three," declared Sir Austin in a voice that spoke of personal triumph and industrious elation. "I don't think that I've met a clearer case of suicide in all my life. Lord, Bathurst, do you want to know what's the matter with you? The spur of the game's growing on you. It's made you super-imaginative. You'll see murder in a Chapel bazaar next."

"Don't tempt me, Sir Austin. 'Twould be altogether too beautiful," murmured Anthony—"the completely beatific vision. The perfect end of an imperfect day. Those things definitely do not occur. One only dreams of 'em. But other things do. And one of 'em's occurred, believe me, here. This Great Kirby motor-car case. A particularly horrible and soul-shattering murder. Of that I don't harbour the slightest doubt. And the fact that so renowned a bloke as the Commissioner of Police himself calls it a clear case of suicide won't alter facts. I'm sorry, sir, but the leopard will still retain his *maculae*. Oh—yes—I'm aware that I'm a damned nuisance. But so are they all—all honourable men."

The Commissioner fumbled for cigarettes. Bathurst's certainty made him uneasy. He became doubly practical. "First of all—how in the name of all God's creatures—did you get an 'inside' on it?"

Anthony became portentous. "The Finger of Fate, Sir Austin. There is a Divinity that shapes our ends. I was staying just on the outskirts of Loxeter. Actually I was putting in a spot of leisure at *The Lion and Lamb*. You know 'em both, sir—the future sleeping partners of Utopia. When the swords all become plough-shares! I was present, one might reasonably say, when the first die rolled from the cup of chance. It didn't roll towards me exactly, but I was aware of its casting. I don't think that I shall ever forget the night when the evidence began to accumulate. The *first* night. I'm going back considerably, of course."

"Tell me," said the Commissioner simply. Although he would have been loth to admit it, he was impressed in spite or himself. Behind Bathurst's occasional levity there lay an unmistakable note of indomitable purpose and Sir Austin was quick to recognise it.

Anthony sat down opposite to the Commissioner, placed his finger-tips together and closed his eyes. "I used the word 'accumulate.' This death at Great Kirby makes the third of a sequence. A very strange and sinister sequence. Unless you and I take a hand I'm very much afraid that there may be a fourth. I shall never cease blaming myself that there have been the second and the third."

The Commissioner stared in amazement. Here was self-revelation. There was no mistaking this for anything but stark truth.

"God, Bathurst," he said, "you disturb me when you talk like that. You've almost converted me in spite of myself."

Anthony expressed his gratitude. "Thank you, sir. It's gratifying to realise that one has uses. I will start by telling you of that evening of mine in *The Lion and Lamb* at Loxeter. Sometimes—even now—when I lie awake at night I can still hear the appalling noise in my ears. For there was a fair in Loxeter on the evening that I slept at *The Lion and Lamb*. A fair that had installed itself on the ordinary and usual piece of waste ground. Lights and noise and that strange unreality that seems to belong to fairs of this sort. I remember that I had passed it during the morning when it was being assembled. The name attached to the concern—*coram publico*—was 'L'Estrange's Travelling

Showground.' I remember that fact as well. I suggest, sir, that the point about the somewhat unexpected substantive, for instance, is well worthy of attention. Not 'show,' you observe, but 'showground.' A rather peculiar use of the word, if I may say so, Sir Austin. Considering how the actual 'showground' changes every time the concern moves. Anyhow, it's probably neither here nor there—although one can't afford to be cavalier with anything. As a show the whole business was pretty meagre. Coconut shy, roundabout, waxworks, a sensation or so—the entire thing comprising about a dozen fixtures and no more. I was in Loxeter for the latter half of October. The 'affair' took place on the twenty-second of October. Nearly a year ago. Can you remember where the girl's body was found? I'm not alluding to the Great Kirby case—I mean in the Loxeter business?"

Sir Austin, startled at the twist that Bathurst had given to the conversation, wrinkled his brows. "In the road. By a hedge. Near a churchyard . . . I forget the name of the church. There was a smashed car in a ditch on the other side of the road."

"Exactly! *When* was the body found?"

"On the morning of the day after—the twenty-third of October."

"Good again. You probably remember the little discussion we had over it. Now for the cause of death. Can you remember the medical evidence? In anything like accurate detail?"

Sir Austin surpassed himself. "Yes . . . very well indeed. I looked into the case myself. The girl's neck was broken. In the same sense, that is, as befalls the victims of our English capital punishment. Her wrist and arms were badly injured where she had been thrown forward on to them. There was dislocation of the spinal column and the girl's shoulder-blades were broken also."

"Shoulder-blades," repeated Mr. Bathurst softly. He looked towards Sir Austin. "What reason was given for the Honourable Phyllis Welby's presence in the Loxeter district? Can you tell me that?"

Mr. Austin shrugged his shoulders. For some reason he felt partly reassured. "Surely, my dear fellow . . . when you ask that, you ask an entirely superfluous question. Any girl that drives a car... now I ask you! How far, after all, is Loxeter from London? Eighty miles?"

Anthony nodded. "Just about. Your position is that the girl had gone for a run in the ordinary way... the car had skidded ... she had lost control... and *voilà*."

"Certainly."

"May I point out to you that the road was perfectly dry? That there wasn't the vestige of a 'skid' mark to be seen anywhere? You will recall, doubtless, how her father, Lord Sturt, at the inquest, insisted on the point being emphasised?" Anthony watched the Commissioner gravely. Sir Austin, a little embarrassed under the keen scrutiny, rose and paced his room. "Well?" insisted Mr. Bathurst.

The Commissioner approximated petulance. "*Anything* may cause a motoring accident. Surely that point doesn't require labouring. Good heavens, Bathurst, they occur almost every day. From the most trifling causes, too! You know that yourself without me telling you. A fly gets in the driver's eye—an involuntary turn of the head—even a sudden sneeze has been known before now to have been the cause of a man's death. You're chasing shadows, my dear boy."

Anthony smiled at Sir Austin's vehemence. "No, sir. Not this time. I will take up the challenge that you have thrown down. The evidence of which I spoke shall begin to accumulate. Do you remember the incident of the girl's money?"

"She had *no* money—or as good as none! Beyond a few coppers, I believe that her pockets and her bag were empty. Also—if you will allow me to have my say—a matter capable of extremely simple explanation! No one need ride rainbows over *that*. Listen to a sane exposition. She had intended to motor out somewhere and to motor straight back. An evening's run. Had probably done many similar runs in the past. Quite conceivably there might occur no need for her to spend a penny."

"It's possible—but in my opinion *definitely unlikely*. A girl of her class and general upbringing—daughter of Lord Sturt—would usually be prepared for emergencies."

"Well," continued the Commissioner, "even then there's another possibility. One that's quite on the cards as I see things. She may have been robbed. After she was dead—I mean. There are plenty of tramps roaming the countryside. Men who would jump at such an opportunity."

"And leave behind the girl's valuable rings and a handful of coppers?"

"It's possible. One never knows. You simply can't lay down hard and fast rules of such a thing as fortuitous theft. My dear Bathurst . . . even now that I've listened to you . . . the case seems transparently clear to me. You shook me for a time, but I've gone back to my original opinion. It was a pure accident. Only the victim knew the real truth of the affair. There are hundreds like it."

Anthony scoffed. "Clear? I'm glad you think so. Because to me it's about as thick as Tewkesbury mustard."

But Sir Austin had found recovery and had regained his confidence. "Even the injuries to the body are perfectly explainable. They were perhaps unusual, I grant . . . but you constantly get extraordinary physical injuries in these car crashes. One occurred the other day in my own sphere of . . . er . . . acquaintanceship. A most extraordinary happening, There was a collision between two cars, and in one of them a man seated next to the driver was just jerked forward by the impact. No more than that. What do you think he got?"

Anthony shook his head. "I'll buy it."

"It broke his neck, my dear boy. Although the odds, I should say, against such a contingency would be about a thousand to one. The doctor who attended the case put it at that anyhow."

Anthony Bathurst turned his back to the Commissioner and looked out of the window.

"All very interesting, but, I venture to suggest, beside the point. What about the girl's hands and arms and wrists? What's your explanation in regard to them? What about the condition of the shoulder-blades? Just the impact of the fall?"

"Certainly! Why not? Why refuse to recognise the simple . . . the obvious? It's a marvellous thing, but people will do it. They always will fly to the extraordinary. Why always seek Abana and Pharpar when there's the stream of Jordan ready and to hand?"

Anthony remained imperturbable under the onslaught.

"Very well, Sir Austin, I will go on. I'm not finished yet. Can you recall the evidence of a certain Miss Margaret Fletcher, the intimate friend of the dead girl? She attended the inquest."

"H'm! I don't know that I do. Why do you ask? Was it frightfully important? As I remember the case—"

"I will revive it for you. And I'll ask you to listen carefully. Miss Fletcher deposed at the inquest that she had been in the company of Phyllis Welby during the morning of the twenty-second of October. They had shopped and had morning coffee together. She was questioned pretty closely about this by the Coroner because one of the Coroner's jury was inclined, judging by the general direction of his interjections, to favour the idea of suicide. But Miss Fletcher stated very definitely that Phyllis Welby was in an 'excited' mood when they had been together. Note the word that she used. When pressed further by the Coroner to analyse this 'excitement' Miss Fletcher labelled it— rather intelligently I thought—the 'excitement of *anticipation.*' The lady became under further pressure even more precise and informative. 'Phyllis,' she said, 'seemed to be on the verge of something exciting, but—' and here she chose her words carefully—'*pleasantly* exciting. In my opinion she was not "afraid." She was not "nervy." She was not "preoccupied." She was not even moderately worried. She was just "looking forward' with a 'certain amount of delighted eagerness.'" They were Margaret Fletcher's exact words. I took great pains at the time to remember them—*verbatim et literatim*—and I have carried the memory of them with me ever since."

The Commissioner still showed impatience. "I still think that you've proved very little. The girl was going for a run in the car and looking forward to the outing. It's the fashion now to magnify most things. Ordinary episodes are taken away from their proper perspectives and exalted into important events. The present generation is—"

"I know it is, sir. It always was. Once again I will continue in my work of 'accumulation.' Following on from—"

"Just a minute, Bathurst. I must ask you to come to the point more. Please! You said a few minutes ago that the girl in the Great Kirby case had been murdered. That was how you started. Are you telling me that this Loxeter girl was murdered in the name way?"

Anthony Bathurst walked from his position near the window and faced the Commissioner.

"Phyllis Welby was murdered at Loxeter. A girl named Vera Sinclair was murdered at East Hanningham and Clare Kent was murdered at Great Kirby yesterday. They have made a tragic trio, Sir Austin. And I am inclined to think that they are three victims of the same man or possibly men. Assuming, that is, that the sex of the killer is male. May I now proceed further with the terms of my indictment?"

The Commissioner seemed lost in thought. Bathurst's words had ruffled the strings of the melody of memory.

"You assert these things—but I still want convincing, I'm afraid. Tell me this. Give me a *practical* suggestion . . . don't depend so much on . . . er . . . mythical . . . theorising. If you are right—how was this Welby girl murdered? I can't for the life of me see the faintest—"

Anthony Bathurst shook his head. "Can't tell you that, sir. Please—no! Ask me something easier. All the same—that's where I castigate myself. I was in Loxeter in the October, as I told you. I saw the red light of murder as plainly and as unmistakably as I've ever seen it . . . and then the Elmer's End abduction case turned up a day or so afterwards to drag me into it and to take all my attention. If you remember, it took me as far as Rangoon." Anthony's persistence came to its highest pitch. "Surely, sir, you must see that the death of this girl Clare Kent is almost similar to that of Phyllis Welby in the Loxeter 'accident'?"

Sir Austin agreed. "The Loxeter verdict was 'Accidental Death.' The East Hannington verdict was 'Accidental Death.' And although Miss Sinclair, like Miss Welby, had only a few coppers on her when she was picked up, the circumstances of the affair were *not* entirely the same as they have been in these other two cases. Have you thought of that?"

"It's a point in your favour, I admit. But not an overwhelming one. I know what you mean. You're referring to the cause of death. Instead of Miss Sinclair's neck being broken as Miss Welby's and Miss Kent's have been, her head had been almost severed from the body. It was presumed by the doctor who was called to the body to have been cut by the broken glass of the windscreen. There was a large jagged piece of 'non-safety' glass picked up near the smashed car that had an edge like a knife, and would have sliced almost anything. Now, sir, may I at this juncture play my ace of trumps?" Anthony leant forward in his eagerness.

The Commissioner was startled into acceptance. "You must. Of course you must. What is it?"

Bathurst came across to him and sat down quietly. "Hear now the personal touch. On the evening that Phyllis Welby is believed to have met her death, I left the bar parlour of the *Lion and Lamb* an hour or so before closing time and went for a stroll on the outskirts of Loxeter. October nights, when they are truly autumnal, hold a special appeal for me. Always have done. As I walked away from the town I heard the noise of 'L'Estrange's Travelling Showground' away in the distance. I saw the dull glow of its lights reflected in the sky. The subdued hum of it all came to me—that almost indescribable medley of sounds that invariably comes from a country fair. You know what I mean, sir—I'm sure that you do. The mechanical monotony of the music from roundabouts and 'chair-o-planes,' the tumult and the shouting that *doesn't* die—until the show closes down and its patrons wend homewards. I walked towards this fair, feeling an irresistible attraction to take a closer look at it. I came up with it and made my way into it, through it and round it. As I told you a little time ago, it was on the parsimonious side. Meagre. It had no generous proportions. Let me see now! What did I patronise? After knocking some nuts down for a group of kids I looked in at the waxworks and then passed on to have an interesting few minutes' conversation with an attractive cove who apparently earned his daily bread by training alligators. Quite a personality this chap, I can assure you. Wore a monocle, if you please. Hard as nails too, I should think. Called himself Lieutenant Tafari. Man who had travelled a great deal—without a doubt. Had knocked about all over the world I should say. Very dark skin. Nationality uncertain. Then, right against one of the booths, I ran up against something that made a big impression on me. Something I have never been able to forget." He paused. His voice grew quieter and he spoke slowly and feelingly. Sir Austin seemed definitely impressed now in spite of himself. He accepted the position and silently awaited what was to follow. "For I came face to face with a girl." Anthony looked up. "She was standing listening to the damned 'hurdy-gurdy' row that was coming from one of those infernal merry-go-rounds. Standing there as she did, with the lads and lassies of Loxeter and district thronging round her, she looked supremely out of place. Not in the picture by any manner of means. Incongruous! Her clothes . . . her poise! She was altogether charming. Everything about her proclaimed her as somebody 'different.' Suddenly, as I watched her, she put her hand convulsively to her throat as though . . . she had thought of something which frightened her . . . or troubled her. I am absolutely certain that she was distressed . . . that she had in the past pushed some trouble away from herself only to find that it had returned to her side. It seemed as though one had caught a momentary glimpse of the girl's soul . . . of a tortured and harrowed soul too. The incident *hurt* me. I passed on. But the momentary glimpse had made a deep impression on me and her memory remained with me. It kept me awake all that night. That and the ever-recurring noise of the roundabout's music. Try how I would, sleep simply would *not* come to me—as far as I am concerned a most unusual experience. 'Stormy Weather.' Prophetic—eh? I often hear it of a night—even now. As a matter of fact it rather *haunts* me, Sir Austin. And shall I tell you why?" Anthony Bathurst's voice held Sir Austin in thrall. Sir Austin nodded. He couldn't trust himself to put his acquiescence into words. Anthony's voice found its gravest note. "Because, when I saw the Press photographs of the girl of the smashed car, whose body was found in the road near St. Rumbald's Church, Loxeter, I realised that the girl whom I had seen at L'Estrange's show was the Honourable Phyllis Welby. Two days afterwards I was called to Elmer's End. A week later saw me *en route* for Rangoon."

Chapter II
DEATH OF A WOMAN

Anthony Bathurst paused. It was the pause of subtlety. He desired to see the effect that his last announcements had produced upon Sir Austin. The Commissioner once again shook himself clear of Anthony's ideas and remained true to himself and to his first instincts.

"Well, Bathurst," he said, "even now you have failed to convince me. Candidly I'm disappointed . . . just a little. If that's your ace of trumps . . . well . . ." Sir Austin Kemble shrugged his shoulders.

"The trouble is, sir, that you don't recognise it as the ace of trumps. You're obstinate and cling to your wretched ditches. How would *you* explain the girl's presence—at this second-rate fair?"

"My dear chap . . . quite easily . . . in exactly the same way as I should explain yours. You heard the sounds, you saw the lights, you were passing, they attracted you—you went in. She was passing. She was attracted as you were. She went in. Good Heavens—why not? She was out in the car, drew abreast of this L'Estrange outfit, heard the sounds, saw the sights and the lights . . . parked the car somewhere handy . . . and went in. As I said, just as you yourself did."

"I've an objection to that. Slight perhaps, but I'll mention it. I'm a man. A girl's different. Especially a girl of her class in a place of that kind. She had no escort, remember! She was absolutely alone. She hadn't the least idea whom she might knock up against—assuming your theory to be correct. Country fairs have an atmosphere of licence." Mr. Bathurst shook his head in definite rejection of the Commissioner's suggestion. "No, Sir Austin,

I can't accept your version. It doesn't fit . . . as I see things. It's against all my intelligence."

Sir Austin expostulated. "You're overlooking something. She wasn't an *ordinary* girl, Bathurst! Get your mind fixed on that point. It's important and, to my mind, explains everything. She was—er—definitely 'modern.' By no means one of your stay-at-home, 'bread and butter' misses. She was not unknown in the ranks of the Gay Young People. She drove a fast car. She had hunted with the Pytchley, she had made her mark at Mürren, and she was keen on flying. She had nerve, Bathurst. And 'guts.' Now—then, what do you say?"

"All that granted, Sir Austin—and I still refuse to budge one step from my position. *J'y suis. J'y reste.* If only because of this one point, Sir Austin. *I am absolutely certain that Miss Welby went to L'Estrange's fair . . . for a reason. That she was not there in the same way as I was.* She may have wanted to find out something . . . or somebody . . . and it's possible that she *may* have had a definite assignation."

Sir Austin waved his hands disclaimingly. "Conjecture . . . conjecture . . . and yet again conjecture. Where are your facts for making such a suggestion? I repeat that there isn't a shred of evidence to support your contention. Not a fragment."

"Very well, sir," continued Anthony, "that's that. We will leave the Honourable Miss Welby for the time being and pass on to the case of Vera Sinclair, the unhappy girl whose death took place near the village of East Hannington in the April of this year. About six months, you will notice, after Miss Welby died. I was through by that time with the Elmer's End case and feeling a bit run down had come back from Rangoon and gone for a cruise to the Canaries. So that, more or less, I came upon the East Hannington affair when the scent was cold. A very different position for me from the Loxeter one. But when I came home and was able to read the facts of the case carefully, weeks after it had occurred—mind you—I took pains to satisfy myself on one point. It was the first step that I took. I will tell you what that point was, so that you may immediately realise its supreme importance. I went to East Hannington and toured round the district. It's quite in the country, let me tell you. Just past the station there's a row of smallish shops, a pub, *The Tinted Venus*, and a few cottages. Then down the road to Bindon Park and past the golf course there are a few really fine residences. Pukka country house stuff. Beyond Bindon Park you come to Altminster, which is a fairish-size place. It's a railway junction and a 'bus route terminates there. Now, Sir Austin, if you have ears, prepare to listen now. Vera Sinclair was found dead on the morning of the eleventh of April. *'L'Estrange's Travelling Showground' was on the outskirts of Altminster for three days of that particular week.* It left on the evening of the eleventh itself. I have not only spoken to several people who patronised the show during its sojourn in the Altminster district, but I have also seen the remains of various Double Crown Posters on the walls advertising its presence in their midst." Anthony cocked his head shrewdly. "Well, Sir Austin? What now? Any change of position? Or are you still a last-ditcher?"

The Commissioner made no answer to the sally. He sat in his chair staring right in front of him. This made a difference—certainly! Anthony, watching him, decided that the time was ripe for him to continue his story.

"Again—this is where I flagellate myself . . . but what in all conscience could I do? I put a cross against our 'Travelling Showground' and did a spot of internal digging. Both by discreet inquiry and personal attendance. L'Estrange himself I have never yet seen. There's a reason for that. He's referred to as 'the Duke' . . . by the various people who tour with the show. From what I have been able to gather, he's not always with them. They tell me he's getting on in years and every now and then leaves the show 'for a rest.' Not alarming perhaps . . . but unusual. We will remember it. To do so, may help us later on. There's a big hefty woman . . . who's almost the biggest noise when L'Estrange is resting . . . called Molly. Don't know her surname. Nobody else seems to know it either. There's Tafari, the bloke with the alligators, whom I told you about . . . several men and women attached to the affair, including a dwarf who looks after the waxworks, a young fellow and girl whose parentages seem to be, to say the least... 'obscure.' The boy's called Lafferty and the girl answers to the name of Rosina. They do odd jobs between 'em... anything that requires doing at the moment. Lafferty's easily recognised. He has an ugly, raw-looking scar that extends right across his left cheek. Powders it in an attempt to hide it. Of the general staff the most important seem to be a fellow named Sargeant, who looks after the 'chair-o-plane' outfit, and another man, Crouch, who runs the roundabout joke. They're a motley crowd from all points of view... as you'd expect... but I haven't yet discovered anything against any of 'em. For instance, none of 'em seem to have been through the hands of the police. Rather unusual, I'm told, in a show of this kind. But there still remains, of course, what I've told you... about Loxeter... and East Hannington... and then, finally, the sickening truth that this mysterious and sinister 'L'Estrange's Travelling Showground' *was yesterday a mile and a half from a place called Great Kirby*... Loxeter, East Hannington, Great Kirby! Yes," concluded Mr. Bathurst sadly, "I thought that this third name would interest you."

Sir Austin's habitual calm deserted him.

"God... Bathurst," he said hoarsely, "you frighten me now. You've converted me... there must be something here more than coincidence. But what *is* it? What devil's problem are we faced with now?"

Anthony shook his head. "Don't know! Can't think! Except on main principles as you've heard. No data—no details. So can't progress. I must go to Great Kirby though. That procedure on my part is most vividly indicated, I think. Don't you agree with me?"

The Commissioner showed reluctance. "H'm! You'd better ... I suppose... but don't forget this, with all your damned theories! As far as I know there hasn't been the hint of foul play in any one of the three cases... yet. So don't rake round ponds and stir up any *unnecessary* filth. Go slow. Be sure with it. For the love of Mike don't stage any of your risks unless you're on a sheer certainty."

Anthony grinned sympathetically. "You are old . . . Father William." Then it seemed that he suddenly became absent-minded. "Three girls—Sir Austin. Each in the early twenties, I believe. Let's have a look at them as they pass in front of us across this screen of tragedy. Have they anything in common? Is there anything that they share or might . . . in some circumstances . . . be expected to share? Phyllis Welby . . . daughter of Lord Sturt . . . society girl . . . already known as a member of the Gay Young People. Found dead, eighty miles from her home, with a handful of copper coins in her bag. An overturned motor-car close by. Then Vera Sinclair . . . a girl of the working class living in the country . . . found dead close to her home with a few copper coins in her possession. And a motor-car close by. Now a third girl . . . Clare Kent. Beyond her name, I know nothing about her—except that again an overturned car is approximate. But I intend to know as much as I possibly can before many hours have passed. Yes, sir!"

Sir Austin put a question. "Where did you pick up your information about this L'Estrange business . . . about the fair being at Great Kirby?" Anthony chuckled. "Sir Austin—you under-rate me, really you do. Since East Hannington, I've known where that hellish 'Travelling Showground' has been to a mile or so from day to day and the places that they've honoured with their performance. Believe me, they haven't moved a yard without me knowing it. Of course I've lain low . . . with two eyes to the future. I may have to do things. Who can tell? Already, as I've shown you, I know quite a lot about this show which is L'Estrange's. And I'm going to know more."

Sir Austin rubbed his jaw reflectively. "This third young lady—Clare Kent—was an actress. Not in the front rank, but very promising, I believe. I happened to read it in one of the papers this morning. Plays the provinces, I believe." Sir Austin checked himself abruptly and a curious expression passed over his face. Anthony noticed it and attacked immediately.

"Well, sir? What is it? You're on to something."

"'Pon my soul, Bathurst—I've just remembered a most extraordinary thing—well—perhaps not extraordinary, but definitely a coincidence. I can't think why it didn't come to me before. You remember the Miss Fletcher who gave evidence at the Loxeter inquest—well, I've just recalled the fact that her people have a country house somewhere near East Hannington. You weren't aware of that, I suppose?"

Anthony's eyes held the gleam that spoke of keen interest and meant so much. "Of course not, sir. Her town address was the only one given when she gave her evidence at the inquest on Phyllis Welby at Loxeter. I hadn't the slightest idea of such a thing." Anthony paced the room. "In my favour again, sir. You must realise that. See how the evidence goes on accumulating! Not only have we the L'Estrange business touching all three 'accidents,' but now there's this Fletcher girl cropping up in two of 'em. Or we'll say 'intimately close' to two of them. If I'm any judge, Sir Austin, it's going to turn out a pretty little case. One of our brightest and best." He stopped in his pacing and swung round on to the Commissioner. "I'll tell you what I'll do with you, sir. I'll bet you a new hat that the fourth girl that dies . . . if the devils beat me to it . . . won't have her neck broken like Miss Welby and Clare Kent. Although she may have a few pence only in her bag when they pick her up. She'll die in the same way as Vera Sinclair died at East Hannington."

Sir Austin stared. There was vehemence in Anthony's voice. Then he saw Anthony Bathurst turn away and go to the door. A minute later he heard Mr. Bathurst's steps descending the stairs. Sir Austin Kemble shivered. These were deep waters, indeed.

Chapter III
DEATH OF AN ACTRESS

ANTHONY—a victim of conflicting thoughts and tumultuous emotions—seated himself at the wheel of his grey Air-flow Chrysler. He bent forward mechanically and wiped a speck of grease from the steering-wheel with a scrap of white waste. Then he tossed away the waste. Still thinking hard he slipped the gears into low. Seconds later he slipped into high and slid expertly in front of a menacing 'bus. He ignored the fierce sparks of violent vocabulary that fell around him. His problem so obsessed him that he almost found himself passing a light that was red. He pulled up just in time. His problem did more than obsess him . . . it fascinated him. Irresistibly! His hands lay almost negligently on the wheel. The road now was wide and grand, the sun blazing hot in its August majesty, and the car moving with smooth symmetry like the shining spirit of speed. Anthony straightened his ankles to operate both brakes and clutch as the Chrysler dipped suddenly down over another sharp rise. The scenery now was England at her best—hills and valleys in alternate and undulating artistry. Anthony's eyes wandered semi-idly to the dial of the speedometer. He saw that he had already travelled a hundred and twenty-two miles, and that he was well in front of his time. He had come some distance since he had spotted the last sign-post. He was now approaching a country of rolling farmland and grateful growth. A thread of silver flashed . . . every now and then . . . away on his left. He was able to pick it out intermittently over many miles. The broad highway of tarred macadam stretched straight and prosaic between fields of barns, hayricks and five-barred gates. How far now, thought Anthony? He searched the road anxiously for destination indications. At length, by a winding lane, his patience was rewarded by the sight of an ancient sign. He descended to read with care. "Great Kirby 37 miles." Anthony got back in his car, gave his starter too much pressure and stalled the engine. He cursed himself for his clumsiness. This was absurdity *in excelsis*. His mind was too much on this L'Estrange business. He must take steps to cleanse it. The miles slipped by as the car sped on its way. Another sign-post! Oh, good! "Great Kirby 9 miles." He turned the Chrysler into the side track indicated by the extended arm. For three miles or so it chugged easily along an inferior road. Then it dipped down precipitately with the road into a miniature valley. The little hills had abandoned their skipping and embraced this valley as rival foster-mothers of an exquisite child. It was a smiling valley of sweet greenness and prim pasture. A finger from the hand of God Himself. One of the nearer hills assumed a disproportionate prominence. "Great Kirby 2 miles" said an earth-stained milestone tucked away in the weed-grown gutter of a ditch. There now came differences of scrub and common. Crossroads and a cow-byre. A chain of ponds. Homesteads and outhouses. The jolting track wended its way and became a perfectly average road. Occasional modern villas . . . half a dozen at the most. The road twisted, turned and curved, and eventually Anthony found himself driving down the unpretentious main street of Great Kirby. It was a quiet little place. Anthony supposed that little happened or was likely to happen therein. But he saw as he drove that it boasted a fine inn—*The Angel*. The cobble stones of the High Street were callous and barbarous. The church which fronted upon the main street was of unusual size in Late Decorated style and with much flamboyant feeling. It was dedicated to St. Gilbert and pointed a lofty and ambitious spire to High Heaven. Anthony descended from the car, pushed open a little wooden gate and looked round the churchyard. At Loxeter, in October, the body of Phyllis Welby had been found lying near a churchyard! He walked up a path. An epitaph on a mis-shapen tombstone caught his eye. It told elegantly of the translation of a Mrs. Ruth Plummer of the year 1741.

> "She drank good Ale, good Punch and Wine,
> And lived to th' Age of One hundred and nine."

Luckier than some of her sisters commented Anthony Bathurst. Three dead in their twenties! He strolled through the grassy paths before returning to *The Angel*. Here he interviewed a young lady of agreeable appearance and capacious bosom, and booked a room. He spent the time before dinner in the lounge, wrote two letters and made the acquaintance of a tall, fair young man who sat in an extremely comfortable chair and between whiles read a magazine of current issue. Mr. Bathurst found his new companion excellent and intelligent company. Indeed, the feeling may be said to have been mutual.

"Pretty slow place this," remarked the young man. "Very little doing indeed. Almost utterly frowsty. A man's got to make his own pleasure when he's stranded here. If it weren't for the future jam on my far ahead bread and butter, Great Kirby wouldn't see me. No, sir, not once a century."

"On the road?" queried Anthony.

"Lord bless you—no. Whatever gave you that idea? Don't say that I've come all over 'salesmanship.' I should wilt at the thought. No—to tell the truth, I'm a lucky young feller. I'm comfortably placed. My father's Sir John Brailsford. I expect you've heard of him. Mount Street—you know. But the Guv'nor's hot upon me doing a spot of work, to keep me out of mischief, he says, so I knock round a bit in the aeroplane business. It isn't hard and it pleases the old man. I've been up to West Lethbridge to-day. I know a lot of chaps at the aerodrome over there. I could have got home but it would have meant a rush and a tight squeeze, so I broke my journey here. Not a bad show, this inn—as country inns go, but the place itself—as a place—is foul! Utterly poisonous! What's your own line?" He grinned expansively. "I'm damnably rude, don't you think?"

Anthony smiled at his frankness. "No more than I was, I'm afraid. It's easily fifty-fifty. In my case—well—I'm up here for hot news."

Peter Brailsford lifted his eyebrows. "No? You don't say so? Oh—good lad. What's doing then in the annals of Great Kirby? A flower-show or the opening of a Maternity Hospital?"

Anthony found this surprising. "Haven't you seen the papers?"

"You bet. They're been my one wild thrill. But I'm not on—all the same."

"Didn't you see any mention of a motoring accident?"

Peter Brailsford's face cleared as though magically. "Oh—I get you. I did read something about it, but I'm afraid that it left but little impression. Every day, it's either that or a 'plane smash. One gets used to 'em. But what's special about this affair? To bring you along, I mean?"

Anthony hesitated. How much could he afford to give away—to anybody? He decided to play for safety. "Not a lot, I expect, when it's all thrashed out. That's being perfectly candid. But the dead girl's an actress which gives her a certain atmosphere.

A Miss Clare Kent. There's a glamour about these people, you know. In the public eye to a certain extent—and all that sort of thing. Means copy."

Brailsford raised his eyebrows. "Not a well-known actress, surely?"

"Oh, no. Chorus work in the West End, I fancy, first of all and then bigger parts in the provinces. Fit-up companies. Very promising all the same. And a lot of people know her by name, no doubt. Hence these tears."

"Oh—I begin to catch up with you. Yes—I see what you mean. You're here for the inquest, I suppose?"

"That's the idea. My name's Lotherington. On the *Morning Message*. Don't imagine for one instant that I expect a scoop. My people wanted a line on it so I popped along. You more or less have to when you get the tip direct." Anthony smiled as he continued. "That's the jam on *my* bread and butter. Now we know each other," he concluded.

Peter Brailsford grinned again appreciatively and cocked his head to one side. "Do I hear the rapturous call to dinner? Yea verily—'tis so! O for the joy and the glory there will be. Fit?"

Anthony fell in behind him and they made their way to the dining-room.

"What are you doing after dinner?" asked Mr. Bathurst, over the inevitable tomato soup.

"Haven't the foggiest," returned Brailsford. "What are you? Anything special?"

Anthony considered. "As far as I can see in this whirl of Great Kirby, we have three possibilities in front of us. One—the billiard-room, fortified by beer in frequently replenished tankards. Two—the local cinema. The picture now showing according to the bill under the railway-arch is 'Love Locked Out,' or 'Should She Have Let Him?' and three—a run round in the car. At the moment, Brailsford, I incline towards the first or the last. Not the second. By the time I have drunk the warm brownish liquid alleged on these occasions to be coffee I shall have probably reached a definite decision on the point."

"The first doesn't sound too bad," commented Brailsford . . . "I don't know that the car ride holds out much attraction for me. Where the hell can you go in this benighted hole?"

Anthony frowned at him in mock severity. "Come, man . . . pull yourself together. Is this the only place then where one can drink good beer. Are there no prophets in Macedonia?"

Peter Brailsford laughed light-heartedly at the implied censure. "Oh—that! To come to the point there's an inn over at Alconbury that's top-hole. About a ten-mile run. Let's see— what's the name of it? Oh—I know—it's the *Fox and Hounds*. I've been in there with some of the West Lethbridge crowd. Bright lads too—most of 'em. When's your inquest take place?"

"To-morrow—midday. And as I shall be indoors for a good part of to-morrow that's the reason that I may take the 'bus' out this evening for a breath of fresh air. Still—we'll see when we've finished feeding. Not a bad piece of chicken—this. I don't think it got shut in the door."

Brailsford nodded agreement. "The poultry in these country pubs is almost always good. You can pretty well rely on it. So it ought to be. You can wring necks on the spot as it were." He suited the action to the words.

Eventually they sat over their coffee. Anthony offered his chance companion a Henry Clay. Brailsford accepted. They lit up. After the pleasing silence which followed, Anthony glanced at his watch.

"Well, Brailsford, what do you say? The time has come for decision. Which shall it be?"

"A run, Lotherington. We twain will explore the countryside as far as Alconbury. Your 'bus' or mine?"

"Just as you like. Mine should be O.K. You'll find plenty of leg-room. Come on, man."

Brailsford followed him out of the coffee-room and they made their way to the inn-yard. The Chrysler sped away and the sounds of Great Kirby receded. But Master Anthony had his objective. His eye searched the clouds for the dull red glow that he knew he must soon find somewhere. "L'Estrange's Travelling Showground" couldn't be far away. Of that fact, he was absolutely certain. The car slid forward at increasing speed. Brailsford chattered inconsequently.

"Make for the Alconbury road," he said eventually. "First right—then second left. The turning should be about here."

The words had scarcely left his lips when Anthony's eyes were rewarded in their, search. They caught the same glare in the sky that Anthony had seen ten months before. He pointed it out to his companion.

"Hallo—what's doing? Looks like a fair or something away over there. What do you say to spending a couple of hours or so there? It might be passably entertaining. Some of these village fairs are good sport."

Brailsford didn't seem too keen on the project. "Oh—I don't know—pretty lousy—most of these country shows—what I've seen of 'em. I don't think you'd find much to interest you there. Still—please yourself—if you're keen—don't mind me. I can make a moderate shot at most things. If you fancy the idea—go ahead."

Anthony nodded good-naturedly. "That's very sporting of you, Brailsford. I certainly do think though—that we might do worse than have a look at things. We can always push on when we've had enough. Fairs and circuses rather attract me, Brailsford, I may as well admit it, I suppose. Most of us have weaknesses—vulnerable heels, you know. They vary from railway engines to a 'Blue Mauritius' and usually date back to the days of our youth."

He turned the Chrysler down a side turning that indicated a direct approach. Brailsford was silent for a time. After a while the noise of "L'Estrange's Showground" came to meet them and assailed their ears. Anthony grinned at his companion in cheerful appreciation.

"Life, my dear Brailsford, vivid and entrancing. Consider its changing pattern. I come for an inquest and find this. In the midst of Death we are in Life. I'll park the car by the gate of this field and we'll saunter in bearing our notes of distinction. What sayest thou, Sempronius? Does the prospect please—or are the women vile?"

"That's O.K. with me, Lotherington. Not that I expect much. I'm not so optimistic as you. I'm confident of its complete and utter foulness."

"What's the odds?" cried Anthony slapping him on the back gaily—"if only the lads have found lassies to woo and to win? For us there's still a tankard of ale at the inn. The people alone at shows of this sort are worth watching, I always think."

Mr. Bathurst and Peter Brailsford mingled with the stream of sightseers who laughed and jostled each other, and eventually came to the tents and booths. Anthony, seemingly nonchalant, had his two grey eyes wide open. He knew the value—none better—of the chance look, of the fugitive fragment of phrase or of the furtive gesture. Any one of these might come his way that night and give him the clue or part of the clue, that his brain was seeking. The clue that might put the threads in his hands and save a life.

It was a dark night now, for August—the moon was waning—and the fair seemed like an oasis of light in a desert of opaque blackness. Anthony and Peter Brailsford slowly and interestedly made the circular tour. They passed the coconut shy, the roundabout with the man Crouch at work, the chair-o-plane run this evening by the woman called Molly, the wax-works with Rosina in charge, the tent of alligators, a flaring show where people rolled coins on to squares and spaces for money prizes, and finally a huge wooden stand from which to an almost sickening altitude swung a boat of human freight. This was supervised by the swarthy Sargeant. Anthony and Brailsford craned their necks to watch it as it swung backwards and forwards. *"Quot homines tot sententiae,"* quoted Anthony, "and that piece of Roman wisdom applies very forcibly, I think, to forms of entertainment. Judging by their semi-hysterical screams, some of the ladies up there are uncomfortable enough to be thoroughly happy. Shall we stroll back the other way?" Brailsford assented.

They came again to the tent of the alligators. Strange and displeasing sounds came from within. Sounds which arrested the attention of both Anthony and Peter Brailsford. There were anger and furious fear in raised voices. There was a violent oath, the words "The Duke," and then the excited chattering hum of the people inside the tent who had paid for the privilege of entrance and who watched what might be. Then there came a noise that seemed to Anthony to speak of indescribable malevolence. A woman's cry cut through it and above it—shrill and staccato. Anthony's hand closed like a vice on his companion's shoulder. "Stay still," he said curtly. The canvas of the tent's entrance parted suddenly, as though it had been thrust aside with tempestuous vehemence, and a man rushed out. Out—and past Anthony and Brailsford. A man who clasped his arm in a fierce eagerness and erosive fear and whose face worked in turbulent and convulsive emotion. He snarled and muttered to himself like an animal, as he ran. Anthony looked and recognised the runner. The man was the man who wore a monocle and who called himself Lieutenant Tafari.

"Spot of bother," murmured Peter. Anthony's face checked him.

Mr. Bathurst pulled a silent Brailsford towards him again and thoughtfully they made their way back to the car. It was best, Anthony considered, that he should not enter the tent that evening and make himself unduly conspicuous. There were duties and industries that lay ahead. He remembered, as he strode along with Brailsford, that again he had seen nobody whom he could reasonably take to be L'Estrange . . . although he had heard those words . . . "The Duke." That he had missed Lafferty as well, the fellow with the scar across his cheek, and also the dwarf who usually superintended the wax-works. But Tafari had run away from something . . . and Tafari . . . a man who in his time had held the world by the throat . . . had been desperately afraid when he ran! As he entered his car after the smiling Peter, Anthony caressed his chin reflectively. Say what you like—this circle around L'Estrange had a definite attraction of its own. For him—if for nobody else. He turned to his companion.

"We will now seek Alconbury," he said, "and honest beer."

Chapter IV
THE INQUEST ON CLARE KENT

Anthony presented his card to the constable on duty at the door of the Central Mission Hall, Great Kirby, and was immediately admitted. The name of Sir Austin Kemble underneath his own, worked wonders. Mr. Bathurst intended that it should. Brailsford, who accompanied him, was impressed by the ease with which the entrance was effected. He expressed himself accordingly.

"You Press fellows certainly get away with it," he remarked a wee bit ruefully. "I can't work the 'open sesame' business where I go, anything like as smoothly as you blokes seem to do. Which is it—you personally—or the *Morning Message*."

"Spare my blushes, Brailsford," returned Mr. Bathurst, making no reference to Scotland Yard—"it's a bit of both as it happens. Let us put it down to the reputation of my paper and my own personal charm working as an irresistible combination. Barriers melt before it. Now you know. Foreign correspondents please copy." Anthony grinned cheerfully.

They took their places just as the Coroner was seating himself. It was the first time that Peter Brailsford had been in a coroner's court. He was aware that the office of coroner was of ancient origin but he had not known until this moment, that the hall in which he sat, in its present condition and usage, so resembled, certainly in external appearances, a court of justice. He noted the details of similarity. There was the raised platform, or dais where sat the Coroner himself. There was the jury box on his right for the 'twelve good men and true.' There was the table for the higher court officials, their subordinates and the various emissaries of the law. There was the witnesses' stand and at the back of the hall, accommodation in the shape of chairs and forms, at the disposal of such of the general public who were sufficiently interested or curious to put in an appearance.

Anthony and Brailsford had found two chairs in the front row—close to the table where sat the officials and the various legal representatives above-mentioned. Anthony had pointed out the two chairs to Brailsford as well placed and they had been quick to obtain them. Of the general public there was but a moderate number. The case on this occasion fell under the head of an ordinary accident and, as such, had but small relation to the sensational. As Sir Austin Kemble had stated previously, accidents of this kind were almost everyday affairs. Peter Brailsford watched with keen interest the swearing-in of the twelve jurymen and observed, too, the general preliminaries which inaugurated the morning's work. Then the Coroner cleared his throat, ostentatiously wiped his glasses and addressed his court. Brailsford craned his neck forward that he might hear the better; it may be noted that coroners are not required as a rule to satisfy the examiners in the art of elocution. Dr. Hotchkiss, it must be confessed, was no exception. But Brailsford, listening intently and intelligently filling in certain gaps, gathered that the death of this young lady, a Miss Clare Glover Kent, was a great shock to everybody and particularly to the Coroner himself. Dr. Hotchkiss inclined his head to an appropriate angle. But in these days when everything was sacrificed on the altar of speed, and human life placed at the mercy of reckless risk, he continually found himself, in his capacity as Coroner, lamenting the passing of lives that were young and full of promise. Lives, if he might be permitted to remark such a thing, without giving offence, that were absolutely thrown away. This young lady, who was an actress of more than ordinary ability, and already becoming to be regarded as a future "star," had been found in the road. Dead. Her car ... which was overturned ... close to her ... her injuries were of such a character ... Dr. Hotchkiss became excessively medical. He described the precise nature of the injuries ... and the jury would be called upon to say how Miss Kent had come by her death. To begin with, he would call John Dexter to identify the deceased.

A well-set-up man went briskly to the witness-stand and took the oath. The Coroner commenced.

The Coroner: Your name is John Dexter? Of Great Missenden, Buckinghamshire? Your address is Appian, Roseworthy Avenue, Great Missenden?

Answer: Yes.

The Coroner (examining his papers): You are the brother-in-law of Miss Clare Glover Kent?

Answer: I am. I married Miss Kent's only sister. Clare Kent was not a stage name. It was her real name. I have viewed the body on which this inquest is being held and I identify it without hesitation as that of Clare Kent, my sister-in-law, late of 19 Marsham Park Road, Lee, Kent.

The Coroner: Thank you, Mr. Dexter. Can you tell us anything about Miss Kent's state of health?

Answer: To my knowledge she was in excellent health. I have no hesitation in saying so. It's true that I have not seen her for four or five weeks, but when I last saw her I should say that she was perfectly well. She had been resting prior to taking up an engagement that opened soon, in the county of Durham.

The Coroner: Thank you, Mr. Dexter. Everything so far is perfectly clear. You may stand down. I hope that there will be no occasion for me to recall you. Call Dr. Keymer.

The police-surgeon, Dr. Basil Mandell Keymer, testified that he had been called to Vista Road, Great Kirby, at half-past six on the morning of August the seventeenth. The body of the young lady, since identified as that of Clare Kent, was lying face downwards in the road itself. Plans were then produced and handed to the members of the jury. She had been dead, said Dr. Keymer, some hours. There were extensive injuries. Dr. Keymer consulted the notes that he had evidently made at the time. He found, he said, that the young lady's right shoulder-blade was broken and the spinal column dislocated. The wrists and the backs of the hands were also badly bruised and lacerated.

Anthony listened to Dr. Keymer attentively and with a certain amount of gratification. Here was news that it suited him to hear. If the other evidence only went as he confidently anticipated that it would, he would be satisfied beyond any doubt that he was not ploughing the sands. Dr. Keymer, in a cold precise voice, was continuing his evidence. Anthony noticed how the occasion was getting hold of Brailsford.

Miss Kent was perfectly healthy, the police-surgeon said—her body was the normal body of a young girl of twenty-three. Every organ was sound, Dr. Keymer concluded.

"Call George Greenwood."

There was a bustle at the back of the hall. A young self-confident person, evidently a local, walked quickly to the stand and looked round the court expectantly. He was duly sworn. Invited by Dr. Hotchkiss to tell his story, he stated that he drove a milkcart from Little Kirby through Kirby-le-Steeple, into Great Kirby every morning of his life. He usually arrived at the last-mentioned place about six o'clock. On the morning of August the seventeenth, he had just passed beneath the railway arch and entered Vista Road when he noticed the body of the young woman lying in the road about a hundred and fifty yards in front of him. When he came up to it, he saw that the body was lying in the road face downwards and he saw at the same time the wheels of a small car showing at the top of the ditch that ran by the side of the road. The car had overturned and the bonnet was at the bottom of the ditch. Greenwood told the court that he whipped up the horse in his milkcart and drove hell for leather for half a mile to the nearest telephone kiosk from where he at once 'phoned for the police and the police-doctor. There were, said Greenwood, distinct marks on the surface of the road, of a skid. The skid was in the direction of the ditch. At this point, Dr. Hotchkiss, with elaborate ceremony, ordered that the various photographs should be distributed amongst the members of the jury.

"It should be pointed out that there had been a slight shower of rain, late in the evening," said the Coroner, "and it is extremely likely, I should say, that the unfortunate young lady, as she drove the car, found the road on the greasy side. Also, I would point out, that particular stretch of the Vista Road, just after it leaves Kirby-le-Steeple, is very dark. Not only do I know that from my own experience—gentlemen—but also I have actually called the attention of the local authority to the fact more than once. I have received, I may say, several replies informing me that the matter will receive attention. Do any members of the jury desire to ask this last witness any questions?" Dr. Hotchkiss beamed on the jury-box. There was no response to his question. He turned again to the witness. "Thank you, Mr. Greenwood. You have given your evidence very clearly. That is all, I think."

The Coroner polished his glasses and proceeded to address the Court.

"You have heard the evidence, gentlemen. It contained nothing, I assert without fear of contradiction, that may be reasonably termed perplexing or unusual. Here we have a young lady who had been out for a day's motoring in the country and who was no doubt returning home. But going perhaps a trifle too fast, and the road being just a little slippery and not too well lighted perhaps, the car had skidded . . . with . . . er . . . fatal consequences. There isn't the slightest question of foul play . . . or of robbery . . . or of collision with another car or of culpable negligence on the part of any other party. The evidence is contradictory to all those possibilities and they can be dismissed from your minds . . . one and all. Miss Kent's car showed no signs whatever of having been hit and she had her jewellery untouched and also her money . . . not by any means a big sum . . . er . . ."—the Coroner referred to his notes—"one and something in coppers . . . but there it was—nothing had been stolen. She had it still in her possession."

Anthony rubbed his hands. Here were crumbs of comfort. Brailsford noticed the action on the part of his next-door neighbour and fell to wondering what it was that had excited Mr. Lotherington. He watched him carefully for any further signs of acute interest. Dr. Hotchkiss meandered on placidly.

"And so . . . in the light of all that we know . . . I am sure that you will have little difficulty, gentlemen, in arriving at a fit and proper verdict."

The Coroner was not disappointed in regard to his confident prognostication. The jury, having viewed the body, behaved themselves in accordance with his expectations and returned a verdict of "accidental death—brought about by the skidding and overturning on a greasy road of a motor-car in which deceased had been driving."

Officers of the law and members of the general public filed from the Central Mission Hall, Great Kirby, quietly and with entire absence of fuss. Everything had transpired as had been anticipated. There had been no sensations—not even the luxury of an "incident."

Anthony excused himself to Peter Brailsford at a convenient moment. "I shall have to send some copy off, Brailsford, if you'll excuse me," he said, "and I want to get the job done before I return to *The Angel*. You understand—don't you? I'll see you later—unless you intend to get away at once. If you do, of course, don't worry about me."

Brailsford nodded and grinned understandingly. "That's O.K. with me, Lotherington. Push on as though I were off the map. As a matter of fact, I'm in no particular hurry as it happens. I'll get along back to the hotel and wait for you there."

As good as his word, Brailsford went off immediately and Anthony lost no time in getting to work on the job that he had mapped out for himself. He made his way back to the room where the inquest had been held and without hesitation walked over to the man John Dexter, who, as the deceased's brother-in-law, had been called upon to identify the body.

"Mr. Dexter," he said, "may I have a word or two with you before you go? I promise you that I won't detain you unduly."

Dexter looked surprised. His face held a frown. Anthony realised that he was a man of strong mind and gave him his card. Dexter's surprise, after he had read it, increased.

"Here?" he asked curtly.

Mr. Bathurst rewarded him with a smile. "My car's outside. May I drive you anywhere? The station—perhaps? We can talk on the way. Or, if you're not returning to town just yet—anywhere that will be convenient to you."

Dexter thrust hands into pockets and gave him a searching look.

"Well," said Anthony half-humorously, "do I pass muster?"

There were a ruggedness and honest-to-goodness about Dexter that rather appealed to him. He looked and acted like a man who knew his own mind and who would stand no nonsense. Anthony, from his first shrewd glances, judged him to be a cool-headed fellow with more than the average leavening of common-sense. He also decided that Dexter, upon closer acquaintance, would prove to be a man who would say what he felt and thought without fear or favour. Dexter coolly looked Mr. Bathurst up and down for a second time and then—evidently satisfied with what his scrutiny had brought him—nodded.

"I guess you'll do," he said bluntly—"and as you suggested it, you can drive me to the L.M.S. Station. That will suit me admirably. I'm going straight home and I can lunch on the train. As you said—we can talk in the car on the way up."

"Good. I'm your man." Anthony piloted him to the yard of the Central Mission Hall, where he had parked the Chrysler and motioned him to occupy the seat next to the driver.

"Now," said Dexter, as soon as the car had got under way, "shoot! I'm in your clutches. What is it that you want to say to me?"

Mr. Bathurst took his time. "You saw my card," he returned eventually, "that should remove all doubts as to my credentials and convince you of my bona-fides, if of nothing else. I want to ask you one or two questions. That's my purpose in life at the moment. I hope that you will see your way to answer them. I think—when you have heard them—that you will. In the first place, I'm going to be perfectly frank and tell you that I'm *not* satisfied that to-day's verdict was a true one. That statement of mine should explain much. I should be interested to hear what you think of things yourself, Mr. Dexter?" He swung the car adroitly round a sharp corner. As he expected and intended, Dexter came to grips at once. "H'm. Is the Yard in on this?"

"Officially—no. I will hide nothing from you. Let us say that I am acting for the Commissioner of Police himself. *But*—in a semi-private manner—you must understand. For the time being, that is. Developments, of course, may mean that—"

"What do you know, then?"

Anthony shrugged his shoulders.

"As regards the case of your sister-in-law, Miss Kent—nothing. Except, shall we say, that she was found dead near an overturned motor-car and that her only cash possessions when she was picked up were coppers. One and fivepence halfpenny, wasn't it?" Anthony shot him a shrewd glance as he spoke. But Dexter was unmoved and unperturbed.

"There's nothing remarkable in that my friend, that I can see. Clare didn't suffer from any embarrassment of riches—believe me. Do any third-rate mummers? She never has done. Very much the other way—in fact. She was thundering glad when she got fixed for this North-country show, let me tell you. She'd been out of a shop for much longer than she found pleasant. The pictures have hit her stuff hard, let me tell you."

"Yet she drove a car, you know," said Mr. Bathurst softly. "Not an expensive car, I grant you. But a car. There's the driving licence and the tax . . . and garaging expenses . . . and the general upkeep. Petrol doesn't exactly prance hand in hand with poverty." Dexter's hand caressed his chin. "I know. The same idea occurred to me. I'll admit as much. But, as I expect you heard me tell the Coroner at the beginning of the inquest, I hadn't seen Clare for over a month and quite frankly I did not know that she *was* running a car. I'd known that she'd *wanted* to, for some time, but *wanting* things and being able to do things are usually totally different propositions. At least—that's been my experience. You see Clare lived in a flat at Lee, near Blackheath. I live in Bucks, as you heard. We were some distance apart—she and I, so that I didn't see a lot of her—as you may imagine."

"Here's a question for you, then. It wasn't touched on as far as I can remember. Did the police tell you the date she took out her driving licence?"

"Yes. I asked the question myself when they first sent for me. I was interested as much as you are. Clare had the licence for the car between two and three months. She applied for it early in May. She had had a driver's licence for a year or so."

"Good. That answers one of my questions. Now tell me this, Mr. Dexter—as far as you are able. What were Miss Kent's habits—generally speaking?"

"Habits?"

"Yes. I'm trying to get a line on any *acquaintances* that she may have made. Or even friendships. Outside her own theatrical circle, for instance. Can you help me in that direction? Do your best, Mr. Dexter. I think that it may well prove to be important."

Dexter considered the question carefully, but eventually shook his head. "I don't know enough of Clare's private life or interests to answer that at all confidently. Beyond the fact that she occasionally went to a night-club—I know nothing. So I'm afraid that it's no use pressing me."

"Your wife—perhaps—Miss Kent's sister—"

"My wife is dead," returned Dexter curtly and rather grimly.

"I'm sorry," murmured Mr. Bathurst—"please pardon me."

"That's quite all right," returned Dexter—"you weren't to know."

"Had Miss Kent any love affairs?" asked Anthony.

"Nothing serious—again—as far as I know."

"Any enemies?"

"None. She was a singularly nice girl. Everybody liked Clare."

"This night-club of which you spoke, Mr. Dexter? Can you remember the name . . . or its locality even?" Dexter knitted his brows. "Now that's a question which I should be able to answer because Clare said . . . now . . . let me think. . . ."

There was silence for some time.

"Here's the station of your desire," said Anthony Bathurst, "Great Kirby. Trains every now and then for London." He brought the car to a standstill. "When's your train? Have you plenty of time?" Dexter looked at his watch. "Three-quarters of an hour—worse luck. I'm a busy man, Mr. Bathurst, and this jaunt down here has come at a most inopportune moment. Time's money with me, I'm afraid."

"With all that time to spare, come and have a drink," said Anthony. "This place doesn't look too bad . . . perhaps you'll be able to remember the name of that night-club under the influence of liquid refreshment. Just a second and I'll run the car down this turning. It should be all right here."

Some moments later, Dexter followed Anthony into the saloon bar of the *Railway Hotel*. The situation of this establishment is unusual. The station at Great Kirby lies at the top of a hill and the hotel, at the side thereof, seems to be perched almost perilously upon the heights. While Anthony was issuing orders at the bar, Dexter walked to the window of the parlour and looked down at the street below. His eyes almost demanded to complete the picture appropriately, the lift that crawls so laboriously up the face of the green-fronted cliff. "What was the name that Clare had—?"

Anthony Bathurst came with filled glasses and joined him. "Well, Mr. Dexter," he queried, "any luck?"

Dexter shook his head. "I'm near to it, but I haven't gripped it yet. Like the old game we used to play when we were kids. Warm you know, but not hot. It'll come to me though, if I'm only patient enough and don't try to force matters. I find that these things generally do. I remember once when I was staying down at East—" He paused suddenly as though an idea had suddenly taken possession of his mind. "I've got it—that name you wanted. Came into my brain like a flash. I remember Clare mentioning it once when she was with me at Great Missenden. The name of that night-club's 'The Purple Calf.' I think, too, that it lies somewhere in the neighbourhood of Bellenden Street."

Anthony nodded his satisfaction and approval. "I know the place well. It has even come under my notice before. It's rather 'rather' you know—as a matter of fact. By no means a Y.W.C.A. Some extremely queer birds congregate there for worms. Still, that's neither here nor there at the moment, is it?"

Dexter made no reply.

"Tell me this," continued Mr. Bathurst. "I know of course from what you have told me and also from my own intelligence that Miss Kent was not wealthy. We're agreed on it. Let me try the idea in a different way. Would you say, if you were asked deliberately, that she had ever been *in desperate need of money*? A need so acute, for example, that it might have driven her to . . . well . . . what we'll call unpleasant remedies?"

"As far as I know, Mr. Bathurst, Clare has never in her life been so badly off as that would imply."

"Forgive me asking . . . has she ever been to you for money? I'm sorry, but this 'money' side of the matter worries me so."

Dexter flushed to the roots of his hair. Anthony found himself wondering at the reason.

"Yes. She has. But only for comparatively small amounts." He attempted further explanation. "You know what I mean. For what I call those *'reasonable'* loans that often take place between decent people, when one of 'em's a bit pressed. But Clare had never let me see or know that she has ever been in desperate straits. That's why I don't think that she can have been. Because, had she asked me, I should most certainly have helped her . . . and she knew that I would have done."

Dexter paused and Anthony was impressed by the look of sadness that had suddenly come over his face. Mr. Bathurst probed again.

"And you can't think of any man in her life who had brought to her a romantic atmosphere? Any man that meant more to her . . . in *any* way . . . than one might have reasonably expected?"

Dexter drained his glass with a curious gesture of deliberate finality. "This may surprise you, but as far as I can remember," he said dramatically, "Clare has mentioned but two men to me during all the years that I have known her. That's an admission for these times, isn't it? But it's true nevertheless. Although she had gone on the boards. She wasn't what I would call 'a man's woman.' And each of these two has been mentioned . . . how shall I say . . . *specially* . . . not casually. I'm a bad hand at expressing myself, I suppose, but I mean that they entered the conversation down a special, particular avenue of reference. Have you got what I mean?" He looked anxiously at Anthony Bathurst for the confirmation that he needed.

Anthony assured him. "I think that I understand you. Tell me who these men were and I may be able to understand you better."

"Ah—I thought you'd ask that. I will if I can. But it's a bit of a task for me, I'm afraid . . . just as that other question of yours was. The first man of whom I spoke was an actor. I can tell you that. Clare had played with him in more than one travelling company. A man with a rather unusual name . . . one of those high-falutin stage names. You know! One they choose instead of their own, to impress the ladies. When they come over all Plantagenet. Now what the blazes *was* this chap's name? Harding . . . Harding . . . I've got it . . . Harding Argyle. His name cropped up somehow like this. Clare had been telling me of an incident that had happened to them in a show one night . . . you know . . . something had gone vitally wrong, either lines had gone west or an entrance had been missed . . . and this chap saved the show by a piece of particularly quick thinking. Presence of mind, you know. I forgot what it was exactly. But Clare did tell me and I know that I was impressed at the time. Splendid 'character' man he was, according to her—that was his name though—Harding Argyle."

Bathurst waited for him to finish and then nodded.

"Yes, I did understand you, Mr. Dexter. And my anticipations weren't disappointed. You had made your meaning clearer than you imagined you had. Now—what was this other name that you have heard Miss Kent mention?"

Dexter smiled ruefully. "No trouble about that. That's an easy one to remember, because, strangely enough, the incident of its being mentioned occurred on the very last occasion that I saw Clare. And it was such that it made an impression on my memory. I'm of the opinion that it would have done the same with most people. She mentioned a dwarf that she had seen . . . some little time before. She was full of it. According to what Clare told me, this man was a most remarkable person. Extraordinarily and incredibly clever too, in many directions. Amongst other things a most beautiful 'copper-plate' writer and an accomplished musician."

Anthony felt the thrill of the chase. Clare Kent's dwarf *must* be the man attached to L'Estrange. Once again, he felt certain, he was to hear of things that mattered.

"Really! You interest me immensely. What was this man's name, Mr. Dexter?"

"Buckinger, Mr. Bathurst, Matthew Buckinger. Clare had seen him somewhere and, as I said, she was full of him. Quite a character, I can tell you, in his own way. He had made a tremendous impression upon her. To tell you the truth I had a rare job to get her to talk of anything else. At the time she was almost obsessed by him."

Anthony looked at his wrist-watch. "I shan't be able to keep you much longer, Mr. Dexter, I'm afraid. Time's getting short—you'll have to be getting along for your train, but what you have told me is most extraordinary. For Matthew Buckinger—let me inform you—was the name of a famous dwarf of history. He flourished, I fancy, somewhere round the year 1700. In the reign of Queen Anne, I rather think. Does this chap whom Miss Kent had met, claim to be a relation of his, do you know? Did you hear anything of that?"

Dexter shook his head. "No. Not a word of that was mentioned. We didn't touch on relationships."

"H'm. One last question before you go, Mr. Dexter. Where did Miss Kent meet him? Can you tell me that?"

"No. I can't tell you that, Mr. Bathurst. I wish that I could. Clare never dwelt on that aspect of the matter."

Dexter followed Anthony's action and looked at his watch rather fussily. "I must go. I really must. I hope that I have been of some material assistance to you. Promise me one thing, Mr. Bathurst. In return for what I have told you. Keep me conversant with anything that comes along which you yourself consider important. I can't forget that Clare was my wife's only sister. Good-bye."

Anthony shook the outstretched hand. "Rely on me, Mr. Dexter. Nothing will give me greater pleasure."

When Dexter had gone Anthony returned to his car and stood by it for a moment, lost in thought. "Buckinger the dwarf," he said softly to himself. "The notorious Matthew Buckinger." As mentioned by Horace Walpole. Was the name a coincidence or of deliberate design?

Chapter V
ENTER SIR JOHN

When Anthony Bathurst arrived back to the comfort of *The Angel*, Great Kirby, he found Peter Brailsford awaiting him in the coffee-room. At Peter's side stood a tall, distinguished-looking man of military carriage, assured manner and silver-white hair. The tall man smoked a cigar, the aroma of which tickled Anthony's nostrils. Peter ushered him forward with some show of eagerness.

"This is a great moment. I must introduce you two chaps," he said excitedly, "because you really ought to know each other. Life isn't complete for you until you do. Lotherington, this is my father, Sir John Brailsford. Perhaps you've heard of him. Guv'nor, this is Lotherington of the *Morning Message*. The chap I was telling you about."

The elder man seemed genuinely pleased to make Anthony's acquaintance. He was courtly, with the manners of the old school, even to a touch of the punctilious. He bowed to Anthony. "How do you do? I am extremely delighted to meet you, Mr. Lotherington. My son has already spoken to me of you in glowing terms. He's quite enthusiastic about you. You seem to have impressed him considerably, for what—I am sure you will forgive me saying it—has been a singularly short acquaintanceship. Moreover, Peter, let me tell you, is definitely hard to please."

"You are both very kind," laughed Anthony—"too kind—and I confess that it's a most pleasant surprise for me to find you here, sir. I never expected to be so fortunate. If I may say so, not only I, but also Great Kirby is honoured." He spoke the latter part of his sentence to Sir John Brailsford.

Sir John smiled genially at the compliment. "As a matter of fact, my dear sir, I hadn't the slightest idea when I went to bed last night that I should be standing here to-day. But I simply felt at a loose end and decided to run down in the car and put in an hour or so with my son here. I knew that he was staying here, you see, because I had had a card from him." He bowed again to Anthony. "I am glad now that I came, I have been more than rewarded."

"Thank you, Sir John. That's very charming of you."

"The Guv'nor's a sun-worshipper and just back from a trip to the West Indies, Lotherington," contributed Peter Brailsford by way of explanation, "so that you'll probably find him in excellent form. We usually do if he's had a particularly good trip."

Anthony nodded understandingly. "Shall we drink, sir?" Anthony gave orders and in time they drank. Sir John Brailsford an old brown sherry of superlative merit, Peter, a gin and ginger-beer, and Anthony himself a pint of beer from a tankard of generous proportions. "Truly," he said appraisingly, "is this inn known as *The Angel*. Craftsman's art and excellent measure—all combine." He turned to Sir John Brailsford. "You like the West Indies, sir?"

"Very much. Besides the appeal of the climate during our own winter, I have had interests over there for years. Business interests. Sometimes I feel that I should like to live there altogether. I may do—one day . . . despite domestic opposition." Sir John's hand went to his head and stroked the plenitude of silver hair that went back—well-brushed—from his high forehead. Anthony was impressed. Sir John had that rare coupling, the brow of the student and the jaw of the relentless fighter. His voice was deep and purposeful. Unemotional, perhaps, at first hearing, but the listener, if he listened to Sir John Brailsford intelligently, soon registered the idea that if Sir John's voice sounded unemotional, it was for the rather unusual reason that Sir John had his emotions under complete control.

"How did you get on after you left me, Lotherington?" questioned Peter Brailsford. "I've been thinking of you. Did you get your stuff off all right?"

"Oh—yes—Everything went as smoothly as possible. I was luckier than I expected to be. Sometimes, you know, in these country towns that are more or less off the map, things are decidedly difficult. They haven't the machinery that London has. I was fortunate in another way as well, as it happened. I ran into that fellow Dexter—the dead girl's brother-in-law. You remember the man, I expect? He was the first witness that the Coroner called. John Dexter. Gave evidence as to identification. I had quite a long chat with him—considering the time at his disposal."

Sir John Brailsford intervened. He looked puzzled. "I'm afraid that I don't quite—"

Peter hastened to make amends. "I'm sorry—it's my fault, Lotherington. I had forgotten. I ought to have put the Guv'nor wise. But I was so pleased and surprised to see him that I jawed and jawed about other things and it slipped me. Fact is, sir," he said, turning to his father in explanation, "we've been to an inquest. Lotherington and I. New departure for me. But it's Lotherington's particular job of work. He actually draws good bees and honey for it. A girl was killed here in a motoring accident. That's really why he's down in Great Kirby. Now you understand."

Sir John smiled at Anthony. "Naturally when you said 'the dead girl,' I will confess that I *was* rather startled. I wondered what was the matter. A sad affair—no doubt. In fact, this toll of the road is one of our greatest present-day problems. As somebody said the other day. Where are we getting to? Our public highways are worse than unfenced railways. Is this craze for speed justified? *Can* it possibly be justified?"

"It's one of the Guv'nor's pet theories," contributed Peter with a wink in Anthony's direction. "We've given him the chance of a lifetime."

"Who was the young lady?" asked Sir John with a smile.

Anthony took it upon himself to reply. "An actress, Sir John. Clare Kent, by name, moderately obscure."

Peter seemed introspectively inclined. To all appearances he was lost in thought.

"How did you find that brother-in-law chap?" he asked.

"Oh—all right. For the purpose that I wanted. He struck me favourably on the whole and I managed to dig out some details that will make good copy. I wasn't with him very long, though. Why do you ask?"

Peter shook his head at the question. He seemed to be worrying himself over something. "Don't know, quite. I suppose that I did it on the spur of the moment. I'm afraid it's a habit of mine—asking damn fool questions. I shall have to break myself of it. But I've a sneaking idea at the back of my mind that I've seen that bloke before somewhere. Can't think where though—his name was Dexter, wasn't it?"

Anthony was interested. "Yes. John Dexter. I'll remind you of what he said at the inquest. It may help you, Brailsford, to connect up. He lives in Buckinghamshire. In the Great Missenden district. He's a widower. His wife was Clare Kent's only sister. Any of that any help to you?"

Brailsford shook his head again. "Afraid it isn't. Absolutely the reverse, in fact. Don't know the district at all. Except where it lies, of course. No—it's not anywhere down there that I've run across him. What worries me, is that so far as I can tell it's a *recent* reminiscence. At any rate, it *seems* to be. That he and I have been somewhere together very recently. That's how I get it. I feel as though I've had a conversation with him."

Anthony looked at Peter Brailsford with deliberate directness.

"Weren't you satisfied, Brailsford, with the verdict of that coroner's jury—or are you just being cryptic?"

Peter rubbed his cheek with a grin. "Do you know—that's rather funny."

"What do you mean?"

"That you should have asked me that."

"Why—exactly?"

"Because I registered an idea as I sat next to you in that front row of uncomfortable chairs that *you* weren't. Am I right, O King?" He cocked his head.

Anthony was amused at the eagerness which Brailsford displayed. "Give yourself a pat on the back, Brailsford. There are certainly one or two points about the affair that puzzle me considerably."

Sir John beamed and rubbed the palms of his hands together. "Now I confess that I find this most intriguing. That's the modern word, isn't it? What is it that you read into this seemingly simple road accident that the police and the authorities generally don't? I've never been 'close' to a mystery in my life. Alas—I shall never grow up it seems. Here am I thrilling to the idea of a crime like a schoolboy devouring his *Sexton Blake*."

Peter Brailsford affected mock resignation at his father's words.

"And I shall suffer for it, I suppose. Our relative positions will be transposed. While you are becoming Peter Pan, I shall unhappily and inevitably approximate Rip Van Winkle. I've been unlucky ever since I can remember. I was born on a Wednesday."

Sir John, however, was in no mood for trifling. He came directly to the point. "What are the features of the affair that trouble you, Mr. Lotherington? You've interested me so much that I'd like to hear them. 'Pon my soul, I would. I thought that my son here described the affair as 'a motoring accident.' But I suppose that you gentlemen of the Press 'hear' things—eh? What's peculiar or unusual about it, anyway?"

Anthony hesitated. In the beginnings of things, when he merely coquetted with "theories"—when those "theories" of his flirtation were unsupported by definite "data," he always preferred to hold them tight in his own brain against all inquiries. In reply to Sir John Brailsford, therefore, he contented himself with the surrender of one point only. And purely tentatively at that.

"Well, Sir John," he said quietly. "I won't deny that you've asked me an awkward question. It's easier, you know, to think things 'vaguely' than to reproduce those thoughts with satisfactory bodies—so to speak. And I've 'heard' nothing—as you have suggested. But one of the points which I find difficult to explain—to myself that is, it's a purely personal matter—is the handful of copper coins found in the dead girl's possession. One shilling and fivepence halfpenny—was the sum I believe. And every coin, I understand, Sir John, was of *copper*. She hadn't, for instance, a shilling—or a sixpence. I will say nothing about a threepenny piece . . . that 'furtive disciple of donation.'" Anthony spoke softly as he made his points and his eyes took on a far-away expression.

Sir John Brailsford frowned. "H'm! You can put me down as dense, if you like, but I'm hanged if I see your point, Mr. Lotherington. That is to say without knowing more of the actual circumstances. Surely the coins that one finds in one's possession at odd times during the day are more or less a matter of pure chance. One day, one thing—another day, another. For instance—we change money. We keep on changing money. That's my experience. What we have given to us . . . in the return part of the various transactions in which we take part just depends—surely! Why, I can remember only the other morning I was in my hair-dresser's—"

Mr. Bathurst interrupted him. He appeared to be devoted to the process of reflection. "The value of evidence, Sir John Brailsford, lies in the power of its accumulation. I have the advantage of you, I know, so that the conditions are unfair, as regards comparison. When you hear more, you will understand better. My advantage accrues from knowledge. Let me transfer that knowledge to you. On the twenty-second of October, last autumn, that is, the Honourable Phyllis Welby, the daughter of Lord Sturt, died as the result of a motoring accident on the outskirts of Loxeter. Miss Welby was a well-known figure in London society. When Miss Welby was picked up, it was discovered—amongst other things—that she possessed, in money, an exceedingly small sum for a lady of her social position . . . all in coins of *copper*."

Sir John Brailsford wrinkled his brows in perplexity. Peter seemed the victim of incredulous amazement. Sir John translated this new interest into words.

"Extraordinary! I begin to understand you better now, Lotherington. As you say yourself—this new feature makes an enormous difference. It puts an entirely new complexion on the matter."

Anthony smiled at Sir John's changed front. "I am glad that I have succeeded in impressing you, Sir John. And I have not yet finished. On the contrary, rather. On the eleventh of April of this year, a Miss Vera Sinclair was found dead at a place called East

Hannington. Again, according to all visible external evidence, as the result of a motoring 'accident.'"

"Good God!" cried Peter excitedly.

"Perhaps," returned Mr. Bathurst. "But we don't know. The devil probably has personality."

Sir John Brailsford stared. "And this last case that you mention—this Miss Sinclair—it was Sinclair, the name, wasn't it—were there similar—?"

Anthony bowed. "When Vera Sinclair's body was picked up, it was found that she was carrying eleven-pence . . . once again all in coins of *copper*. I *think* it was elevenpence. But that is immaterial. At any rate, I am certain that the value of her money amounted to less than a shilling."

For a time neither Sir John Brailsford nor Peter spoke. The terms of Anthony's full indictment had stunned them.

"Well, gentlemen," he said quietly—"I think you see now why I am interested in this affair at Great Kirby. It has its points, hasn't it?"

"I should think it had," cried Sir John. "Have you told the police? Don't *they* suspect these things?"

"In reality, Sir John, 'these things'—using your own phrase— are somewhat different in the appearance which they present when told as I have told them to you, than they appear to the eye of authority. I have exaggerated, perhaps, the significances, in order that you should perceive them the more clearly. All that makes a vast difference, you must admit. Besides—who am I to hold theories? A humble reporter whose copy as likely as not never sees print. So give the police time to collect themselves. It never does to stampede them into action. For all you and I know, they may be looking into one or two matters even now."

"The inquests don't suggest that that's likely," contributed Peter with a shake of the head.

"The verdicts, do you mean?"

"Yes. They've all been 'accidental death'—haven't they? Well—if that's—"

"That's true. But even that fact may mean much less than you imagine. On occasions, you know, the police have a knack of hiding their real intentions. They're very clever with it. The history of crime has taught us that fairly frequently. I could quote you innumerable instances."

Sir John Brailsford nodded his understanding. "Oh . . . yes . . . that is so, I know. I've noticed it myself. There are notorious examples of such happenings. There was Alloway . . . the Iford murderer of Irene Wilkins, and another instance of similar action on the part of the police was the Browne and Kennedy Case."

"Yes. And it may be so in this instance, Sir John. As I just said—who am I to assert otherwise?"

Sir John's appetite had been whetted. He desired more. "What are the other points about the affair that have struck you, Lotherington? You've interested me so much that I—"

Anthony shook his head deprecatingly. "I'd rather not dilate on them, Sir John—if you will excuse me. They're much too vague and too undefined altogether. They're merely wraiths of thought . . . wisps as you might say . . . just floating about in my mind without proper direction or controlled impulse. Whether they will ever become definite and worthy of recording is problematical. But, all the same, a fourth girl may die . . . and be found with still more . . . copper coins." Anthony shrugged his shoulders and laughed whimsically. "Well—goodbye, sir. I'm pleased to have made your acquaintance. Good-bye to you, too, Brailsford, for the present, at least. I'm returning to town almost immediately." The two men shook hands with him. "I shall read your account in tomorrow's *Morning Message* with great interest, Lotherington," said Sir John.

Anthony laughed again. "It will be quite bare. So that I'm afraid that you may be disappointed, sir. No trimmings. No embroideries. No hints. No veiled innuendoes. No suggestions. And not the slightest soupçon of sensation."

Sir John raised his eyebrows at Anthony's emphasis. "No?"

Anthony smiled. "Not yet, sir. Give me time! Consider the building of Rome. . . ."

"I see. Why yes . . . of course. 'Pon my soul, Lotherington, you've made me as interested as yourself in the matter. Your enthusiasm's infectious, my boy—I'm damned if it isn't."

"I'm sorry, sir. But it's partly your own fault, you know. Look what you've done! What did you want to ask questions for?"

Sir John laughed heartily. "Ah . . . well. Goodbye. Promise me this, though. Keep Peter and me in touch—generally speaking, that is. Will you?"

"That's on, sir. Good-bye." Anthony waved his hand to him as his car made pace out of the village of Great Kirby. Sir John Brailsford and his son Peter waved the farewell back to him.

Chapter VI
BUCKINGER

Anthony, upon his return to town, dined at his flat with fastidious selection and characteristic appreciation. He then repaired to his bookcase—an action which he had deliberately delayed until after dinner.

"Buckinger," he murmured to himself. "Mr. Matthew Buckinger. I shall be more than interested to read what I may of him." He took down his gazetteer, went back to his armchair and turned up the second letter of the alphabet. He found the name "Buckinger" with but little trouble and read the following. "Matthew Buckinger was in many respects perhaps the most wonderful dwarf in history, if only for the fact that he was, in many connections, unique. But 29 inches in height, he was born without hands, without feet and without thighs, on the 2nd of June in the year 1674." Anthony nodded to himself approvingly. He had been right then in what he had said to Dexter. He read on. "His birthplace was near Nuremberg in the Marquisate of Brandenburg, in Germany. He was the last of nine children by one father of one mother. To these parents were born eight sons and one daughter. Buckinger himself was married four times and had issue eleven children, one by his first wife, three by his second, six by his third and one by his fourth wife. He performed such 'Wonders' as had never been done by any but himself. He was skilled to play on various sorts of Music to admiration. Among them were the Hauteboy, the Flute in consort with the Bagpipe, the Dulcimer and the Trumpet—over all of which instruments he had obtained clear mastery. He also designed intricate machines that played almost all kinds of sweet Music. He was no less eminent in the art of Calligraphy, in the Drawing of Coats of Arms, and 'Pictures to the Life' with a pen. He was able to play at Cards and Dice, he performed incredibly clever tricks with Cups and Balls, Corn and Live Birds and could play at Skittles and Ninepins to a great nicety. He was also the author of several other performances to the general satisfaction of all spectators. His picture was most curious. His arms were extraordinarily short and ended in stumps of hands with only rudimentary digits. His legs similarly ended abruptly, but with an indication of division. He dressed with extreme smartness and in the height of fashion, usually affecting a stylish coat adorned with handsome braid. He also wore a full-bottom wig. He is reputed to have left to his heirs a remarkable portrait of himself which he described in his private papers as his 'effigies.' In this portrait, the wig, to which reference has been made, is perhaps the most remarkable feature of all. It is most elaborately curled and on each curl is most minutely engraved a text taken from the Bible. The longest of these curls holds the words, 'As a sheep before his shearers is dumb.' If Matthew Buckinger were indeed the artist of this portrait, as is commonly reputed, the claims made for him by his contemporaries do not seem to be so very extravagant. This account is taken almost *verbatim* from an article about him which appeared in an old magazine on the 29th of April, 1724."

Anthony Bathurst returned the book to the bookcase and lay back in his armchair. A curious coincidence certainly. Why did this man of L'Estrange's call himself Buckinger? And how and why in the name of goodness or evil had Clare Kent come into contact with him? He had impressed her so much that in the words of John Dexter, her brother-in-law, she had been "full of him." That she had met him and witnessed some of his "performances" of which Dexter had spoken seemed moderately certain. But where had she met him? Where *could* they have encountered each other? The longer that Anthony considered the question, the more positive he became that the point of meeting must have been either in or at "L'Estrange's Travelling Showground." He knew that Phyllis Welby had been there. Out of the best of all knowledge, He had seen her there! Well, then—Clare Kent must have been there too. Taken all in all, matters were clarifying. Not a lot, perhaps, but enough to be evident. But it was borne upon him most forcibly that there were several things that he absolutely must do before the stream of Time rolled very far onward. With pen and paper he listed them. Main principles first, *(a)* He must attack the Welby case, *(b)* He must attack the Sinclair case and *(c)* he must hammer away at the Clare Kent end of the tangle. Arising as subordinate out of these three lines of main campaign, he must *(1)* interview Margaret Fletcher, who not only knew Phyllis Welby and had been with her just prior to her death, but who also lived at East Hannington. *(2)* He must try to find connections of Vera Sinclair, *(3)* he must endeavour to find a certain person by name of Harding Argyle, and *(4)* he must have a look round the premises of this sinister night-club in the neighbourhood of Bellenden Street, which rejoiced in the appellation of "The Purple Calf." In addition, he decided that "L'Estrange's Travelling Showground" must perforce receive from him a certain measure of additional attention. There was that little matter of Tafari, for example. Anthony Bathurst filled his pipe and extended his lithe length in the armchair. Elimination! Concentration! Reflection! The harnessing of thoughts to the chariot of the brain. The organisation of ideas. He had always argued that mental process can never be static. Its action is not like the action of water that flows steadily between banks, but more akin to a central and almost circular movement. Like to a stone that is tossed into a pool and produces an ever-widening succession of circular ripples. He surrendered himself to an exercise in concentrated thought. The copper coins . . . the fair with its lights and garish noise. Phyllis Welby there, as he himself had seen her . . . the overturned cars . . . the bodies in the road with their dislocated spines, broken shoulder-blades and cut wrists. Girls. Young girls. Not girls belonging to the same society set. These were differences that hit you. First, Lord

Sturt's daughter, then an ordinary girl from a country district, and after them, a moderately-successful actress. Anthony puffed steadily at his pipe. Clouds of tobacco smoke floated around him and seemed to make a halo about his head. The injuries to these three girls. He must consider them again. Phyllis Welby—dislocation of spinal column, broken shoulder-blades, and marks on wrists. Vera Sinclair, head almost cut off by jagged glass, but *no* marks on wrists. Clare Kent—the latest of the three—as Phyllis Welby—dislocation of spinal column and the curious marks on the wrists. What else was there? Had the cars all *belonged* to the dead girls? There had been no question of the car in the case having been "supplied" as it were to set the stage and colour the picture for any one of the murders. That is to say as far as he knew. Again—where was this man L'Estrange himself? Why hadn't he been seen by Anthony on any of his visits? Had he purposely kept himself out of the way? Tafari—again! Here was yet another problem. Why had Tafari of the alligators run from the tent on the evening when Anthony and Peter Brailsford had visited L'Estrange's show? Mortal terror had shone in his eyes and Anthony Bathurst was certain that Tafari wasn't the man to run from mere shadows of fear. And Buckinger! A dwarf! Clare Kent had said that he could do marvellously clever things. A musician! A character in his way! A man who had charge of a collection of wax figures and who added to their attraction by reason of his own grotesqueness. Loxeter, East Hannington and now Great Kirby. The coincidence was far too remarkable to be resisted. He must be somewhere near the truth if only he could strike the right path. Those coins of copper that had so singularly persisted in the trio of cases ... they *must* mean something if the science of deduction had ever told him anything at all. *Had* there been anything of importance that had escaped him? *Was* there any point of vital consequence that he had overlooked? No case in which he had ever been engaged had entirely failed to illustrate the value of his own analytical methods. He had demonstrated the truth and soundness of them many times. To Sir Austin Kemble himself time after time. To Inspector Baddeley of the Sussex Constabulary in those strange affairs of the Considine billiard-room murder and the "Creeping Jenny" mystery, to Chief Inspector MacMorran of Scotland Yard and even to the famous Monsieur Le Gonidec, the Chief of Police of the Sûreté Générale. In this last reference, there was the occasion when he had solved the bizarre case of the "Orange Axe" and there was also the time when he had been privileged to give Le Gonidec considerable assistance in the affair of La Rothière, the execrable assassin of the Boulevards. When he had pointed out to Le Gonidec the damning significance of the clotted cream on the wheel of the car, the case was as good as over. Those coins . . . copper coins always . . . no silver . . . no notes . . . in the possession of these three murdered girls . . . murdered . . . he felt sure. That last fact definitely *not* within the region of guesswork. In the province rather, to use the words of the immortal wizard of Baker Street, "where we balance probabilities and choose the most likely. It is the scientific use of imagination, but we have always some material basis on which to start our speculations." If by any process of elimination or exhaustion he would be able to . . . suddenly Mr. Bathurst's senses tautened . . . most people belonging to the social stratum of two at least of these three girls, carried in their money, copper, silver and more often than not, currency notes. And these three girls had been left with copper coins only! Again and again he had come back to it. An idea came to him . . . his thoughts ran riot now with it . . . of course, he whispered to himself . . . that might be the explanation . . . it was on the cards certainly . . . he rose from his chair and went to his directory of London. He badly wanted more knowledge of Bellenden Street, and the surrounding property. His fingers came to the place. Bellenden Street . . . Morstan Street . . . Zionist Street . . . Petersfield Street . . . he searched them all thoroughly for the name he wanted . . . Coverdale Street . . . ah . . . at last . . . there it was—"The Purple Calf, Coverdale Street, No. 12." Anthony Bathurst put back the directory on its shelf and looked at his wrist-watch. What he saw there brought him to an instant decision. There was time for him to put in an appearance there that same night. Reversing Caesar, "The Purple Calf" appealed to him—to "The Purple Calf" he would go.

If he were to die to-morrow, that is what he would do to-night. Mr. Bathurst went to his room and started to change immediately—for he had dined alone and in comfort.

"Emily," he 'phoned downstairs, "tell Pollitt that I shall require the Chrysler."

Chapter VII
THE PURPLE CALF

Anthony parked his car in a Coverdale Street garage right at the west end of the street. The proprietor of the establishment seemed desperately anxious to impart inspired information. He spoke in a coarse whisper. "I suppose you'll be wantin' the Calf, sir? Yes? Number 12, sir. That's right. Straight up on the left. You can't miss it." He cocked an eloquent eye in Anthony's direction and became even more communicative. "Pretty hot place, too, sir. If you haven't been there before, that is. Bit of most things along there—so they tell me. Still, I expect you know as much about it as the next man. Thank you, sir."

Anthony smiled to himself as the man pocketed the gratuity; he then strolled quietly up this Coverdale Street. Judging by the number of cars parked in the garage that he had just left, "The Purple Calf" was doing good business that evening. When he arrived at the door of the "Calf," Mr. Bathurst found that the place was very much as he had anticipated. He had known something of its reputation for some time. There had been that case of Captain Andrew Forbes and "The Spiked Lion." Mr. Bathurst attached himself to a table next to the foot of the staircase.

The head waiter, who quickly arrived in full sail and complete obsequiousness, pointed out with much declamatory gesture, that this position which Anthony had chosen was by no means a favoured one. Anthony waved his objections to one side and in the grand manner ordered kippers and a bottle. The head waiter was immediately impressed by Mr. Bathurst's superb understanding and relayed the order to an underling with the fine careless rapture of keen appreciation. The cabaret show was just on the point of beginning and Anthony watched the preparations for it with keen interest. His attention was soon riveted on a woman with petunia-coloured hair who was haranguing a thin, supercilious-looking waiter with some measure of vehemence. A rather feeble cabaret show started and ran to its welcomed conclusion. Then dancing started. With a difference here, however! The band was excellent and the floor soon became covered with swaying couples. Anthony sat and watched ... and waited. But he knew not for what. Had he been interrogated, his answer to the question would have been "for anything or anybody that happens to turn up."

He finished his meal and ordered a second bottle of wine. The band played on and from the head waiter at regular and beautifully-calculated intervals, there came rapidly gesticulated orders. Mr. Bathurst scanned with interest the faces of the various dancing couples as they swept by his table. But he saw nothing in any one of them that excited his particular curiosity. After a time, however, Anthony noticed something that seemed just a little out of the ordinary. Something with regard to the conduct of the head waiter. Unless Mr. Bathurst were very much mistaken, this waiter-chap was shooting continual and regular glances towards the other end of the room. Anthony, under the pretence of perfect nonchalance, watched him more carefully. He wanted to make sure that this idea of his was right. Yes ... once ... twice, and yet again ... it happened, three times in quick succession. A quick, sharp, shrewd turn of the head with an accompanying look that might have been a signal for something. Anthony lit a cigarette with well-calculated fastidiousness, placed it in an inordinately-long holder, rose from his seat and sauntered along the side of the room. Coquettish invitations archly conveyed by the eye or by a movement of the head met him from all directions. He smiled with cynical tolerance upon them all without fear or favour ... but ... for the time being at least, Mr. Bathurst passed on. Later on perhaps. . . . When he came to the middle of the room he was surprised to find that his eyes were unable to pick out the head waiter. Look where he might, the man had vanished. But his disappearance was but momentary for piloting himself gently through a wedge of dancers Anthony saw the man again. He was now seated at a square, flat table, with his eyes bent assiduously over a long thin black book. Every now and then he nodded to himself with a show of satisfaction. This table was placed in a small recess or alcove right at the end of the room, and from where he stood, Anthony's eyes could discern behind this recess a door with a covering of green baize. Above this door a small electric light turned red and Anthony saw the head waiter watching this light with an industry and assiduousness that approximated fervour. As Anthony watched all this, the light over the door changed its colour to amber and immediately this took place the head waiter sprang to his feet and almost raced down the room to the flight of stairs. The dance band played with verve and zest. The dancers developed a greater gaiety and an increased irresponsibility. "The Calf" was being fatted for prodigal sons and their sisters and also for the Hours and Houris of Pleasure. The daughters thereof gathered themselves together, so that they might use their red lips and love ere love flew beyond recall. Anthony, in the rôle of onlooker, deliberately summoned himself to his highest pitch of mental and physical efficiency. He felt, that at any moment now, something might happen that would demand all his powers of intellect and in all probability help him towards the solution of his problem. Why exactly, he thought this, he didn't know. Possibly it travelled to him, by that sixth sense of instinct—the usual avenue of such happenings to most of us. His eyes still followed the quickly retreating figure of the head waiter. The man was in a seemingly devilish hurry. Anthony turned adroitly to avoid contact with two enthusiastic dancers . . . and at that moment there came the lightest of touches on his arm. He turned again . . . in the opposite direction from the way of the waiter . . . and saw an extremely charming little lady regarding him provocatively with lovely and challenging eyes.

Mr. Bathurst bowed to this new delight. It has been recorded of him by more than one chronicler . . . and truthfully . . . that in dress-clothes Anthony Bathurst cut an ideal figure. Also, that to the sex he was almost irresistible . . . when he so chose.

Tall and clean-limbed, broad-shouldered . . . keen-cut face that betokened the intelligence of the born thinker . . . grey eyes . . . with that lean hardness which always speaks eloquently of supreme physical fitness. . . . Anthony made an appeal which many ladies, in their time, had found undeniably attractive. In this gallery we may remember Pauline, Lady Fullgarney, Cecilia Cameron and even Rosemary Marquis. The girl's eyes were still holding his after he had bowed to her. "Charmingly pretty," he thought . . . "and exquisitely turned out even for a place like this . . . but why does she want to speak to me . . . and also, most important of all, perhaps, *who is she?*"

Then the girl found speech and simultaneously took his breath away. "You must forgive me for what must seem to you like the most awful cheek. But the coincidence was so remarkable that I simply couldn't resist it."

Anthony was thrilled to hear that her voice was an added charm in her equipment. The girl was almost too good to be true or maybe too true to be good. But the word which she had used surprised him.

"Coincidence?" he echoed after her. "I'm afraid that I don't understand."

"Come over here and talk," she said with a quick movement of the head, "please."

"Or over there?" returned Anthony, nodding in another direction. "I have a table over there, by the staircase. It's moderately comfortable and if one sits well back and tucks one's feet in, one isn't disturbed too much. What do you say?"

The girl nodded brightly. "Suits me," she said. "I know the table you mean. Letting you into a secret, I have sat there myself."

"You come here a lot, then," remarked Mr. Bathurst quietly. They reached Anthony's table.

This time a different waiter presented himself in the guise of obedient servant. Anthony raised his eyes to his companion. She continued the previous conversation.

"No. Not a lot. But I have been here two or three times in the past. Order me a Clover Club, please."

Anthony added the order to his own demands. This girl who sat at his side was beautiful, beyond a doubt. Her bare white neck glistened under the soft glow of the lights. She was quick and ardent of life, eager, vivid and anxious. He took in again, to his infinite satisfaction, *le tout ensemble* of desiring eyes, shell-pink of smoothest cheek, rose-red of parted lips, and heavy black cloud of hair.

"I am proud," said Anthony in his most gallant manner, "to be in the position in which I now find myself . . . but I confess that I am a little puzzled also. You spoke of coincidence. The word seemed uppermost in your mind. You shall tell me more. That little more . . . and how much . . . ?" He paused and looked at her inquiringly. For a fleeting instant the expression in the girl's eyes changed. The raillery and sophistication gave place to something deeper and more real. Light-heartedness or its simulation yielded to serious purpose. Her eyelids flickered. The mask was down even though its lowering was to be of scant duration.

"Yes," she said quietly . . . "coincidence . . . and to me, untutored, and not too used to such happenings, a most marvellous coincidence. For this is the second time, sir, that I have seen you to-day."

Anthony took the shock and deliberately steadied himself. These hours at "The Purple Calf" were not destined to be wasted after all. He affected disinterestedness.

"Really? Well—what of it? And is such a thing so strange? In London of all places? The largest city in the world?"

As he came to grips with her the dainty colour in her cheeks darkened a little. She lifted her glass to her lips and drank. Then she smiled and shook her head.

"No. Looked at in that way—it isn't. But you haven't got it right. I shouldn't have waylaid you if things had happened as ordinarily as that. You're miles out. It's because they happened so differently that I felt that I must speak to you. You see—I'm interested—very very interested. When I tell you all the circumstances, you'll understand. I saw you for the first time this morning. At no less a place than Great Kirby. In the Central Mission Hall, Great Kirby. At an inquest on the body of a girl named Clare Kent. The verdict was 'accidental death.' She was killed . . . according to the jury at Great Kirby . . . in a motoring accident. As far as I know I had never seen you before in my life. Until then! Then, in the space of a few brief hours, I see you again . . . in a place many miles from Great Kirby . . . and in a place, too, where I don't think you really belong. That's why I prattled of coincidence. Please acquit me immediately of anything like foolishness."

Now that she had supplied him with the facts, she recovered a little of her former manner. Anthony came to a quick decision and decided to walk warily. Although she had had her voice well under control, it had nevertheless wavered a little on its lowest notes. But he knew that she had spoken with deliberate intention and meaning for she had so carefully marshalled her sentences. For a moment or so he was irresolute as to his opening gambit. He had expected something from the encounter, it is true . . . but nothing like this. The girl finished her cocktail and put her glass between them. She was waiting.

"Suppose we are frank with each other," he suggested . . . "perfectly and utterly frank. Yes?"

She nodded in quick agreement. "That is what I would wish myself. I would not ask for any other condition. My name is Margaret Fletcher. What's yours?"

Anthony hesitated—but for a split second only.

"Bathurst," he said quietly, "A.L. Bathurst."

Margaret Fletcher's hands went to her lips and her eyes opened wide in surprise. "Not Anthony Bathurst?" she said in a hushed, strained voice. "*The* Anthony Bathurst?"

"I cannot contradict you," came the reply . . . "much as it is my most earnest desire to give you the best in Life. I regret extremely that the name should strike such terror at your heart. Please commence by forgiving my negligences and ignorances."

"It isn't that," she said, "even taking you seriously—as I know you don't mean me to. It's just . . . oh—I can't explain."

"I will attempt to help you then. I can do so—easily. I have been concerned with you, Miss Fletcher, since October last. Ten months to be exact. I'll tell you why. On the 27th of October you interested me. On the 11th of April I decided that it would be as well if we met. On the 17th of August I realised that we positively *must* meet. You knew Phyllis Welby. You were probably the last person—"

She put a restraining hand upon his arm and checked him. "Don't say any more—please! I am beginning to understand. Well?"

"Well?" His eyes commanded her.

"What do you want?"

He shrugged his shoulders. "That's hardly fair, you know. In the circumstances."

"What's hardly fair?"

"Asking me that."

"Tell me this, then. What are you doing here?"

His grey eyes twinkled attractively. "The same as other people apparently."

"Oh—you're hopeless. I wish you men weren't so sure of your own strength. I'll try again. Why did you go to Great Kirby?"

"Why did you?"

She stamped her foot. "Heavens! And you agreed to be *frank*," she said between set teeth.

"So did you." Anthony smiled maddeningly.

She half rose from her chair. Anthony gently pulled her down again. "Come now—it's not so bad as all that. Silence at times may be extraordinarily eloquent. What can you tell me about Vera Sinclair?"

"S'sh," she said with a peremptory gesture and a quick glance round. "You mustn't be so indiscreet. I feel that you take an awful risk mentioning names like that . . . in here." She lowered her voice, fingered the stem of her glass, and without looking at him, almost whispered . . . "I *was* right, then. You *do* know something, after all. Tell me, please, Mr. Bathurst—what do you suspect?"

Anthony replied quietly and unemotionally. The conditions were of definite purpose and intention.

"I have heard of Phyllis Welby . . . of Vera Sinclair . . . and of Clare Kent . . . how the three of them died . . . *and I am not satisfied.*" He spoke the last words incredibly softly.

Miss Fletcher's fingers worked convulsively. "Oh, thank God I was right," she murmured . . . "you are an ally, and not—but why are you *here*? In this place. What do you suspect that has made you come *here*? To Coverdale Street?"

Anthony deliberately chose his words. "There was a man named Dexter at Great Kirby. He was Miss Kent's brother-in-law. He gave evidence. He was the first to give evidence. Do you remember him?"

She nodded. "Oh—yes. Of course."

"Dexter told me things . . . after the inquest. Momentous things. I made him. Don't think that Dexter got talkative generally and used a megaphone. I intercepted him and asked him questions of malice aforethought. About Clare Kent. He talked. I must have been irresistibly persuasive. Amongst other pieces of information, I gleaned that the dead girl had, upon occasion, come here. Hence these actions of mine. I followed scent."

Margaret Fletcher turned her head slightly to one side and looked at him shrewdly. "That's rather unconvincing—considering everything. You met Dexter—you say—at Great Kirby. Which makes me wonder. Because it means that you went to Great Kirby *before* you met him. You probably didn't know that he was going to be there. Something took you to Great Kirby. What—Mr. Bathurst?"

The dancing by now was taking on greater pace and "The Purple Calf" was growing fuller than ever. The band played with enthusiasm and seemed on top of its form. Anthony beckoned again to a waiter who hovered near and ordered more drinks.

"I will tell you. I was in Loxeter when Phyllis Welby was killed. Last October. Unfortunately though, I was abroad round about the time when Vera Sinclair died and I was prevented from returning until some time afterwards. But I read enough into the two "accidents" to expect a third case of a similar kind. As you know . . . I have not been disappointed. Most distinctly has my expectation been realised." He interpreted her look. "Oh yes, Miss Fletcher . . . I thoroughly agree with you . . . I censure myself. *Mea culpa* and *Peccavi*. Each an excellent exercise. Have no illusions on that score—I simply ask you to grant me one concession only. That shall be my sole apologia. It's different 'suspecting' evil and being in a position to identify it and destroy it. That second condition takes time and *may* depend upon opportunity. But we're getting hold a little now."

"Who's 'we'?" she instantly flashed at him.

He smiled. "Call it either the royal or the editorial plural—I leave you a free and unhampered choice. Pick whichever you prefer."

She ignored the semi-evasion and pressed her point home.

"Do you mean the police?"

"You may understand that *actually* I hold no official position whatever. I simply 'meddle with crime.' That, I believe, is how the superlatively clever describe it. You know the people I mean—they usually 'sit on committees' and 'believe in service for others.' Whatever that may mean. I have my own version, of course. This activity is the pre-eminent English vice. You've no idea how your insinuation disheartens me. I'm Irish, you see, and possibly over-sensitive. But with all their faults the Irish have ideals which few English people can understand. In all my career I've only met twenty-two Englishmen who valued 'doing' things more than 'having' things. No, Miss Fletcher, at the moment I am playing a lone hand." He glanced quickly at her and fancied that he detected a look of something like relief pass across her features. Anthony continued. "Now—to our preliminary bargain. Frankness for frankness and confession for confession. A Childe Roland for a Bath Oliver. What do *you* suspect? Or—possibly—*know*?" He changed his voice purposely to a steadier and harder note. Long lashes that fringed lovely eyes grew moist beneath his probing.

"Phyllis was my friend. The closest that I had. That I have ever had. As I've no doubt you know, I was with her just before . . . she went to Loxeter. And because I knew her so well I am certain of one thing. Her visit to Loxeter was vitally *important* to her. I *know*, from her manner beforehand, that it was something very different from an ordinary everyday visit. It held greater consequences."

Anthony nodded understandingly. "I remember the evidence that you gave before the Coroner's jury. I remember your actual words. You said then that Miss Welby was 'Looking forward.' Candidly, *I took pains* to remember your actual words."

"That is so, Mr. Bathurst, I did say that." She paused and looked distressed. "Oh—it's a long story and I'm telling it the wrong way round. I'm perfectly hopeless at being lucid . . . and . . . clear. I always seem to begin in the middles of things. Let me try to sort things out for you so that you may understand better. I live with my people at a little country place called East Hannington. The nearest town's Altminster. Stephen, that's my brother, he's my half-brother really, but I call him my brother, comes here pretty regularly—comes up to town on purpose to come here. He and another boy with whom he's been friendly for some time now. This other boy—whom I've never met—lives in town, so that the place is quite handy for him. Stephen met Phyllis here . . . in 'The Purple Calf' . . . over a year ago. I didn't come here then. Don't think that. My first visit is only a fortnight old. That surprises you—doesn't it? I'm not absolutely sure, but I think that Stephen was in love with Phyllis. As far as a girl can tell in the case of her brother. Any old how . . . I can truthfully say from what I know now that they were attracted by each other. I'm dead sure of that. And the affair between them— or whatever understanding it was—developed. After a time, Stephen brought Phyllis to East Hannington. To our place. We often have little house-parties there and she came quite a lot." Margaret Fletcher leant forward eagerly across the table. "Am I interesting you?"

Anthony Bathurst smiled encouragingly. "Go on. You're doing splendidly. My luck almost takes my breath away. Some of my blank squares are actually filled in already."

"Phyllis often begged me to come to 'The Purple Calf' with them. It seemed to me that she wanted company. I always refused. For one thing, I didn't think that Stephen was desperately keen on having me as an attachment and secondly I love the countrywide and open air. Night life and late hours don't agree with me too well. So I stayed away and refused to honour the place with my gracious presence. Let me see. Where had I reached? Last August and September . . . all the latter end of the summer, in fact, Phyllis was at East Hannington staying with us. In all, she stayed for six or seven weeks. She and Stephen would pop up to town in the evening. Not every evening—I don't mean that—but fairly frequently. Three or four times each week—on an average. Then . . . one morning . . . I noticed something about Phyllis that made me 'think things.' It was a morning after the night before . . . a night when I knew that she and my brother had been here at 'The Purple Calf.' She was . . . depressed . . . downcast, and her looks showed it too. But the phase passed off and before the end of the day she became more or less herself again. Some time elapsed . . . a fortnight I should think perhaps . . . and then one morning I observed that she was moody and dispirited again. *And again, Mr. Bathurst, it was on a morning following upon a visit to 'The Purple Calf.'* But by the end of September all her depression had gone and as a natural result I paid no more attention to it. She got back to all her old spirits." Miss Fletcher paused, to proceed almost at once. "You see— when the Coroner at Loxeter asked me those questions about her at the inquest, I didn't feel that I *could* go back all those weeks. I mean about Phyl being dispirited and depressed. Who would have understood? There seemed no point in my doing so. It would have seemed so irrelevant—so beside the point . . . when all that she might have been suffering from was a headache or a bilious attack. Well . . . she was killed, poor kid . . . and I've thought about her death ever since. More than anyone will ever realise. I had but two facts to go on. The one about which I have just been telling you . . . and one other . . . the one which has really brought me here."

Anthony at once put his curiosity into words. "Which was . . . Miss Fletcher? Believe me, I'm desperately anxious to hear it."

She gave her body a little shake as though the idea of which she wanted to rid herself had been a physical attachment.

"Don't be too sure. You may be absurdly disappointed when you hear what it is. It may have nothing more to do with the case than I have myself. But you must know that one morning I came up to town to do some special shopping and to have a photograph taken. Let me see—when would it have been? I think that it was in the early autumn." She made a mental calculation. "Yes. I thought so. It was the first week in October. I had been to a photographer's, in Berkeley Square, and I was coming down Hay Hill. Phyllis, much to my surprise, was walking along but a few yards in front of me. I had not the slightest idea, you see, that she was anywhere in the neighbourhood because Stephen had told me that she had gone to a friend's place to stay—near Albyns. Now listen to this . . . because here comes the whole point of the story. With Phyllis, as she walked in front of me, was a man . . . a man whom I had never seen before." Anthony leant towards her for the complete revelation. Miss Fletcher continued her narrative. "A strange-looking man . . . and yet, without a doubt, a man of rare distinction."

"Describe him, Miss Fletcher, please . . . with as many details as you can supply," said Anthony softly.

"He was a very dark man. On the tall side. A foreigner, I should say, from the half-look which I was able to get at him. Yet I can't say what country would claim him. You can take it from me that he was a man of most unusual type. Oh . . . something else . . . he wore a monocle." She put a hand on Anthony's arm and lowered her voice. "If you want to know these things, the head waiter has been watching us rather closely for some little time. I don't like the look in his eyes. Mr. Bathurst—there are many mysterious features about this place called 'The Purple Calf.' More than once I have found them frightening me. Dance with me . . . please. It may serve to distract their attention."

Anthony smiled at the sudden request. "Alas . . . I am no dancer, Miss Fletcher. Don't tell me that you are too terribly disappointed. Surely there's a place where we can gamble . . . or at least watch others equally spiritually engaged. Wherever it is . . . we can go there and come back. It will do something to remove us from the head waiter's vigilant eye. There's bound to be a . . ."

She beckoned him to follow her. "How silly of me. I had forgotten for the moment. Of course. Come down this staircase."

Chapter VIII
"AND GUIDE US WHEN PERPLEXED"

NINE stairs down the staircase towards which Miss Fletcher had directed him, Anthony knew that their movements had been signalled by certain of "The Purple Calf" entourage and that they were actually being followed. He put his arm within Margaret Fletcher's with an air of careless proprietorship.

"Commonplace chatter and saccharine nothings from now onwards," he whispered to her . . . "little more than that. Mere prattlings and more prattlings of small consequence. You have my permission to become offensively unintelligent. I'm afraid that you are right. We have aroused an unhealthy interest. The explanation must be that we are a particularly handsome couple."

They passed into a room where *chemin de fer* and baccarat were being played. The door of the apartment was ostentatiously labelled "Refreshments," but Margaret Fletcher walked towards it confidently and pushed it open.

"This is only my third visit to the 'Calf,' but there's one thing, I've found my way about pretty well. I was born with the priceless bump of locality. What will you do? Which would you prefer? Play or watch?"

Anthony gave question for question. "Is this place ever raided, do you know? I love to be herded together." As he spoke, a big, square-shouldered man drew abreast of him in the doorway, and deliberately stared him up and down. Anthony watched him . . . lazy-eyed and nonchalant. The man seemed to be on the point of speaking but it is a distinct possibility that a certain lurking gleam in the grey eyes of Mr. Bathurst may have served to deter him.

Margaret sensed atmosphere and played up gallantly. "Oh . . . yes, it was a perfectly marvellous show, I believe. So Stephen told me. He saw the *première*." The big man moved away. Miss Fletcher allowed herself to be serious. "A raid's nothing like as bad as anyone might be inclined to believe. But a thrill of thrills all the same if you're feeling in the right mood. The police appear on the stairs there." She pointed behind her at the staircase which they had just descended. "At any rate, some of them do. Others, Stephen says, walk pompously about in pairs, and take, equally pompously, the names and addresses of the social sinners. These obtained, they are put with appropriate ceremonial garnish into a note-book, to be learned and conned by rote. Stephen made me die when he told me about it. I positively curled up with laughter. The night he was here and the police, came down after the manner of Sennacherib, there were no less than nineteen Hepplethwaites from Manchester. And sixteen of these nineteen called themselves 'Joshua.'" Margaret shrieked. The door closed behind them and they approached the gaming tables to stand on the fringe of the crowd. The big man, who had favoured Anthony Bathurst a moment previously with such a show of attention, had come back and now moved a few paces in front of them.

"We'll watch, I think," remarked Anthony. "Lookers on you know" . . . he added significantly. As unobtrusively as possible they drifted up to the players. As they came into the circle of play, Anthony was conscious of much bustle and noise. Margaret flung conversational commonplaces and fatuous frills at him which he parried and returned in like manner. He has said since that he was badly scared that he would be taken for a Member of Parliament. Half an hour went by in this fashion. The big man alternated between immediate proximity and moderate distance. But he was at no time very far away from them. It was clear to Anthony that the man intended to hear all that they had to say.

"Where's your car?" asked Anthony of his companion. "I'm going to be terribly ungallant and suggest that you're looking *épuisée* . . . and I think I've seen and heard enough for one night. Matters certainly aren't exciting."

"In a garage at the end of Coverdale Street. But don't worry about me getting home if that's what you're thinking of. Stephen's going to drive me home. It's about time he turned up. Even now he's later than usual." She looked at her watch in order to check the statement. "Yes . . . it's half an hour past his usual time."

"Is he a punctual sort of bloke in the ordinary way . . . this brother of yours?" asked Anthony.

"Very," she replied decisively. "Stephen is absolutely reliable and efficient in everything he undertakes. In fact he stands out among the men of my acquaintance for those qualities. Most of them are hopelessly sloppy and unreliable. Mediocrity flourishes like the green bay these days."

"Will he come down here?"

"He may. He does sometimes. Not so much though since Phyllis died." She wrinkled her brows in thought. "Somehow I don't think he will to-night. I think that he'll probably stay upstairs. He may even be there now. Let's go back there . . . we may find him. Are you fit?"

Anthony, thinking hard, took her arm and piloted her through the crowds at the various gaming tables. As they walked, he whispered, "Before we go upstairs . . . let me say this, I may not have another chance . . . as favourable . . . to arrange anything . . . I'll meet you here again . . . I must . . . not to-morrow night . . . say the night after . . . quick . . . can you manage it?"

She bit her lips. "The night after to-morrow . . . yes . . . I think I can."

"Say nothing to anybody . . . about me . . . or meeting me . . . very well then . . . we'll leave it at that."

They came to the top of the staircase and reached the room above. Margaret's quick eyes scanned the crowd of loungers and dancers. "I can't see Stephen . . . he doesn't seem to have arrived yet . . . but never mind . . . don't you wait. I'd much rather you didn't. I shall be all right. He's bound to come. He won't fail me—he's never let me down yet." She smiled assuringly and gave him her hand in farewell.

Anthony took it appropriately and then suddenly turned to go. His turn was quicker than an onlooker might have anticipated and the big man with the square shoulders, who was still shepherding him, had to display unwonted alertness to avoid an awkward collision.

"Your pardon," murmured Anthony mellifluously, "but from your attention to me this evening we might almost be cousins. Cousins—'a state of consanguinity.'"

"I beg your pardon," growled the man.

"You most certainly should," said Anthony... "it was undeniably indicated."

The man scowled uncompromisingly. "I don't mean that. I didn't hear what you said to me."

"Oh... that. Don't grieve over your loss... it's immaterial, I assure you. I was merely alluding to our condition of evident consanguinity... that was all."

The man drew back a trifle and muttered something under his breath. Anthony fancied that he heard offensive words... "bloody fool."

"In the circumstances and considering my last remark," he said, "I must congratulate you on the appropriateness of the adjective. There is so much in the selection of the right word. Good night."

Outside "The Purple Calf," he made his way slowly down Coverdale Street towards the establishment where he had left his car. He assessed values... raked the ashes of remembrance ... then shook his head in perplexity.

"Curiouser and curiouser," quoth Mr. Bathurst. But suddenly he smiled and rubbed his hands.

On the whole he had most certainly made progress.

Chapter IX
HEARTS A'FLUTTER

There was bustle in fields that morning. Men, boys and women moved with alacrity about their individual tasks. L'Estrange's Travelling Showground was on the move again. The tents had been folded and the tent-pitchers were far from silently stealing away again. The cavalcade started and gradually got under way. It passed through the northern outskirts of Friningham itself, some miles beyond Great Kirby, and had for its next objective the neighbouring town of St. Leydon. But, even to the most casual of observers, it would have been noticeable that something unusual was afoot. The normal atmosphere of the retinue was changed and another had taken its place. Rumours were rife. There were regular times in the routine of L'Estrange's when the ordinary atmosphere *did* change and this was assuredly one of them. Men whispered soft words to each other behind the backs of their hands. But the softness had menace not music. And always the whisper was in the same words. "'The Duke's' back. And Lafferty." Some, to whom this shred of information was passed on, asked countering questions. "When? Have you seen him yourself or has somebody told you?" Most of the questions received head-shakes and mumblings for answers. But Sargeant, the man who worked the "chair-o-plane," told Crouch that the "Duke" had interviewed him and had given him certain instructions. Crouch told Buckinger at the first opportunity that came and noticed that the latter shivered and went pale at the news. "Look slippy this morning, Bucky lad, or the Duke'll know the reason why. Sargeant says he's white at the gills which don't spell healthy weather for us truly—by no means." Crouch chuckled at the Buckinger's discomfiture. The latter went off to Big Molly, who, for some reason, had always had a certain fondness for him. No matter how Big Molly was feeling, she always found time for little kindnesses to Buckinger. So the news of the "Duke's" return came to the women of L'Estrange's. To Molly, to Rosina and to Annabel. "The 'Duke's' back. The 'Duke' himself. A week before his time. Lafferty, too! What's afoot? What will it mean? Who this time?" Faces paled and snatches of song died on the lips of those who had conjured them. It can be said with little fear of contradiction, that only one member of the show heard the words that spoke of the "Duke's" return entirely unmoved. Reference is made to the man who trained alligators, the swarthy, cadaverous Lieutenant Rame Tafari. When Tafari heard the news, he screwed his monocle more tightly into his eye, wiped his lips daintily with his handkerchief and smiled sardonically. He adjusted the bandage on his arm which the movement had slightly displaced and became fluently profane. His profanity ended, he resumed his air of indifference, rolled a cigarette and looked across the fields lazing fallow in the haze of the morning sun. Their reddish yellow tints coloured the landscape.

"So he's back, is he, the cunning swine?" he muttered to himself, "and all his filthy retinue shiver in their shoes at the mere thought of it. What a bunch of yellow streaks! God . . . what scum! Ah . . . well . . . this time we shall see who's the better man. . . . I fancy that I remember a proverb of this atrocious country about the comparative value of laughing last." The thought had barely passed through his mind when he saw the young man Lafferty coming towards him, between the vehicles, as the line of them slowly turned and negotiated a corner of the long, flat, winding road. The unsightly red scar across the young fellow's cheek, always heavily powdered, looked more prominent than ever, as he came into Tafari's view. His slightly opened mouth intensified his suggestion of simplicity. Tafari smiled grimly at the savour of reminiscence.

"Morning, Lieutenant," said Lafferty as the two men came face to face. It was the custom at L'Estrange's to give Tafari the title under which he appeared on the bills. It was universally known that Tafari liked it and that fact alone counted for a lot. Nobody knew, with any degree of accuracy, whether it had been assumed or not—but the "Duke" himself used it in early days . . . and that—believe me—was an excellent precedent for the remaining members of the show to follow in the "Duke's" suit. Indeed, the same thing may be said with regard to most activities that held sway at L'Estrange's. The "Duke" was "Sir Oracle" to his servants and there were few dogs there that had ever barked when the "Duke's" mouth had been opened.

Tafari's lip curled in pointed and almost contemptuous indifference as Lafferty fell into step abreast of him.

"Good morning, Lafferty. So you're with us again—eh? Life has taken on an added savour. 'Pon my soul, even the birds are singing more sweetly. I myself breathe freely again."

An ugly light flashed in Lafferty's eyes but it died down as quickly as it had flickered into being, and his answer, when it came, was given with all his usual sullenness. It might have been that Lafferty had deliberately checked an impulse, on the other hand, it may have been that Tafari's assertion of personality and projection of individuality were the stronger and that Lafferty recognised the fact, and his consciousness of inferiority encompassed him. For a time, he made no reply to Tafari's stinging satire. Then he embraced discretion and eschewed commonplaces for essentials.

"The 'Duke' sent me along to see you," he said in his hoarse, strained voice—the voice that shouted in front of the booths most afternoons and every evening when and where 'L'Estrange's' had 'pitched'—"he wants you punctually at midday—he says. At the first halting place, I was to tell you. And you're to bring your book without fail, he says. 'The book that you've kept since April.' You know what that means. Is that O.K. with you, Lieutenant?"

"That is O.K. with me, my excellent Lafferty. I, Rame Tafari, shall be present at the ducal interview. With book. And record." He rolled another cigarette with the utmost nonchalance and then turned deliberately to his companion. "You'll be gettin' dizzy soon, son . . . won't you?" Tafari's voice was dangerously quiet and even.

"What do you mean?" queried Lafferty.

"Well . . . suppose we put it like this, so's you can understand me better. The 'Duke' and you! You and the 'Duke.' Joint counsels. The 'Duke' and the dustman." Tafari burst into turbulent temper. "What are you doing now, you scarred bastard, but givin' me orders? Me—Rame Tafari who before now . . . has—" Tafari paused. The blaze of burning wrath that had sprung so suddenly into flaming fire subsided almost as quickly. "Scram"—he said bitingly . . . "before I amuse myself with you, you hell-deserving brat." He put the cigarette that he had just rolled, to his lips, lit it with a steady hand, and puffed its smoke deliberately into Lafferty's eyes. Then Rame Tafari turned on his arrogant heel and strode away towards the rear of the L'Estrange cavalcade. He liked that particular position . . . he could see all that was to be seen without being observed himself.

For an electric moment, there seemed to have been born of this last insult a new Lafferty... the promise of a man who one day and that not very far distant, would throw off the fetters of servility which were now shackling him and bloom in his own strength. He quickened his step so that he should keep better pace with the lumbering wagon at the side of which he was walking. As he moved forward, he had caught sight of Buckinger a few paces in front of him. Lafferty overtook the tiny figure and called sharply to him.

"Bucky, I want you."

Buckinger turned at the voice and slowed his pace down to allow Lafferty to overtake him. Lafferty repeated to him the message that he had just delivered to Tafari.

"The 'Duke' wants you at midday, Bucky. You and some of the others. At the first stopping place—he told me to tell you. Bring your book—so that the 'Duke' can see all the details since last April. Understand?"

Buckinger nodded, and suggested a curious sagacity. "How is he, Lafferty?" he asked anxiously. "Is he—?"

"How d'ye mean, Bucky?"

The little body seemed to shrink in fear. "What sort of temper is he in... that's what I mean, boy? You know!"

Lafferty drew the back of his hand across his face and wiped away the sweat that had beaded his brow.

"He ain't exactly sweet, Bucky... but on the whole I've known him worse, more vicious. What's come to all of you these days? What's bin doin' while the 'Duke's' been away. Seems to me you're all shiverin' in your shoes what I can see of things... like a pack of snivellin' kids, I call it. Reckon the 'Duke' and me's been away too long... that's what's been the matter."

Buckinger shook his head and gave his body a little twist that hinted at defiance. "It's different for you," he said. "The 'Duke' treats you differently from us. You've got a graft somewhere. Besides..."

"Besides what?" demanded Lafferty curiously and a little truculently.

Buckinger looked round with some show of apprehension before he brought himself to answer.

"Well . . . things haven't gone too well . . . have they . . . that's what I was meaning?"

"How do you mean?"

Buckinger pushed out his lower lip and shook his head again in an excess of Socratic wisdom.

"If you don't know, Lafferty, then I don't. Not on your life! Oh . . . no. My second name's 'Blue Points.' There's one thing I've learned from being with the 'Duke' all this time . . . and that's to keep my mouth shut. Some people never learn it. And they always pay the price."

Lafferty made no reply. The truth was that there was no adequate reply of which he could think.

Buckinger harped on. "Who's to go to the 'Duke' as well as me—eh, Lafferty? *All* the others—did you say?"

"Who are *all* the others?"

Lafferty's thrust was shrewd and well-pointed and Buckinger knew it. It told him that Lafferty was by no means the dull fool that many judged him to be.

"The usual trio—I mean. Of course I do. You know that very well. You're closer to the 'Duke' than any of us. What else could I mean, Lafferty?"

"I'm not good at guessing, Bucky. Never was. Give me names—real names—that I can get my teeth into and which I can understand."

Backinger's leering little face, with its loose folds and creases, puckered and frowned like the soft wrinkled flesh of a monkey.

"Tafari . . . the clever Tafari . . . and you yourself, Lafferty . . . and Miss . . . Miss—I forget the name . . . let me see now, what was it?"

"Clever . . . clever Bucky," returned Lafferty . . . "but not quite clever enough. Cut it out. Get that. Leave the pretty girls alone. They spell trouble for the likes of you."

A gleam of displeasure passed across Buckinger's features as he realised the comparative failure of his endeavour. He was getting nowhere and the time at his disposal was extremely short. He showed his yellow teeth. Buckinger hated to plough sands. "Tafari was right, then. He said you'd come over all high-hat, Lafferty, and I'll say he told us the truth for once. Go your own way, though . . . and I'll go mine . . . time will show which is the better one and then one day maybe you'll be sorry."

After the delivery of this parting shot he skipped along in front of Lafferty. When he had gone a dozen yards or so however, the latter fired a return volley at Buckinger.

"Don't forget, Bucky," he cried, "at midday. The first time that we stop. And if you take my advice you'll mind your step. The 'Duke's' a bit touchy."

The line of vehicles lumbered on . . . through an occasional village with straggling outskirts . . . past stretches of green . . . along winding ribbons of white roads. "L'Estrange's Travelling Showground" made neither haste nor hurry. Why should it? Those conditions belong to towns . . . not to the open spaces. It travelled at its own pace and in its own custom. Shortly after twelve o'clock, when the sun was high in the sky, word was passed down L'Estrange's line that a halt was to be made as soon as it should be convenient. It came from the man who led the venture. It travelled quickly. "At Everetts' Corner. A mile and a quarter to go. Three tents." So the message was sent. The distance that the leader had named was covered before the hands of the clock had crawled to the next hour. The men and women of the equipment went to their respective places and duties, with the calm celerity of smooth habit. The tents were pitched, pegged and roped. Pots and pans were utilised and in an amazingly short time, rations were passed round. Before he could make progress with the share that came to him, Rame Tafari found himself tapped on the shoulder. He turned quickly to greet the acquaintance. As he expected, he found the lad Lafferty at his side.

"The 'Duke,'" said a smiling Lafferty softly . . . "now! Buckinger's already gone in. The 'Duke' wants you and him to be there together."

Rame Tafari ostentatiously dusted the shoulder which Lafferty had tapped, with his uninjured arm.

"Don't put your filthy hands on me again," he said, "or it'll be the worse for you." He brushed Lafferty to one side without ceremony, and stalked like the great Lord of Luna towards L'Estrange's tent.

Lafferty followed him at a respectful distance. Tafari, without checking his pace, passed into the tent.

L'Estrange . . . the "Duke" . . . sat at a small table. His right hand plucked impatiently at his shaggy beard. There was a row of black notebooks arrayed in a studied formation in front of him. Buckinger sat, or rather perched, at L'Estrange's side. He looked, as far as Tafari could judge, both uncomfortable and unhappy. The "Duke's" eyes fell on Tafari's bandaged arm. He jerked his head towards it, sharply.

"What's the matter with you? Trouble?"

"Nothing to worry about." Tafari was off-hand.

L'Estrange glared and thrust his head forward at his Lieutenant. "What got you? Or was it just your own damned carelessness . . . as usual?"

Tafari's lip curled according to its habit. "Listen! And I'll tell you things. I told you not to worry. The explanation is eminently simple. One of my white mice got out. I went after it . . . and it savaged me. Still . . . the wound's going on all right. No complications likely to set in. My blood's clean. It's not merely blue—it's pure azure. Good job it wasn't your boy friend, Lafferty, who got bitten. You don't know what might have happened to him. Bad blood festers so." As he spoke, Tafari's eyes met the "Duke's" steadily and unwaveringly. They refused to yield an inch of ground in the silent battle that was being waged. L'Estrange's voice cut crisply into the silence.

"I'd advise you, Tafari, from the bottom of my heart . . . not to get fresh with *me*. You can try it with Buckinger, if you like, or with Lafferty, but draw the line when you come to me. If you don't the climate won't suit you. Things'll happen. Sit down."

Tafari bowed and took the seat that L'Estrange had indicated. He crossed one leg over the other with easy coolness. Buckinger, doubly apprehensive now that he had heard the recent conversation, moved to the side a little to allow Tafari elbow-room.

"Produce your book, if you please, Tafari," said L'Estrange. "I'm concerned with business now. The book that should start somewhere about the end of last April."

Tafari, making no reply, produced the book which L'Estrange had requisitioned. As he laid it on the table he looked straight at the man who was instructing him.

"This is the book that you require," he said quietly, "I started this when we were at East Hannington. On instructions received from you. You can tell that by the date. The others were destroyed . . . also by your orders."

L'Estrange bent over the book . . . pushed his fingers through his untidy beard and examined several pages.

"H'm," he said . . . "h'm. Not so good—eh?"

Tafari shrugged his shoulders and the two men glared at each other. Buckinger watched them anxiously . . . and maintained a discreet silence.

There were times when Buckinger embraced silence eagerly and this was one of them.

CHAPTER X
AIRS AND GRACES

ANTHONY Bathurst, debonair and distinguished, entered the precincts of "the Purple Calf" for the second time in one week and immediately he crossed the threshold became hopefully defensive. The time at the moment of his arrival was but seven minutes past nine, which was much earlier, it will be observed, than had been the time of his previous visit. He handed his coat and hat into the charge of the attendant in the gentleman's cloakroom, received his check for same and, as he turned from the counter nonchalantly, lighted a cigarette. He had scarcely tossed away the match which he had used, when the telephone behind the attendant rang persistently and he saw the man drop a coat across the counter and dart across to answer the call. The attendant listened, nodded, and spoke. "I didn't quite catch. What name did you say?"

Anthony, but a few yards away from the counter, saw the man look round in his direction rather furtively. The attendant essayed reply. "No. Alone. Very good, sir. I understand, sir. 'Oo's likely to want him—any idea? Oh . . . I see. That's all right, sir. 'E shall be h'informed . . . at the proper time. Leave it to me, sir. That shall be attended to."

Anthony saw the telephone replaced and the man return to his ordinary duties. Then, without looking behind him again, Mr. Bathurst sauntered into the restaurant proper, passed the seat that he had occupied on the previous occasion when he had visited the "Calf," and wandered lazily over to the bar. Adroitly evading the *maître d'hôtel*, whom he had noticed from the corner of his eye bearing down upon him in full sail, he reached the bar, beckoned to an attendant and gave an order.

"I have need of you," he smiled. "Give me a cocktail, Rudolf, will you? I feel this evening that I want a special one. I don't think I'll have my usual 'Clover Club' this time. Or a 'White Lady.' I'll try that new one of yours instead. What do you call it? Tell me, I've forgotten."

Rudolf grinned appreciatively and showed a line of regular white teeth. "Mossyface Kick, sir. Vare good, too. Becoming vare populaire with all our patrons. Especially amongst the ladies. You like it, too—eh?"

Anthony nodded gaily as Rudolf picked up the cocktail-shaker and got to work on his own special preparation. Eventually he delivered the goods and Anthony took his cocktail over to a table. Twenty minutes past nine! A waiter crossed from the bar to the next table at which there were seated a lady and gentleman. The waiter carried a tray with a bill and change. Anthony noticed a ten-shilling note lying on the top and, as far as he could tell at the distance, four silver coins . . . three half-crowns, he thought, and a florin.

"Your change, sir," he heard the waiter say. The waiter placed the tray on the table and bowed.

"Thank you, waiter." The guest pocketed his change and handed a coin to the waiter. At that precise moment, Anthony was acutely conscious of a distinct stir in the lower apartments of

"The Purple Calf." Several people were on the point of entering. He turned quickly towards the door and saw, amongst others, the girl whom he wanted to see . . . the girl whom he had come to meet—Margaret Fletcher. The *maître d'hôtel* met her as she crossed the floor and, to the accompaniment of a grandiloquent bow, handed her a magnificent spray of dark-red roses.

"Oh . . . how beautiful," murmured Margaret in ecstasy . . . "are these really for me?"

"Oh . . . yes, my lady. Quite. Madame, if I may say—looks vonderful. I give beauty to beauty. That is how it always should be. If she would only permit me. . . ."

Margaret kept her head and her poise admirably. "Please don't trouble. I am quite well looked after, thank you. You see—I am not unattended—as you appear to think—I have an escort. This gentleman is waiting for me."

Anthony rose at the words. The *maître d'hôtel* saw this and backed away. There was something about Mr. Bathurst . . . his height perhaps . . . or his broad square shoulders . . . or possibly the gleam in his grey eyes . . . but definitely something. . . that gave the man pause. And also food for subsequent thought. Mr. Bathurst gallantly took Miss Margaret Fletcher's arm and escorted her to his table . . . and the general excitement that had so suddenly simmered, just as suddenly subsided. A waiter was at their side instantaneously.

"Get me a cocktail, please," whispered Margaret.

"Two 'Pink Columbines,'" said Anthony. The alert waiter vanished.

"Well?" . . . said Anthony . . . to Miss Fletcher . . . "Any news for me?"

"None," she returned crisply. "Disappointing, isn't it? . . . I've come, though, as we arranged the evening before last. Does it matter so very much?"

"It doesn't matter two hoots. All things take time. Is your brother here?"

Miss Fletcher shook her head. "No. But he's coming on later. That's certain."

Anthony sought certain assurances. "You've told nobody about our meeting? Either to-night or the other time?"

She shook her head again. "I haven't said a word to a soul. I've kept absolutely quiet, just as you told me to."

"Good. It may not happen . . . but if you are forced to introduce me to anybody . . . introduce me by the name of Lotherington . . . say that I'm a reporter on the *Morning Message*. Call me neither Bathurst, Miss Fletcher . . . nor even . . . Beaumont. Got that?" He grinned.

She nodded. "I know the theatre well."

His next words surprised her. "Oh . . . a really marvellous show. I wouldn't have missed it for worlds. Raymond Massey superb. He seemed to have such an intense sympathy with the part that he was playing. I received the impression that he sincerely believed much that he was given to say. Which makes an enormous difference to the playing of any part. Thank you, waiter. Put them down there, will you? And bring me change of this." The waiter took the pound note which Mr. Bathurst proffered him. "I'm sorry if I startled you, rather, but no chances now," said the latter quietly . . . "we're on the track of something big . . . believe me. Wait a minute and I'll tell you more. Hold on for a second. He's coming back."

Margaret could hear the band starting in the room behind. She looked at the centre doors. Anthony checked his change and dismissed the waiter. Then he smiled at her understandingly.

"No, Miss Fletcher, I regret to inform you that for this evening tangos are taboo. The valse *verboten*, and the foxtrot merely futile. In other words—the flowers are not for you to pick. Or me. Your recreation is to be in another direction. Shall we say in the kitchen garden?"

She fluttered interested eyes at him. "Explain . . . please. I hate being left in the dark."

Mr. Bathurst bent more closely towards her. "You can refuse, of course . . . or say to me 'on what compulsion must I?' . . . but somehow I don't think that you will." He drew his head back and eyed her . . . deliberately appraisingly.

"My dear man," she said, "I am not in the Garden of Eden. When you look at me—"

"I feel as though I might be," returned Anthony, "or at least in the vicinity—shall we say—of a Paradise. Of man's first disobedience—"

Miss Fletcher began to mock under her breath. "Do not trust him, gentle maiden. . . ."

"That's torn it," said Mr. Bathurst. "My hopes are dashed to the ground. There must be a perfect and complete understanding between us. Any other condition is . . . frankly . . . impossible. On this occasion, you have simply got to come and play with the gypsies in the wood."

Margaret Fletcher smiled at him. She looked marvellously sweet and her eyes held both allure and invitation. Her dark hair was still clouded round her head. Except in her face, she carried no jewels . . . but her eyes shone like stars as she looked at him. Anthony saw that her lips were red and that her throat was soft and white.

"Tell me something," he murmured to her. . . . "Is it possible that anyone could wish you harm?"

"Idiot," she murmured . . . "to be beautiful it is necessary that one should suffer. Of all true Gallic proverbs—the truest. You of all people . . . should have been taught that."

"Then without doubt am I becoming a veritable Adonis. Needs must. Listen to me. Interrupt me not. Do not fling conversation at the man at the wheel. It is indecently foolhardy and invites deadly peril. You remember where we went last time we were here?"

Miss Fletcher nodded. "Only too well." He felt her small shoe against his. It was at that moment that he noticed she was dressed in a perfectly wonderful shade of blue. Blue, it may be mentioned, is Mr. Bathurst's favourite colour. She propped a superb chin on white arms. "White and indefinite blue," he murmured.

"Once upon a time," continued Anthony . . . "I had an idea. It was brought up and nurtured with care. It was a one ewe lamb of ideas. Perhaps you would care to listen to it."

"There is nothing that I should like better . . . or even as well," murmured Miss Fletcher in return.

Anthony looked round carefully, lowered his voice almost to a whisper, and embarked upon explanation. Margaret Fletcher listened with rapt attention. Suddenly she drew back from him shrewdly.

"You're not lost for it, are you . . . Mr. . . . er . . . Lotherington? How do you know I won't turn on you and give the show away completely?"

"I don't know. I admit that I don't."

She shrugged her shoulders cynically. "You seem to have a considerable amount of faith in human nature, Sir Galahad. Anyhow, go on."

Bathurst obeyed. He spoke at length. When he had finished, the lines of his mouth were grave and set. "Well?" he demanded of her.

Over his shoulder Margaret Fletcher saw—some distance behind him—a waiter and two men closing in upon them. She rose imperiously and fixed Anthony with flashing eyes and a pointing finger. Anthony realised with unerring instinct that he had said enough. Very possibly—more than enough. The waiter, who had by now come very close, drew back in some measure of alarm. There was anger in the lady's eyes and he knew enough of the world to avoid this adroitly. Two wives had tutored him and a daughter.

"Get out of here," cried Miss Fletcher . . . "and don't you dare make such a suggestion to me again."

Mr. Bathurst, shocked and surprised, looked at her incredulously.

"Why . . . you must have misunderstood me . . . what on earth are you talking . . . !"

Miss Fletcher gave him no time to finish. "Get out of my sight . . . do. I have no wish to discuss the subject any further."

Anthony, sensing that this spelt finality, bowed and turned away. He walked as far as the main door of the apartment. He stood in the doorway. He saw that Margaret Fletcher had recovered her equanimity and was shaking hands with two young men. Each of the men had his back to Mr. Bathurst. Each was tall—one very tall. One was fair . . . the other, the very tall one, was dark. Suddenly, as Anthony Bathurst watched this group of three, the very tall, dark man turned and looked across in Anthony's direction. Judging by her gestures, Margaret seemed full of annoyance and expostulation. Anthony took stock of the dark man.

"He looks," he said to himself, "like a pagan, suckled in a creed outworn, and safely weaned."

The man who had looked across at Mr. Bathurst was certainly a noticeable fellow. In any company. Besides his height, he was very thin, very dark and decidedly saturnine. If anything, he gave the impression at first glance of being taller than he really was. Also, he suggested a quality of faun-like elusiveness. Anthony wasn't sure whether this was the effect of his piercing black eyes or of his haunting, almost furtive smile. Anthony saw him laugh in Margaret's face. The temper with which she had assailed him had now died down and only the embers were left to her. But although Anthony saw the laugh come to birth on this dark man's face, he wasn't sure whether he laughed with Margaret or at her.

"No," said Anthony to himself again. "I must correct myself . . . certainly not a pagan . . . but a faun . . . his hair is long and tumbles about his brows—to hide his horns perhaps. And a marvellous talker, too." Anthony observed the dark sallow face light up under the flow of thought like the sun of the early hours that dissipates the mists of the morning. "Hear him," communed Anthony, "reproving the men and women of his generation. Also their modes and manners, doubtless. I know his like too well." Anthony passed through the door and left the restaurant proper. His last glance afforded him a sight of black brooding eyes fixed on the other man in that same group of three. He made his way to the cloakroom and surrendered the check he had taken for his coat and hat. Mr. Bathurst thought over the events of the evening . . . his amazement at Margaret Fletcher's vehemence. He had been unprepared for such uncompromising completeness. Mr. Bathurst reached the street. He turned and looked back.

"Good-bye," he said under his breath, "for the time being, at least, to 'The Purple Calf' . . . but not to 'The Purple Calf's' sinister secret."

Then once again Mr. Bathurst counted his change. He had been charged nine shillings for his two cocktails.

Chapter XI
RIEN NE VA PLUS

Had Anthony Bathurst, as he walked from the doorway, been able to hear the conversation that was passing between the group of three, he would have been still more intrigued. The tall dark fellow was speaking.

"This is my sister, Brailsford. I am aware, you see, that you have never met her. The omission must be repaired. Your separation has endured too long. Margaret . . . a friend of mine . . . Peter Brailsford."

Margaret smiled at the introduction and murmured conventional words. Peter Brailsford nodded happily.

"Weren't you with somebody, Miss Fletcher? When Stephen and I came in? Or am I mistaken?"

She frowned and bit her lip. "A man was annoying me . . . if that's what you're referring to, Mr. Brailsford. Although I had refused him several times, he would persist in asking me to dance with him. I was forced in the end to tick him off rather severely."

Stephen Fletcher intervened, a frown on his dark features.

"Who was it?" he demanded curtly.

Margaret hesitated. To admit that she knew might lead to unpleasant questions . . . questions which she was in no mood to answer. She lied.

"How should I know? The man was a perfect stranger to me. It's astonishing what gets into the 'Calf' these days."

"I shall complain to the management," remarked Stephen sourly. "That sort of thing must be put a stop to. My sister . . . indeed."

81 | THE CASE OF THE PURPLE CALF

"Well, I'm a comparatively optimistic bloke, generally speaking, but I don't fancy you'll get much satisfaction out of that. You and your management. So far I've not run up against any of 'em. Always seem to be well in the background."

Stephen's sourness stayed with him. "Don't know why Margaret must come here. Never used to. Entirely new idea. Ridiculous. Sensation hunting. Dedicates herself in a fervent fanaticism . . . and expects Heaven as a reward. She has unusual capacities for happiness . . . for a modern girl that is . . . she has ardent zest . . . an overplus of natural curiosity . . . and really rude health. But ignorant . . . oh, Brutus, Cassius and all the company of conspirators . . . she brings tears to my eyes! So charming and yet so fatuous! Behold me weep . . . I cry and dissolve in mist."

Margaret dissembled. "Oh well . . . Stephen . . . you need not make such a fuss. It hasn't happened to me before and it may not happen again. As the papers say of these things, the incident is now closed and the man who annoyed me has taken himself off."

Stephen nodded. "All right, then. We'll say no more about it." He turned to Brailsford and pointed to the crowds that were now gathering in "The Purple Calf."

"Dancing, my dear Brailsford, since the war, has become the new religion."

"I should hardly call it that. A craze . . . certainly . . . but—"

"Why not?" demanded Stephen, "what's your exact point of objection? You confuse the meanings of words . . . that's your trouble . . . the same as it's the trouble of hundreds of other people . . . religion is a habit of mind . . . not something that is taught by somebody else . . . like the ablative absolute or the differential calculus." He paused. Peter looked a trifle puzzled. Stephen went on. "We were all tremendously religious when German bombs dropped on us. And this dancing craze . . . this night-club enthusiasm is 'big business,' my boy. Believe me, Brailsford . . . it is. In the past religion has often meant 'big business.' The whole line of history teaches us that. I'll supply you with a specific example. The Levantine sophist saw 'big business' in Christianity and ran it in Europe for all it was worth. Ever since then, the only real hope of religion has been in what lurked of sheer paganism . . . in the forests of Germany . . . in the Tuscan uplands . . . and most of all . . . in the damp Irish swamps." Stephen Fletcher rubbed his hands.

Margaret leant forward towards him and tapped him on the arm. "Stephen dear . . . enough of all this. Oh, how you weary me. I really think that the man who annoyed me was vastly more amusing than you are." She became imperative. "Take me to the card-room—please. I would gamble. I feel that to-night I can win heaps and heaps of money. Coming with us, Mr. Brailsford?"

"Delighted, Miss Fletcher. As soon as you like. I told Stephen as we came along that I meant trying my luck to-night." There was a twinkle in Peter Brailsford's eye.

The three of them at once made their way down the staircase to the gaming rooms. Stephen piloted his sister and Brailsford to the big table which stood to the left of the entrance door. This was the baccarat table where it was usual for play to run pretty high. The present occasion seemed to show no exception to this rule. The size of the crowd round this table when they entered, indicated that play was running high this evening. This crowd was at least four deep. Margaret, on its verge, was forced to stand on tip-toe to see the faces of the players. Even so she was unable to see the man holding the bank. The green table round which the crowd of players and spectators thronged was covered with notes. Brailsford, from his greater height, was able to see the face of the man who held the bank. He recognised the man with a start of surprise. It was the man who had given evidence at the inquest at Great Kirby on Clare Kent when he had been there with that journalist fellow, Lotherington. The man who had identified the dead girl as his own sister-in-law! The man whose name was John Dexter. It was evident to Peter Brailsford that Fortune herself sat at Dexter's side on this particular evening. The croupier, unsmiling and impassive, piled the bank notes at Dexter's elbow. Dexter, like him, betrayed no excitement or thrill. His face was immobile. Not a tremor showed on it. Eyes, lips and jaw were alike steady and unwavering. As Brailsford watched, Dexter turned up yet another winning card and the croupier raked in the winnings to Dexter's side.

"*Faites vos jeux, messieurs,*" he cried again. "*Le jeu est fait.*" The cards were stacked once more. Margaret seized an opportunity to push her slim smooth way through the crowd. Her hand held a pound note. She went to the cloth and rather impudently staked her money. Stephen shook his head at her restrainingly, but Margaret refused to heed him. The cards ran against her. Her note was quickly swept away and gathered to Dexter's previous winnings. Other notes followed in its unhappy wake. In spite of Stephen's continued protestations, Margaret played on with a fine courage and a finer optimism. Occasionally she won a little, but generally speaking the tide of disaster flowed steadily and unwaveringly against her. Four times in the space of a very short time the bank changed hands. But no matter who held it, Margaret's ill-fortune refused to desert her. Heedless of Stephen's entreaties and Peter Brailsford's kindly-given advice, she persisted, and the amount of her losses rose higher and higher. After a time her calmness deserted her and anxiety began to show itself unmistakably in her face.

"God, Margaret," expostulated her brother, "you can't go on! Pull up, for the love of Mike. You must have lost a small fortune already."

"I'm going to get back what I've lost," she said, stubbornly, between clenched teeth, "my luck must change before long. It's out of all reason that it can go on like this."

"Can't it," returned Stephen with gloomy pessimism, "you've no idea what luck can do when it feels like doing it. Before now I've known the *Daily Mail* nap go down at least two days in succession."

Margaret pressed forward to the green-covered table again. She counted the notes that remained to her with a feverish anxiety. Fourteen pounds only. A quick calculation told her that she had already lost over eighty pounds. Knots of people, scenting the sensational, were beginning to watch her and her play. News travels quickly and the room became more crowded than ever. A young lady at the baccarat table was playing with reckless fortitude. Her pluck, it was freely whispered, was altogether disproportionate to her luck. A note from her fingers fluttered to the table. Again fortune frowned and the cards ran against her. Dexter, back with the bank again, turned up a "natural" and the croupier relentlessly harvested the stakes. Margaret bit her lip with vexation . . . tossed her head and played on. Gradually and with unbroken persistence her dwindling resources dwindled more. She came down to her last note. Stephen and Peter Brailsford shrugged admonitory shoulders.

"You're a plucky kid," said Stephen, "and a born gambler . . . all the Fletchers are . . . but your luck's dead out, girl. You ought to have taken my advice and chucked up the sponge long ago. When you're cleaned out, Peter and I will see you home."

Margaret took her courage in both hands and played her last effort. It met with the usual fate.

"You will observe, Margaret," said Stephen, "that your notes have all gone the same way home. All the whole collection! In the same direction! Alas, that in your infantile obstinacy you refused to be guided by your Socratic brother." But he, Peter Brailsford, and the crowd of people who watched were astounded at what followed. For Margaret Fletcher's *sangfroid* and indifference suddenly and completely deserted her. Her eyes held the haunting dread of fear. She stood there, the cynosure of neighbouring eyes, of eyes that were inquisitive and almost actively interrogative, her lips quivering with emotion, fingers clasping and unclasping. Even Stephen, the arch-exponent of nonchalance and cynical indifference, was spellbound at what he saw in his sister's demeanour.

"Margaret," he cried—his voice unnaturally shrill—"control yourself—do!"

Her hand went convulsively to her brow. Her face flushed. Then the change came and it clouded over. Her supple slenderness swayed and seemed unstable. For a split second there was an oppressive silence that overhung and almost engulfed the room. Then Margaret Fletcher screamed, and having screamed, pushed past her brother and his friend Peter Brailsford and rushed headlong from the room. The crowd of watchers, silent and spellbound while the drama lasted, burst into a babel of excited conversation as the door closed behind her. Stephen beckoned to Brailsford with a peremptory gesture.

"Follow me," he cried curtly.

Brailsford, amazed and wondering, obeyed him.

The evening, for him, had ended very differently from his expectations.

Chapter XII
CONCERNING VERA SINCLAIR

ANTHONY Bathurst came to the village of East Hannington at a few minutes past seven in the evening of what had been a glorious August day. A day when the ripeness and mellowness of the month were there for all to see and understand. It was the second occasion upon which he had visited East Hannington. He had been there on the eighth day of June. In accordance with his usual practice he entered and sought the hospitality of the village inn. Its sign was uncommon. It rejoiced to call itself *The Tinted Venus*. As he had expected, with an anticipation that approached certainty, the bar-parlour was unreasonably full. The sturdy and slow-thinking men of the Essex countryside were already beginning to gather for their evening's social contribution. Anthony ordered a beer and at the same time wished the *habitués* a cordial "good evening." Conversation for a time was desultory. Nothing held centre stage for any length of time. But Anthony, by a series of carefully seeded remarks, eventually brisked the talk up considerably. It went from the weather to agriculture. Anthony always believed in adjusting conversation to the average and general "experience" of the listeners.

The layman requires an entirely different attack from the expert. "The touch of Midas" will convey far more to him than the Shakespearean statement that "all that glisters is not gold." The mere mention of giddiness will mean more to him than a didactic dissertation on incipient vertigo. Suddenly Anthony tangented to questions of locality and direction.

"Can you tell me," he said with a show of keen interest, "where I am . . . exactly? I know that I'm in the village of East Hannington . . . of course . . . from the various motoring signs that I've passed . . . but beyond that, I can't say that I know too much about my general locality. And even the name, East Hannington, doesn't mean a great deal to me." He laughed genially at the last sentence. "I must ask your pardon for that remark. Don't think for one minute that I'm belittling East Hannington . . . will you? Nothing is further from my thoughts. Now gentlemen, drinks on me . . . all round. Will you take the order, landlord?"

The landlord, beaming at the vista which Mr. Bathurst's generosity conjured, would and did. Several horny-handed sons of toil volunteered information regarding geography. Anthony listened attentively. At times he punctuated the various statements with courteous noddings.

"Oh . . . thanks . . . then I know where I am now. I know the Bindon Park golf course that you mention. I rather fancy that I played a round on it some few years back. And beyond Bindon Park, you say, I shall eventually come to Altminster—eh? Well, that suits me."

"That's so, sir," said a grey-beard. "Go past the golf course and then bear to the right. You can't miss the Altminster road. There's a big house just where you'll be turning round. It's called 'The Cranes.' Belongs to Colonel Fletcher. One o' the best known of the gentry what's livin' in this district."

Anthony wrinkled puzzled brows. The action on Mr. Bathurst's part was deliberate. "East Hannington," he said apparently to himself, "now I come to think of it, the name seems familiar to me. East Hannington! Now when was it that I heard that name before? H'm . . . bless my soul . . ."

Several of the onlookers showed signs of amusement. One of them grinned broadly. "East Hannington reached the semi-final of the Essex Junior Cup last season. Reckon's that's what's getting you, mister. Match were played on neutral ground at Chelmersley. 'Gainst Little Beddoes. East Hannington lost by the odd goal. The ref. were fair rotten. The winning goal were yards offside." The man spat in an excess of contempt. Anthony smiled and shook his head.

"No—it's not that. That's not what I was thinking of. I should have remembered at once if it had been that." He shook his head for a second time as he raised his tankard to his lips. "No—it's something that I saw on the news-page of a London paper. Goodness gracious—my memory's getting worse than ever. Dear me—it's most annoying. I keep getting near the idea . . . only for it to elude me again."

A hard-featured man who up to the moment had made no contribution to the conversation looked up with deliberate intention and began to speak equally emphatically.

"I reckon I know what you're thinkin' of—guv'nor. Your mention of the newspaper started my old wits a'movin'. They're slow . . . but when they do start . . . they're pretty sure." He looked round the knot of his companions and addressed them generally. "Don't none of you chaps cotton on yet?"

Heads were shaken. Tankards were put down. "What are you gettin' at, George?" said the man who had recalled the ill-fated semi-final at Chelmersley. "I'm hanged if I can—"

George dallied before he came to the supreme moment of his triumph. "What about Ted Sinclair's girl—eh? I'll lay a shillun' that's what the gentleman's referrin' to. Downright sure of it, I am! Wasn't the account of her accident and the inquest what followed in all the London papers? *Now*—do you remember?" George beamed effusively.

Many nodded corroborations came from the group. The landlord, who had left the bar and come nearer, appeared to be listening intently. Anthony judged that the tide in his affairs should now be taken at the flood. He immediately joined in the chorus of agreement.

"Our friend George is right," he said decisively. "One word from him served to put me on the right track. That was when he mentioned the name of Sinclair. I remember the case well—it's come back to me. I'll prove it to you, if you like." He made a pretence of remembering. "It was a motoring accident. That was it. Near here. I remember well that the village of East Hannington was mentioned in the account of the case that came to my notice. The poor girl's neck was badly cut by a piece of broken glass that was found in the road near her body."

The landlord pressed yet farther forward and stood with the group of men. Once or twice, he looked round anxiously as though seeking somebody.

"Don't exactly want Ted Sinclair to come in and hear this. You know what I mean. He was rare upset you know at the time—natural-like—and I reckon grief of that kind don't need revivin'. It's best left alone. I've been through the mill myself."

"That's all right. You needn't worry, Tom," said George, "you won't see the colour o' Ted Sinclair's money this evenin'. If you want to know he's gone into Altminster on a matter of business. As it happens I met him on my way down here and he told me where he was off to."

This statement appeared to be final and Anthony noticed that the landlord, apparently satisfied by George's declaration, returned to his former position behind the bar.

George continued. "Yes, mister. That were a sad case and no error. Especially to us chaps here what use the *Venus* at all regular-like. A village like this 'ere is small—you see. Everybody knows everybody else's business mostly. Ted Sinclair's one of us, as you might say, and we all knew Ted's Vera since she were a baby. All them things make a rare lot of difference." He shook his head sagely.

Another man nodded agreement and took up the parable. A thin-faced man, with an untidy straggling moustache who kept wiping his mouth with the back of his hand. "Tell you another who was mighty upset when Vera Sinclair was taken. Besides Ted hisself." He paused to look round but for a moment only. "Young Stan Langford. That's the young chap what I'm referring to. He was sweet on Vera. I reckon they'd have got hitched up together in the end if only things had turned out all right for 'em. Good steady, straight young feller he were . . . and is . . . Vera might ha' done a deal worse."

"Ay . . . Albert . . . I reckon I can say you're right there. Stunnin' lookin' girl was young Vera Sinclair," added George, "the kind of girl what people turn round to look at twice when they've passed 'er. Would ha' made her mark on the pictures . . . or in one of them fashion shops you hear about. Fine figure, a real good-looker and highly intelligent. Plenty up top," George tapped his forehead with due solemnity. "And when I say these things I reckon I know what I'm talking about. None better." George wagged his head wisely. Anthony thought that he detected a clear opening.

"Does this young Langford still live in these parts? Or did he clear away from the district? After the accident, I mean?"

George shook his head at the last two questions. "No. He never cleared out. Though I expect he'd ha' liked to have done. He's still knockin' around. His father works on the railway . . . up near Altminster. One of the repair gang. They live in one of them cottages close to the big house of Colonel Fletcher's. . . . 'The Cranes' . . . the one as I was tellin' you about. Young Stan's doin' a bit of electrical engineerin'. Pretty clever chap he be . . . with his fingers. All the Langfords are what you might call mechanical. Times is very different to when I were a young 'un and no mistake. There wasn't much choice of occupation for a lad in my young days, I can tell you. You worked on the land. Where your old dad had worked in his time and where his father had worked before him. Right back for generations. As for now—why some of the jooveniles round here pick and choose like the gentry themselves. It's the so-called education that's done it. And how do they finish up—nine cases out of ten? At the Unemployment Exchange—that's *my* name for it. On the dole! Week in and week out. Livin' on charity." The lines of George's mouth expressed his sturdy disgust. Anthony showed signs of agreement with George's declaration.

"There's a good deal of sense in what you say, sir. Times are certainly not what they were. But there—they never are. And probably never will be. That's the way of the world. We all have to pay homage at that altar. Well—I must be getting along. I've stopped here longer than I intended to—as it is. It's your fault, you know. You made me too welcome." He waved to the chorus of good evenings, made his way out, and turned his car towards the road that led to Altminster. He was toying, let it be said, with an idea. As he passed the Bindon Park golf course, he came to a decision. According to the information that he had just gleaned in *The Tinted Venus*, Colonel Fletcher's house, "The Cranes" was on the bend of the road . . . on the corner as it turned in the direction of Altminster. And in the row of cottages just beyond it, was one that was inhabited by this young fellow, Langford, of whom mention had been made. If he could catch him in and were able to have a seasonable word with him, Mr. Bathurst considered that he might very well learn and hear something to his advantage. Anthony negotiated the corner skilfully, cocked an appraising eye at "The Cranes," the exterior of which pleased him immensely, and in due time reached the particular row of cottages which he had been seeking. They lay well back from the road and—approaching Altminster—on the left-hand side of it. Each had a long straggling front garden, devoted, in more cases than not, to the utilitarian cultivation of vegetables rather than to the decorative growing of flowers. A middle-aged woman wearing a plaid shawl across her shoulders and a moustache upon her upper lip, leant over the garden gate of the third cottage of the row. Anthony slowed up the "Chrysler" and came to a halt just in front of her. Mr. Bathurst raised his head before alighting and doffed his hat. The woman folded her arms and awaited his coming. From her point of view this visitor belonged to the class that placed the word "trouble" in her vocabulary. For her—*inter alia*—they represented such contingencies as law . . . and order. . . .

"Excuse me, madam," said Mr. Bathurst, in his most gallant manner, "but I wonder if you would be able to help me? I am trying to find a gentleman by the name of Langford. Am I right in believing that he lives in one of these cottages?" Anthony smiled engagingly.

The woman recovered herself and nodded slowly. "Yes, sir. You're quite right, sir. You haven't got very far to go. It's the last cottage but one." She pointed somewhat vaguely towards the end of the row. "Is it the young feller you're wantin'—the son— or old Jonas Langford?"

Anthony replied to her question with another smile. "I want the young man. Young Langford. Stanley—his name is."

The woman moved her head almost as though she had been expecting the terms of Anthony's answer.

"Then you're in luck's way, sir—and no mistake! For I see young Stan himself go into his place less than a half-hour ago. And he ain't come out again, neither. So if you're quick and pop along now you'll be bound to catch him."

Anthony thanked her again and drove the car slowly towards the end of the row. When he came to the Langford abode he made his way up another long garden path similar in every respect to all the others and knocked on the door.

An unusually tall young man with high cheek-bones and very fair hair answered Anthony's knock. His height, no doubt, was accentuated by his excessive thinness, but even taking this into consideration, Anthony judged him, by a rapid comparison with himself, to be somewhere near six feet five inches. He was a young giant—there was no gainsaying that—but Mr. Bathurst could see at a glance that the boy had outgrown his strength. Everything about him declared "length." His neck, his fingers and even his ears and his nose. He seemed surprised when he saw the man who had knocked on the door of his father's cottage.

"Have I the pleasure of addressing Mr. Stanley Langford?" inquired Mr. Bathurst cordially.

"Yes, sir," the young man replied.

Anthony came to the point. "Would you be good enough to give me a few minutes' conversation with you?"

Langford looked a little bewildered before he eventually acceded to the request. "Step inside, sir . . . into the front parlour."

"Thank you."

Young Langford stepped to one side and pointed the way for Anthony Bathurst. "In the room on the right, sir, if you don't mind. Take that chair by the window, sir. That's the most comfortable. What was it you wanted to see me about, sir?"

Anthony took the chair indicated, and regarded him kindly and sympathetically. "I don't know that that's an easy question for me to answer. Because I want you to understand that I have no desire to hurt your feelings, Langford," he said. "Believe that of me . . . please. But I'm afraid that before this interview is finished it may have proved necessary for me to do so. So that I'll begin by asking your pardon."

Langford stared at him.

"I can see that you are puzzled," went on Mr. Bathurst, "and wondering what on earth we're going to talk about together, aren't you?"

Langford nodded rather eagerly. "I am that, sir. Is it about the voting? For Parliament or the local Council?"

"No, Langford. Heaven forbid! Harbour no fears in that direction. Do I look like a canvasser? My dear boy—I'm clean-shaven. I've come to East Hannington with a special object in view. When I came, I had no idea that I should meet you. Candidly, I didn't even know of your existence. But a call at *The Tinted Venus* down the road there, and a few haphazard words spoken inside there, put me on your track . . . and here I am. Your welcome guest, I hope. Fact is—I'm doing a job of investigation." Mr. Bathurst paused significantly and looked at him.

"About what, sir. I don't know that I've any—"

"Yes—you have. None better. It's because of your special qualifications, too—qualifications that nobody else in the world has. I want to ask you one or two questions about a young lady whom you used to know."

Langford's eyes flashed and he started up in agitation. "Not. . . you don't mean . . . ?"

Anthony spoke quietly. "Yes, Langford. You are right. None other. I've come to talk to you about the late Vera Sinclair."

Langford assumed his previous attitude on the edge of a chair and then put his elbows on his knees and propped his face in his hands. It was evident that he was affected. For a time Anthony respected his silence. Then he decided to break more ice.

"I want your help, Langford. The best help that you can possibly give me. That means that I want you definitely on my side. Now, if you're going to be on my side . . . you'll have to be *against* somebody else. That's obvious isn't it . . . and speaks for itself. Would you like to know the name of your opponents? If you would, I'll tell you. The forces of evil, Langford! Evil so black and so repulsive that it didn't hesitate to array itself against three charming girls. I wonder if you understand *quite* what I mean. I used the word—'three.'" Anthony watched him with acute interest for he had chosen his words with deliberate intention.

Suddenly the lad looked up. "Do you know, sir," he said exceedingly slowly, "I'm wondering too . . . *what you mean.*" Langford's voice shook with emotion.

"I'm glad of that. I want you to do that. Very much. The more you wonder, the better I shall be pleased."

Langford rose from his chair and looked Anthony Bathurst straight between the eyes. "Are you trying to tell me, sir," he said deliberately, "that my Vera was the victim of foul play?"

Mr. Bathurst didn't answer in terms of words. He simply nodded.

Langford stood and pulled himself to his full height. "Do you know, sir," he continued, as the entire realisation of the affair took possession of him, "the thought of that has haunted me . . . for months now—waking and sleeping. I can't tell you why it has. It just has! I can't give you any facts . . . or even *one fact* that 'ud be a reason for my thinkin' so. But there it is . . . I have thought it . . . and I'm not goin' to deny it now that you've put it to me, as you might say."

He seated himself again and relapsed into a moody silence . . . staring vacantly almost, out of the window.

"And I haven't facts either, Langford—that's the devil of it," declared Mr. Bathurst, "so that you and I are in the same boat." He rose and put his hand on the young fellow's shoulder. "Tell me," he said with encouraging and inviting sympathy, "all that you can about Miss Sinclair. Everything. Her habits. Her ideas. Her fancies. Her ways. What she liked. What she disliked. You know what I mean. Then perhaps . . . who knows . . . I may be able to disentangle the threads . . . and separate the clear truth away from all the falsehoods that are twisted round it. You see, Langford, that's my job in life. And sometimes I have been lucky enough to help people."

Langford stared at him with wide-opened eyes. "I know nothing special, sir . . . or practically nothing. So what can I possibly tell you?"

"Tell me plain things, then, Langford. Don't bother your head about special things."

"Vera was an East Hannington girl, born and bred. Daughter of a fellow named Ted Sinclair. He's a railway man. Same as my old Dad is. Members of the same shift very often. Been workin' for the line these thirty odd years. Good straight chap, too. I've never heard a word spoken against him. I'd known Vera ever since we were kids and had gone to the Council School over at Altminster together. But don't get me all wrong, sir. Don't think from that that Vera was an ordinary sort of girl . . . 'cos she wasn't. Not by any manner of means. She was the finest lookin' girl for miles round. People used to turn round and look at her." Langford held up his head proudly.

"Go on," remarked Anthony, "you're talking as I want you to talk. You're telling me things. Soon perhaps you may tell me something . . . that will count and eventually help me no end."

Langford shook his head as though he had been discouraged in some way. "The only thing that I *can* tell you as you call it . . . that's like to be of any help to you I mean . . . is that Vera changed a bit when she changed her job. I *did* notice that—to be sure. At the time, too. Not afterwards when I might ha' been thinkin' things over. But on the other hand there might very well be nothing in the matter of the jobs. 'Cos I suppose you can call a change of occupation a natural thing to happen to any young girl."

"Tell me all . . . *all that you think*," Anthony prompted him softly.

Langford's mind went back to the contemplation of the past. His eyes took on a far-away look as he entered the realm of reminiscence. "Vera used to be cashier in a creamery in Altminster. Quite a decent shop, kept by people of the name of Hardy. They had a good business in Altminster . . . been established in the town for years and years. Vera was more of a friend to them than an ordinary employee. Well . . . suddenly . . . I was as much surprised as anybody, I think . . . Vera left Hardy's place." Langford played with a silver chain that was looped across his waistcoat and his speech slowed down considerably. "And the funny thing is, I'm not sure where her new job was . . . or even what her new job was. Do you understand what I'm telling you, sir?"

"Almost, I think. You mean that whereas she habitually gave you her confidences, when she changed her job and left the Hardy people at the creamery, she did nothing of the kind. In other words, her confidences ceased and she kept certain information from you."

"That's it, sir. That's just what I do mean."

"And yet in all other respects, relations between you continued on the same footing as they had been when Vera was employed at Hardy's?"

Langford took time to find suitable words. When he found them ultimately, a flush was on his cheeks. "I should like to say 'yes' to that . . . but if I did so . . . it wouldn't be telling the absolute truth . . . quite! We still had our understanding, she was still my girl. As far as a fellow like me can tell, Vera didn't fall in love with any other man . . . or anything like that. I don't mean that at all. But I'm not going to deny that the fact that she wouldn't tell me where she was working . . . I put the question to her several times, sir . . . *did* make a difference to me . . . and to the feeling between us. It was only natural that it should. I fought against it but it was no good."

Anthony thought hard over this last piece of information. "Did you see her as often as you had been in the habit of doing?"

Langford slowly shook his head. "Nothing like so often, sir. You see it was like this. She would be away from home for long spells. When that happened . . . of course . . . I only heard from her. By letters."

"Kept any of them, Langford?"

"No, sir. Not a single one. I hadn't the heart to. When Vera was killed, I burnt all the letters that she had ever sent me. I didn't seem to have any interest in anything, and I couldn't see any use in keepin' any of 'em. You see—I'm not over-sentimental. But there was nothing in any of them, sir, that could have helped you. I *can* tell you that for certain. They were all just ordinary-like."

"Where did they come from, Langford, these letters? Any one place in particular?"

"No, sir. From various places. Dotted about the country like. That was one of the things which I noticed first of all. I can remember some of the post-marks. From Oakengates, Much Wenlock, Kidderminster, Alcester, Kinver, Droitwich, Stratford-on-Avon, Banbury, Bicester, Aylesbury . . . all sorts of towns, sir."

Anthony mentally noted the names. "Did she seem happy and contented?"

Langford paused and considered the question before replying. "That's hard to say, sir, but in my opinion . . . no! I always got the idea that there was something on her mind as you might say."

"Tell me this, Langford. When Vera was killed . . . did you know before her death that she was in this district . . . close at hand? Had she informed you of that?"

"I knew . . . in a way. And yet in a way I didn't. She had written to tell me that she was coming along these parts. About a week or so before. It was somewhere about Easter time. Because I can recollect that on the Good Friday I was knockin' about on my own. But Vera's letter, you see, didn't say the *day* that she was coming and I was hopin' and expectin' to hear from her again, when I should receive news of her that was more definite."

"And you didn't?"

The young fellow shook his head. "Not another line . . . nor yet word, sir. Nothing! The next thing that I heard about my poor Vera . . . was from the papers. That she had been killed. The morning after it had happened."

Langford's face twitched with emotion. Anthony rose from the chair in which he was seated and looked out of the window. He stood with his back to Stanley Langford for a space of some seconds. Was there any point in the conditions of Vera Sinclair's new "employment"? The trouble had first cast its shadow, according to this young chap here, when the girl had changed her occupation. What was it that had caused her to make this change? If he but knew that . . . the thing with which he had begun to coquette in relation to Clare Kent and the Honourable Phyllis Welby scarcely seemed to fit the case of this East Hannington girl, Vera Sinclair.

And yet . . . Anthony Bathurst turned and confronted Langford.

"Ever heard of a travelling circus . . . 'L'Estrange's Showground'?"

Langford's eyes were dull as he looked up at the question. The name seemed to have conveyed but little to him.

"No, sir. I don't think that I have. Why?"

Anthony stimulated him. "Cast your mind back again, Langford. To that tragic month of April. After Easter had come and gone—you will remember. Wasn't there a show somewhere near Altminster about that time . . . that went by the name of 'L'Estrange's Travelling Showground'? Think, Langford, think!"

The semblance of a light came into Stanley Langford's eyes. "Yes," he answered slowly . . . "now you mention the name . . . it's all come back to me. I believe that there was. Somewhere round about the time when Vera's accident took place. But I don't understand. Why do you ask, sir? What can that have to do with . . . ?"

Anthony ignored the question that Langford put to him. "You didn't visit the show by any chance, then?"

"No, sir. For two reasons. First—I was workin' late round about that time. And second . . . there was Vera's affair—itself. But why do you ask?"

"Oh . . . never mind for the moment. I just wanted to make certain about it—that was all. Do you happen to know anybody about here who did patronise the show?"

"No, sir. I never heard tell of any. No doubt there were some that did go . . . plenty, I expect, if you could only find 'em . . . but I wasn't takin' much notice of things just then . . . as you can guess."

"Can you tell me this? What occupation was ascribed to her at the inquest? Can you remember?"

"Cashier, sir. Just an ordinary cashier—I do remember that. Just as though she'd still been with Hardy's at the creamery. Nobody at the time seemed to worry about that sort of thing. Even her father, Ted Sinclair, never said anything at the inquest about her having changed her job."

"Were you aware that she had bought a car?"

"Oh . . . yes. But it was a cheap one . . . and Vera had always been a girl able to save."

"Had she a car when she worked for Hardy's?"

"No, sir. She bought it soon after she left there. I remember her writing a letter to me in which she told me that she was buying it. 'Treating herself,' she called it."

"Was she in comparatively comfortable circumstances . . . as regards money . . . as far as you know, that is?"

Langford shook his head. "Just ordinary-like . . . had a few pounds saved up, I should think . . . I never knew a lot about her financial affairs . . . she wasn't one to talk of things like that. But as I told you, sir, she could always manage to save a little. Now that I come to think of it I should have said—" Langford stopped with an abruptness that surprised Anthony. A curious look took possession of his eyes. Mr. Bathurst prompted him.

"Well . . . what would you have said?"

"Why, this, that just about the time that Vera left Hardy's creamery she seemed to have *less* money than usually. Once or twice I noticed that she refused to fall in with certain suggestions I made to her . . . about going to places, I mean. You know, pictures and so forth. Really, I thought that it was this that made her take on the other job."

"I see," commented Anthony quietly. "That certainty must be regarded as a possibility. Now tell me this, Langford. There's a Colonel Fletcher lives near here, I believe. His house is called 'The Cranes,' isn't it? Do you know him?"

"By sight, sir. Very well. Not in any other way, of course. He's not like us villagers, sir—the Colonel. He's a gentleman."

Anthony smiled at Langford's naive statement. "Tell me about him. All that you know. What's he like?"

99 | THE CASE OF THE PURPLE CALF

"He's a big tall gentleman. Military looking. I've never spoken to him or anything like that. Just touched my cap and said 'good morning' to him sometimes when I passed him."

"A son and a daughter, hasn't he?"

"Yes, sir. Mr. Stephen and Miss Margaret. But Mr. Stephen Fletcher's mother was Colonel Fletcher's first wife."

"Did Vera Sinclair know the Fletchers? Did she come into contact with them? In any way of which you can think? Direct or indirect?"

Langford looked astounded. "Why no, sir. They're gentry. How could she have done?"

"Yes. I know all about that. But the gentry, as you describe them, may come into *contact* with the rest of us . . . in various ways. We can work for them, serve them, even rely on them for some things . . . did Vera Sinclair touch the Fletchers in *any* indirect way that may suggest itself to you?"

"No, sir." Langford was definite in his denial. "At any rate, if she did—I never heard tell of it. I can't see that she could possibly have done so, sir."

Mr. Bathurst rose at Langford's final denial. "Thank you, Langford," he said, "I don't think that I need trouble you any further. It is becoming increasingly evident to me that I have much to do before I can hope to see this case finished. But I'll tell you this. Vera Sinclair was murdered! Murdered as clearly as if she had been deliberately shot through the heart or slowly poisoned."

Langford paled at Anthony's sternness. Anthony Bathurst put a firm hand on his shoulder. "And I'm going to put a rope round the neck of the callous brute that murdered her. Be sure of that."

Langford heard the wheels of his visitor's car returning into the distance. He sat in his room . . . with bowed head. This stranger who had visited him had so poignantly brought back the past. When his father returned to the cottage he was still in the same position. He had not sought Sorrow. The grey lass had chosen her own way and come to *him*.

Chapter XIII
GREEN-ROOM GOSSIP

Mr. Bathurst entered the Gainsborough Theatre by the stage-door. Certain preliminary arrangements, adroitly executed, had made this a possibility for him. He quickly passed through several dark passages, up and down various short flights of stairs and eventually found himself outside the door of a dressing-room upon which had been fastened a printed card that bore a name—"Harding Argyle." Mr. Bathurst raised his hand, knocked quietly on this door, and awaited response.

"Come in," said a florid voice.

Mr. Bathurst obeyed the request. As he entered, he saw that a man was seated in a chair facing a mirror positioned on the eye-level. Every now and then, this person leant forward, apparently anxiously, and peered steadfastly into the glass. Suddenly he seemed to remember that his privacy had been invaded and he turned languidly to face his visitor. Anthony saw a stout young man, with fat, puffy cheeks and blue protuberant eyes. Taken on the whole, however, the face was not ill-natured. It was redeemed by an expression of comic bewilderment. In repose it appeared to clothe itself with a strange wondering smile which looked as though it belonged to its owner by rights and should be permanent. The head was big, the hair light and straight and unusually close-cropped. The man's mouth was large and taken in conjunction with his cheeks, looked as though a whole apple had been stuffed into it. As he surveyed the man who had called upon him, Harding Argyle deliberately picked up a snuff-box and tapped it with his right hand.

"Good evening," he said, "as I told you in my previous message, if you care to wait here while I make-up, I can give you exactly twenty-two minutes. Bathurst is the name, is it not?"

"Yes. Anthony Bathurst. Thank you for the opportunity. As for the time and the day—"

Argyle interrupted him with a surprising gesture and a strange grimace to point its meaning. "The better the day, my good sir, the better the deed. Often have I heard that told. I read Russian novels and am a moderately capable exponent of the writing of mechanical verse. Why should I refuse other activities that may prove to be pleasing?" He carefully and pensively rubbed cream into the folds of his fat face and sang.

> "Flitter, flutter, fairy fingers,
> Sure 'tis poetry that lingers
> In your frolics, silent singers!"

Mr. Bathurst listened with amusement and without audible comment.

"The lighting in this damned hole," continued Mr. Argyle, "is unconscionably bad and foully inadequate. The dimmers are vile and the 'foots' appalling anachronisms. I imagine that they came from the Ark when Noah was S.M." As he spoke, he set his head a little to one side and inspected his appearance critically. Then he threw his head back, half-closed his eyes and broadened his mouth into a capacious smile. Anthony determined to let him talk . . . for a time. "The mummer's is a strange and precarious life, my dear sir. Bed till midday. Rehearsals . . . upon occasions. Taverns where throng lewd fellows of the baser sort who at times grin like a dog and run about through the city. Clubs. Strange beds in dirty rooms. The tuning up of the orchestra. Applause. Condemnation. Suppers! Then bed again at cock-crow. And through it all the stench of this abominable greasepaint . . . which, nevertheless, I love beyond expression . . . and indeed could never live without." He cocked his fat face at Anthony with a cunning shrewdness. Anthony assessed him with care. The man returned Anthony's comprehensively critical survey with a cool and calm assurance. Anthony saw how the fat stumpy fingers curled and crinkled round his cheeks as he smoothed and evened the grease-paint which he was applying to them. Seconds passed in silence. Suddenly Argyle turned from the looking-glass into which he had been peering, put down the liner which he had been using and rapped out a question. He seemed in a twinkling to shed something that had been intensely artificial and to become real. Anthony recognised the peremptory tone.

"Well . . . and what is your real business with me Mr. . . . . er . . . Bathurst? I'm more or less ready now and I will confess that I am moderately anxious to know."

Anthony judged that it was high time that he came to grips. He made a sudden decision to try a long shot and countered with relentless force.

"I wanted to ask you a question, Mr. Argyle. As I told you in my first communication with you. Who killed Clare Kent?" But if he sought reward in the shape of immediate enlightenment, disappointment lay in wait for him.

Harding Argyle showed unmistakable signs of genuine astonishment. Anthony's question had brought his mind to a standstill, as it were.

"My dear fellow," he said coolly and imperturbably, "do explain your troubled self. I haven't the slightest idea of what you're talking about. Please be more explicit . . . if you expect me to carry on an intelligent conversation with you."

Anthony still struggled. "Surely you should have found me explicit? After all, you must have understood my question. Let me repeat it. I said to you—'Who killed Clare Kent?'."

"Clare Kent?" Harding Argyle spoke the name after Anthony somewhat incredulously. "Is Clare Kent dead, then?"

Mr. Bathurst nodded. "Yes, Mr. Argyle. Am I to understand from your remark that you were unaware of the fact?"

"That Clare Kent was dead, do you mean? Of course I was unaware of it. Hence my question to you. What otherwise would have prompted that?"

Anthony hesitated. The man whom he had taxed seemed genuine enough. Argyle noticed his hesitation and proceeded to make immediate capital out of it.

"Besides—what have I to do with Clare Kent when all is said and done? Why come to me about it?"

"Simply this. I was referred to you as having been one of her most intimate friends. That was the reason why I came to you."

103 | THE CASE OF THE PURPLE CALF

Argyle frowned. Anthony noticed the sudden ugliness which the frown gave to his face.

"Just a moment—if you don't mind. Let's face facts and get this straight. Let's get *you* straight in addition. Are you a detective? From Scotland Yard? Now—out with it."

Anthony shook his head. "I have no strictly official connection with Scotland Yard, if that's your meaning. Although at times I co-operate with the police authorities. Indeed at the present moment I am investigating the matter of Miss Kent's death with their full knowledge and consent. Do those facts satisfy you, Mr. Argyle?"

The man addressed shrugged his shoulders rather grudgingly. "I'll guess they'll have to. The best thing that you can do is to put me wise to all that you know. Tell me the facts. I'm completely in the dark—remember. When I've heard the details, maybe I'll do a spot of talking." He looked at his watch. "I can give you a quarter of an hour before my call. Jump to it, Mr. Bathurst."

Anthony realised that the man was talking sound sense. He told him of the girl's death. Of the various details connected with it. Of the inquest and the result thereof. But he carefully omitted any reference to the man Dexter, and made no mention of any statement that Dexter had made. Argyle listened carefully and attentively. Eventually he looked up at Anthony. As he did so, a tap sounded on the door of the dressing-room. "Mr. Argyle."

"There's my call," he said. "I'm not on for long first act, so that if you care to wait here till I'm off I'll talk to you later. All right?"

Anthony nodded his assent.

"That's O.K. with me then," said Argyle. "You stay here and I'll come back to you." Argyle walked to the door of his dressing-room and turned to deliver a last piece of advice. "See how I trust you," he flung at Anthony, "leaving you the run of my room. How many men in my position would do that? But there—I went to school with Mary's little lamb."

Mr. Bathurst smiled and watched his host's retreating form and then thoughtfully scratched his cheek. It was true, he admitted to himself, that this man whom he had come to interview, definitely puzzled him. He endeavoured to recall Dexter's exact words in relation to him. Harding Argyle, in the opinion of the dead girl, Clare Kent, had been a splendid "character" actor and a man, too, "who had once saved a show from a 'flop' by a particularly clever piece of quick thinking."

Mr. Bathurst held silent communication with himself. He realised that the man with whom he was dealing was of no ordinary type. This man had undoubted gifts. If the best results were to be obtained, cleverness and craftsmanship would have to be met and matched with the same qualities. A travelling actor! Continually, perhaps, "out of a shop." When "fixed," playing most provincial towns and a good many considerably smaller places. Mr. Bathurst mused thus for some minutes. At length, he heard a burst of applause from the house and his musing was cut short by the return of Harding Argyle. That gentleman entered unobtrusively and took his seat opposite to his mirror.

"You will excuse me a moment. I'm sweating like a pig. I must 'powder off.'" Argyle pressed the powder-puff against his face. Then he turned again to Anthony. "Now laddie," he said with more than a hint of patronage, "get this! And once you've got it don't forget it. I haven't seen Clare for months. I had no idea that the poor girl was dead. I'm damned sorry to hear it. She was a thoroughly decent kid. A good pal and a good companion when you worked with her. What you have told me about her death is both a shock and a surprise to me. But now I'll tell *you* something. I've never been in Great Kirby in my life. So I'm afraid, Mr. What's-your-name, that you've had your journey for nothing. Or next to nothing."

"You don't read the papers carefully, I take it?"

"I don't read 'em column by column. Not on your life. To tell the truth it's the sporting page that commands most of my serious attention." He grinned affably. "Not entirely to my profit I can assure you."

Anthony accepted his statement without comment. He harked back. "Returning to what you said a few moments ago, Mr. Argyle, you stated that you hadn't seen Miss Kent for months. May I ask you if you were aware of any of her movements?"

Argyle became round-eyed. "Certainly not. What are you hinting at? Why on earth should I be?"

"You didn't correspond—then?"

"Good Lord—no! Clare and I were never more than ordinary friends. Hardly that even. Call us acquaintances and you'll be much nearer the mark. Just an actor and an actress who had played in the same company at odd times and then passed each other in the night. The last show we played together was 'A Man of Few Words' on its West-country tour. We finished at Truro. I was resting for some time after that and I've no doubt that Clare was in a similar position. That's the luck of our game, you know. I haven't heard a word of her or from her between the last 'Treasury' at Truro and your walking in on me this evening."

Anthony considered possibilities. "In the meantime, then, Miss Kent may have been financially embarrassed? Would you subscribe to that probability?"

"I couldn't say for certain—but no doubt it's extremely likely. At the same time she was unlucky not to have made good. She had a wonderful gift of mimicry. She didn't get near the people she imitated—she got absolutely inside 'em. Right into their skins. And that's what counts in our game. More perhaps than in any other profession. Poor old Clare." Argyle shook his head with a sympathy that seemed to Anthony, watching him carefully, eminently sincere. He asked Argyle another question.

"During the time that you were in daily contact with Miss Kent—did she run a car?"

Argyle shook his head emphatically. "A car? Laddie—you've some sure imagination. Cars weren't in our line in those days—believe me. We walk to most of our assignations. Of course, like Digby Grant, we occasionally *have* money—I admit—and a tram fare is not then beyond us. But cars, now—"

Argyle wagged his head.

"It would be logical, then, seeing that Miss Kent was driving her own car, when she went to her death, to assume that, although she hadn't been playing for some little time, her financial position must have materially improved."

Argyle bit his lip. He seemed a trifle annoyed.

"It would seem so—I'll grant you that." Anthony shrugged his shoulders as the man made the concession.

"In that case, then—it raises an important consideration, doesn't it?"

"You mean, I suppose—from whom did the money come?"

"Exactly. What else?"

"H'm—easier asked than answered—conjecture's pretty useless."

"My dear sir, in the absence of definite fact—one is forced back on to conjecture. And sometimes, Mr. Argyle, a chance conjecture may lead one to the truth."

"Equally—conjecture may lead one astray. Surely you would admit that. If you've had any experience at all you must know that."

"And yet," said Anthony softly, "it is a disgraceful thing to stumble twice against the same stone. What happened to Miss Kent between Truro and . . . Great Kirby?"

A half-smile came into being and played round the corners of Argyle's creased mouth. "That, my dear sir, is what you have to find out."

Anthony's eyes held challenge. "More than that, Mr. Argyle. It is what I'm *going* to find out."

Argyle made a curious movement with his hands—as though he were attempting to push something away from him. Anthony took a further step forward. His grey eyes held Argyle. "Miss Kent's death was more than it seemed on the surface. More indeed than I have so far allowed myself to tell you." He paused, weighing his words. Argyle's eyes searched his face for truth. Anthony decided to give it to him. "It was the third tragedy of a series. She was the third girl since last October, Mr. Argyle, to be found dead beside an overturned car. Her predecessors in this dread triangle of terror were a Phyllis Welby—the Honourable Phyllis Welby—daughter of Lord Sturt—and a Miss Vera Sinclair. These two girls met their deaths at Loxeter and East Hannington respectively."

As Anthony finished his sentence, Argyle passed his hand across his forehead. "When?" he asked.

"Miss Welby died in October. Miss Sinclair in April. You will understand now, Mr. Argyle, why I confess to such an absorbing interest in these matters." But Argyle paid no attention beyond repeating the names of the three towns that Anthony Bathurst had mentioned to him. "Great Kirby . . . Loxeter . . . East Hannington. East Hannington . . . Loxeter . . . Great Kirby. In only one of them have I ever been—Loxeter! So I can't get a proper mental picture. A proper mental picture that would help me. Of the other two." He stood up, looked across the room and held out his hand to Anthony Bathurst. "My time's up. I'm wanted again in a few minutes. You have been the bearer of most astounding news. And sad as well as astounding. Good-bye. And good huntin'."

"Thank you," said Mr. Bathurst. "Both for your information and for your good wishes."

He paused in the doorway.

"It's possible, I suppose, Mr. Argyle, that we may even meet again."

Chapter XIV
SHOCK FOR STEPHEN

It will be remembered that a girl named Margaret Fletcher had screamed in a gaming-room of the establishment known as "The Purple Calf." More than that, her half-brother, Stephen Fletcher, had heard the scream and when Margaret had run from the room in her agitation he and his friend, Peter Brailsford, had followed her. But they had failed to find her, for Margaret had returned home. The days that came after were a nightmare to Stephen. Strive though he might, he was unable to escape from the trouble that overshadowed his sister. She carried it with her during those days so obviously and so unmistakably. He found himself watching her, her actions and her movements . . . once . . . twice . . . and then repeatedly. When he sought an avenue of intelligent approach, to his surprise and amazement, Margaret fended him off. But her visits to "The Purple Calf" grew more frequent. Many times she went there without him and, as far as he knew, unescorted. Then, one morning when he came down to breakfast, he found a note awaiting him. He opened it hastily and read it. A glance at the writing told him that it was from Margaret and that his worst fears of her were at last realised. For the contents of the note ran thus:

"My Dear Stephen,

As Father is away on one of his holiday tours I am addressing this to you, because I suppose that in his absence I must regard you as the head of the family. In a way I'm glad that it should be so because I find it easier to write this to you than I should have done to write it to him. Perhaps you understand me better than he has ever done. At any rate, we will leave that as the chief explanation. I am glad, too, that he is away, for another reason. Because it's just possible that my trouble may be all over and done with by the time that he comes home. In that case, you see, he will have been spared it all and need know nothing whatever about it. You will have guessed yourself from what you know and from what you may have since added to that knowledge, that things are not so good with me. Stephen, dear Stephen, I have been both reckless and improvident. To put the matter in a nutshell I have lost heavily at 'The Purple Calf' ever since I first started to gamble there. Honestly, Stephen darling, my luck has been outrageously bad and nothing has seemed to go right for me. I've waited and waited for my luck to turn. I thought that it *must* by all the laws of average. I prayed that it should! The tide of fortune has flowed steadily against me right from the very beginning. I have paid away every penny that I had to spare . . . I have borrowed from friends whom I *could* ask . . . and from some whom I was a fool to approach, and I am terrified to think of the amount that I owe . . . which, at the moment, I am utterly unable to pay. I know that it's no good coming to you for it and I simply can't face Father over a matter like this. I have given I.O.U.'s for the amounts that are still outstanding. That was over a week ago now and I have already had two scarcely-veiled hints that my chief creditor is neither willing nor prepared to

THE CASE OF THE PURPLE CALF

wait very long for the money that is due to him. A remark which accompanied the latter of the hints was too beastly for me to repeat here. I have therefore, Stephen dear, decided to take my courage in both hands and try something desperate. No, dear Stephen, don't let your thoughts immediately fly to the worst. I'm not contemplating suicide or anything like that . . . yet! I'm simply following my secret heart and attempting to execute a plan, the idea of which has come to me during the past few days and which I hope may eventually turn out to be my salvation. If I can work it out as cleverly as I have every hope of doing, there is just a bare chance for me to come through my trouble. A week should tell. A week to ten days. By the time that you read this letter of mine, I shall be miles away. And for the time being at least—*safe!* The crucial test for me will come later. It will demand all my nerve, all my courage and all my resources of will-power. Please God that I come through it all safely. If I do—I shall come home with banners flying and bugles blowing. If I don't—now listen to me carefully. If, in say, ten days' time you have heard nothing more from me . . . and I haven't returned to 'The Cranes' . . . please take this letter to a Mr. Anthony L. Bathurst. You will find his address in the telephone directory. Have no fear of meeting him . . . on the score of divulging any secrets, I mean . . . and be absolutely frank with him with regard to any question about me that he may ask you. I've met him . . . don't worry . . . it was at 'The Purple Calf' of all places . . . and I have thought since that if you appealed to him on my behalf, he would do all that lay in his power to help me—and to help us. If Father should return from his trip before I am back home again, I leave it entirely to your discretion—how much of all this that you tell him. I think it would be for the best if you concocted a story that I had been invited to stay with somebody. With Lord and Lady Sturt for example. It might serve to keep him quiet for a few days at the very worst. *Au 'voir*, Stephen dear, or should it be good-bye? *Moritura te saluto*. This is a long letter—the longest, I think that I have ever written, but remember this, Stephen, in extenuation and make the necessary allowances. *It may well be the last that I shall ever write.* Still—who cares? Good job, too! Good job, twenty-two! Death, after all, may prove to be a marvellously great adventure. I don't know that Life is such a joy-ride after all. With all my love, Stephen—*toujours à toi*,

Your Sister,

MARGARET."

Stephen Fletcher's hands were trembling by the time he came to his sister's signature. His glittering, cynical outlook on life was temporarily arrested and many personal adjustments had to be summarily carried out. The letter that he had just read brought him sharply back to stark realities. But in justice to him, it must be admitted that his first thought was to blame himself for the semi-tragedy that had so unexpectedly enveloped his sister. There was one thought from which he could find no escape. If it hadn't been for him, in the first place, Margaret would never have gone to "The Purple Calf." In all probability would never have known of the place's existence. He cursed himself bitterly for all his sins of commission and omission.

He lit a cigarette and read the letter for a second time. For any indications which he had possibly missed but which, if found, would be more positive than those which he had already assimilated. But even on a second reading, the main features of the story appeared plain and commonplace enough. Gambling losses, debts of honour and dishonour, were ordinary occurrences that surrounded "The Purple Calf." Stephen Fletcher had known several similar cases within his own range of acquaintance. Affairs that had finished in disgrace and then tragedy. But why on earth hadn't Margaret given him her confidences before she had reached the present pass? Anything would have been better than this. It *was* sheer tragedy—not merely semi-tragedy as he had visualised it previously. Stephen Fletcher had frowned when he had come for the second time to the unexpected reference to Anthony Bathurst. He regarded Margaret's suggestion in this respect as approximating an affront to himself. What in the name of goodness could this fellow Bathurst do that he himself could *not*? He lowered his dark eyebrows in his criticism. "Devil take me," he muttered to himself. "It's a nice kettle of fish altogether, but why in the name of all that's reasonable must we drag in outsiders?" He read the letter for yet a third time. This time he was even more affected than before. His eyes glistened and his breath came fast. Feverishly he turned the page over. For at last he had learnt something from it. Was it possible that he could learn more? His mind cast back eagerly and impatiently for clues and evidences. A fragment of memory came to him. What a consummate fool he had been not to have considered it before. There had been that evening at "The Purple Calf" when Margaret had been annoyed or insulted by somebody. The man had been a stranger. He remembered how she had dismissed the matter somewhat lightly when he had taxed her with it.

"The incident is now closed." They were the words which she had used. It had occurred, he recalled, as he probed the past, just before he had arrived at the "Calf" one evening, with Peter Brailsford. Stephen began to shed much that was superficial. He left the world of phantasms and fantasies, wherein he had dwelt for so long, and re-entered the state of men and deeds. The world of hot loves and wild burning hates! The world of elaborate conspiracies and distrustful, open-mouthed fools. He tossed away the stub of his cigarette and pored, quick-breathed, over Margaret's message. Anger and resentment now showed in his glittering black eyes. He walked to the window of the breakfast-room and looked out on the beauties of nature. He looked across to where the Cran had its source. A dark meadow, a winding river and a line of elms—such made up the landscape at which Stephen Fletcher looked that morning. To the westward he could see the faint gleam of white cliffs where the sea lay, blue-dark in their sombre shadow. The morning sky was as blue as the deep water of Torbay itself and the sun rode high. Fletcher longed ardently to be under those white cliffs where he could watch tiny waves chasing each other in undulating glee before the breath of the gentlest of south winds. He saw and heard a wild duck flap boisterously from the rushes of the Cran. That duck had no dark problem to contemplate such as he had! Then he saw something else which caused him to jerk back his head in surprise. He saw a car drive up and stop at the gates. A young man slid from the driver's seat. Stephen mocked cynically. "Orpheus, no doubt," he murmured to himself, "in search of the lost Eurydice." The man was Peter Brailsford. But his step was a little less brisk than usual and the hot morning sun could not be held totally responsible for this difference in his gait. For Peter's eyes, too, were duller than usual and the cheeks less fresh. Stephen's mouth twisted curiously as he watched him from the window. "Margaret, evidently," he whispered to himself, "has cleared up the arrears of her correspondence. And le Bon Pierre has become queasy in consequence and lost temporarily the sweet savour of this transitory world. Weep not, Peter! The lusts of the flesh will return to you—ere long."

He heard Crench go to the door to admit the caller, and then Peter Brailsford's voice. Stephen opened the breakfast-room door and greeted him. He looked straight at Brailsford and smiled at him.

"Your most obedient servant, my dear Peter," he observed with soft pleasantness. "Why are we thus honoured so early? Why do you disturb *les heures immaculées*? As a matter of fact, Margaret has not yet come down for breakfast." It seemed to him that Peter Brailsford winced as from a sharply-struck blow.

"Margaret?" he queried with unsteady voice, "you haven't heard, then? I thought it might be so."

But Stephen was Stephen and still showed the world a smile.

"I have a letter here," said Peter. "I brought it specially to show you. Read it."

"A letter?"

"Yes. From Margaret—your sister. For God's sake don't stand there like that as though nothing at all mattered. Read it. When you've read it, you'll understand that we've got to do something—quickly."

Stephen took the letter to the window for better light. The terms of Margaret's letter to Brailsford were very much as he had anticipated. He knew his sister's moods and temperament so well. He looked over the top of the letter to see if Brailsford were watching him. Peter suddenly felt an irrational anger consuming him. This Stephen Fletcher—Margaret's half-brother—

Stephen handed back the letter. His detached attitude almost made Peter Brailsford shiver.

"She doesn't say much—this sister of mine." Stephen was choosing his words deliberately. He continued. "Why your undue anxiety, my dear Peter? Do you read more into her words than I can? Do you *know* more than I do?"

"I don't understand what you mean! What are you hinting? All I know is what that letter says. That Margaret is in the cart over something pretty badly and that she's taken fright and bolted somewhere. That's serious enough in all conscience, isn't it?" Stephen shrugged his shoulders non-committally.

"Women always exaggerate. They're eternal creatures of hysterical hyperbole. Things are never normal with them. Invariably 'terribly.' I really don't see what you're going off the deep end about. Don't you worry. She'll come back all right—when it suits her."

Peter stared at him incredulously. "You're taking it all damned lightly, Stephen—aren't you?"

"What do you suggest that I do, then? Go mad and bite somebody?"

Peter showed signs of impatience. "Inquire—investigate—find things out. She may be desperate. We can't sit still and fold our arms—can we?"

"Where do we inquire? At the Post Office? Or broadcast an S.O.S.?"

Peter hesitated before replying. Stephen followed up. "Isn't that the last thing she would want us to do? Judging, that is, by the terms of her letter? Publish her troubles and shortcomings in the streets of both Gath and Ascalon? For Heaven's sake, use what brains you have, Peter."

In this respect it must be conceded that Fletcher held an undoubted advantage. In this way. He had seen Brailsford's letter, but the latter hadn't seen his. He wasn't aware, in fact, that Stephen had even received a letter. Margaret had told him much more than she had communicated to Peter. For instance there had been no reference to Anthony Bathurst in the letter that Margaret had written to Peter Brailsford. Stephen eventually came out into the open.

"As a matter of interest to you, Peter, I may as well tell you now, that I, too, have heard from Margaret. By this morning's post. The gentle creature timed her epistolary effort with the matutinal coffee. The whole thing is definitely disturbing, I admit, but I see no reason why we should lose our heads over it. In fact, I can assure you that I have no intention of losing mine." He walked forward and pressed a bell-push.

Peter thrust at him. "Has she told you more than she has told me?"

Stephen Fletcher shook his head. "Not a thing. That counts, I mean. She is certainly more verbose in her effort to me, than she has been to you, but the main points are substantially the same." He turned to the maid whose figure showed in the doorway. "Clear away, Rogers, will you? And tell Herapath that I shall want the car. In half an hour's time. Have a whisky and soda, Peter?"

Brailsford nodded. "Well—it's a trifle early—but there's no point, I suppose, in refusing."

Stephen walked to the sideboard and did the necessary. "Never is, as far as I know. Say when."

"When."

"There you are, then."

Peter looked hard at Stephen prior to drinking. "You know, Stephen, you're a cool card, upon my word. You've taken this in your stride. I imagined that you'd be worried like hell."

"Is that why you rushed here to tell me? Showing your kind consideration—eh?" Stephen's smile was indulgent.

Peter Brailsford made a petulant gesture. There was a sign of anger in his eyes. "Oh, curse you, Stephen, for a cold-blooded fish. You know that's not true."

"What is truth?" returned cynical Stephen.

"You ask me?"

"I ask you."

Brailsford was frankly puzzled. "Oh—an end to this bandying of words. *Everything* demands action from us. I'm going to leave no stone unturned to find out where Margaret is. What's become of her. Everything. If you don't stir yourself—I'm going to. And that's that."

"Interesting. Very. Any plans? Glad to hear 'em if you have." Stephen seated himself with a parade of comfort and looked up at Peter in invitation. The latter responded.

"I've no plans at the moment. I haven't had time to make any. But that doesn't say that I shan't have any in a week's time. I was going north on business for the guv'nor, but I'll give that trip best and get to work on this Margaret tangle. Let me tell you this—'they laugh best who laugh last.'"

"Or perhaps those that don't even laugh at all." Stephen lit a cigarette with a perfectly steady hand.

Brailsford stared at him. "What do you mean by that last remark?"

"Well—what I'm wondering is this. What has Margaret's sudden flight into Egypt to do with the death of Phyllis Welby? Or possibly—if I like to choose my words more carefully—with the *murder* of that rather charming young lady?"

Peter shook his head. "You've taken me out of my depth. I can't help you there."

"No? Ah well—I'm not really surprised at that. But I wonder if a certain Mr. Anthony Bathurst will be able to?"

Chapter XV
WHERE IS MARGARET?

Stephen Fletcher came from the outskirts of East Hannington to Anthony Bathurst's flat in London on a morning that dawned with spiral mists. The early hours were of autumn. He passed the white walls of the monastery of St. Aloysius glittering near the waters of the Cran, under a grey horizon of cloud. He passed dull red roofs and drab walls. Fields and meadows, on the swell of hills, had lost the generous plenty of summer and were now approaching a condition of bareness. In the dim light of this grey morning they seemed to look all alike as Fletcher's car swept arrogantly by them. In the hollows of the land the menacing mist hung heavier. Stephen shivered as his senses reacted to it. Visibility was not good, as may be imagined, but he kept the car going at a consistently good pace. He contrasted the countryside as he saw it now, with the country-side of spring. The touch of that magic season on an English hedgerow. Thorns white-garmented! Deep, still, streams with blazing king-cups on their banks and the soft spring breeze heavy with the scent of English flowers. Branches filled with the sweet-smelling sap of springtime. True autumn would be here soon and England's deep-bosomed fields smiling in the golden haze of an autumn day. From where would Margaret see it? If she were yet alive to see it! Stephen drove on—almost fiercely. The miles slipped behind him. Mean streets were now in front of him. In due time, Stephen Fletcher halted his car outside the flat of a certain Anthony Lotherington Bathurst. The latter, back from his interesting encounter with Harding Argyle, received him curiously and gestured him to a seat. Mr. Bathurst held his visitor's card between thumb and finger and awaited that visitor's pleasure.

But Stephen Fletcher was undeterred at this and took his time. "I haven't the felicity of your acquaintance, Mr. Bathurst," he said eventually, "and I am not here upon my own behalf. I think that it is only right that I should start by telling you that. Let me say, rather, that I am here because I am acting under instructions. When I add to that statement that the instructions come to me from the lips of a lady—you—as a man of the world—will understand, I am sure. I am—as you will have seen by now—Stephen Fletcher, of 'The Cranes,' near East Hannington." Anthony nodded silent acquiescence. Fletcher went on. "I know but little about you. I take you almost entirely on trust."

Anthony regarded him semi-humorously. "That condition is mutual, then. We meet, one might say, on strictly level terms. By no means a bad idea. That's always a good basis on which to start. Well, Mr. Fletcher?"

Anthony's attack meant that Stephen was slightly disconcerted. But he recovered quickly, in accordance with his invariable habit, and proceeded to develop his story on the lines that he had meant to use originally.

"You will observe, Mr. Bathurst," he said, "that my need is not my own. I am suppliant for another. An apostle of supreme altruism."

"The lady of whom you spoke—I take it!" Anthony's question was a smooth interruption.

"Yes. My sister. To be strictly accurate—my half-sister—Miss Margaret Fletcher."

Stephen watched for the effect that this name would have upon the face of the man who had questioned him. But Anthony gave him little sign that the name was familiar or even previously known to him. He repeated it aloud—after Stephen. "Margaret Fletcher."

"Yes."

Anthony's face cleared. "I think that I have traced an association. Margaret Fletcher was the friend of the girl who died as the result of a motoring accident last year. At Loxeter. The Hon. Phyllis Welby. Am I right in assuming that this is the lady of that connection?"

"You are quite right, Mr. Bathurst. My sister gave evidence at the inquest on Miss Welby. But I didn't come here to discuss that. The point is that my sister has disappeared and I have come to you upon her own instructions."

Anthony wrinkled his brows. "One moment, please. Let me understand this clearly. You say that Miss Fletcher has disappeared—and yet that you come to me acting upon her instructions. Am I right?"

"Absolutely." Stephen permitted himself the luxury of a smile. It pleased him to see this man Bathurst even temporarily mystified. The latter came again.

"Perhaps you would be good enough to explain."

Stephen handed Margaret's letter to him. "There is no need for me to do that. If you read this, it should tell you all that you want to know."

Anthony took the letter and read it twice. First rapidly—then slowly and with more sustained concentration. He folded it, replaced it in the envelope and returned that to his visitor. The latter, in turn, replaced it in his pocket-book without further comment.

"It means this, then. You have heard nothing, I take it, from Miss Fletcher, since you received that letter?"

Stephen Fletcher bowed. "Your deductions are marvellous."

Anthony smiled. "Well?"

Fletcher moved his shoulders awkwardly. "I have simply carried out her instructions. The rest is surely up to you. I have played the part that she allotted to me. Now it's your turn."

"Against your inclinations?"

"Perhaps. More than perhaps. Most probably. I may as well be perfectly sincere."

"'The Purple Calf'—Miss Fletcher refers to the night-club of that name in Coverdale Street?"

"Obviously."

"Do you go there yourself, Mr. Fletcher?"

"Yes, I go there occasionally."

Mr. Bathurst's eyes held a tremendous question. He translated it into words. "Were you not aware then, of this trouble that was overshadowing your sister? If its genesis can be traced to 'The Purple Calf'?"

Stephen Fletcher made a gesture of annoyance. "That's asking too much. I'm not tied to my sister's apron-strings—neither do I hold Margaret's hand. She has her own friends and moves in her own circle. This is the twentieth century, Mr. Bathurst. The days of the duenna and the chaperone belong to the past."

"You were not aware then, that Miss Fletcher was gambling heavily? And losing?"

"I knew that she occasionally had a flutter at the tables but I hadn't the slightest idea that matters had come to such a serious pitch. If I had known, I should have put my foot down—naturally. But what's the real point behind your question?"

Anthony shook his head as though Fletcher's query annoyed him. "Merely this. That I must get right into the heart of things. Who can tell me relevant facts better than the missing lady's brother? Can you think of anybody yourself?"

Stephen realised very clearly that Mr. Bathurst had turned the tables on him. He contented himself therefore, with a direct denial. "No."

"That's understood, then! Do you agree to put the case into my hands, Mr. Fletcher?"

"You've read Margaret's letter. The point lies therein. It is *her* wish. I've never said that it was mine."

"Data, then, my dear sir! Facts! Evidences! What have you to tell me?"

Stephen smiled cynically at Mr. Bathurst's insistence.

"Nothing. Beyond what you have already heard. I know nothing—suspect nothing or nobody—in short am as ignorant of the whole wretched business as you yourself are. Don't rely for a scrap of help on me. For once you have a real problem to solve." The spite in his voice was ill-concealed.

The lines round Anthony's mouth and his jaw were firm and set. "You mean that you cannot make the slightest suggestion as to your sister's whereabouts?"

"Exactly. I am overjoyed that you have at last appreciated the fact."

Anthony rose and bowed to his visitor. "In that case, then, Mr. Fletcher—there is no need for me to detain you any longer. To do so would waste the time of each of us." He smiled sweetly as he walked to the door.

Fletcher gave suavity for suavity. "Two minds with but a single thought, I perceive. I always said that Margaret had strange reactions."

"I notice that you use the past tense, Mr. Fletcher." Anthony opened the door for Stephen's exit. Then he walked to the window and saw Stephen go to his car. As he watched and wondered, Mr. Bathurst saw something that made him watch and wonder more. A man on the other side of the road was gazing up at the window of the flat. As Fletcher started his car, this man who watched ran quickly to another car and brought it into a run almost immediately behind Stephen Fletcher's. The two cars gathered pace, the one still behind the other. Helped by his memory, Anthony recognised the man who followed Fletcher, with but little difficulty. It was Lafferty, of "L'Estrange's Travelling Showground"! The plot thickened!

Chapter XVI
THE TEETH OF TAFARI

Rame Tafari removed a toothpick from his mouth and lounged towards Lafferty and Buckinger. "Good morning, gentlemen," he said with an icy geniality, "at the cost of personal disturbance, might I have a word with you? Or even words?"

Buckinger looked uneasy, but Lafferty stood his ground courageously. "Well?" he inquired truculently, "what is it that you want? Do you talk to me or to Buckinger?"

Tafari smiled and the smile revealed his white even teeth. "On that point, I am indifferent. To either. Or to both. It's a question of the cap fitting. For all I know, your two heads may be of the same size."

"Very good," returned Lafferty.

Buckinger made no reply. He felt that silence left a greater margin of safety.

Tafari continued and tapped his riding boots with a switch as he did so. "What I'm going to say to you, Lafferty, and to you, Buckinger, is no concern of the 'Duke's.' Get that into your heads and when you've got it, fix it there firmly. If I'm any judge, there's probably plenty of room for it. *Don't run squealing to the 'Duke.'* But the lady's name is Rosina." There was sheer malevolence in his tone as he uttered the last sentence. "I have observed on more than one occasion in the immediate past, that you, Lafferty, and in a somewhat lesser degree, you, Buckinger, you misbegotten hound, have each found enjoyment in the company and conversation of the lady whom I have just mentioned. Which, if I may venture to say so, is a most indiscreet practice on your part. Indiscretions, you see—particularly, blazing indiscretions, are often visited with unpleasant consequences."

THE CASE OF THE PURPLE CALF

"I am not frightened of you, Tafari," said Lafferty stoutly—"even if Bucky is. And I don't want to have anything to do with your Rosina—either—if you want the truth."

Tafari took a stride forward and caught Lafferty by the shoulders. "*You* don't want to have anything to do with my Rosina, don't you? You flatter yourself, Lafferty. You ugly whelp! Take this piece of advice from me before I tear you in half. Toy with the 'Dukes' last darling—or Crouch's latest conquest—or Sargeant's favourite strumpet—but don't presume to touch—with your finger-tips even—that which is Rame Tafari's. Neither when he desires it nor after he's tired of it. Get *that*, Lafferty, my lad." He turned suddenly and kicked Buckinger with vicious violence.

The latter cried out bitterly and stumbled for shelter as fast as his legs would carry him.

"Rosina," went on Tafari, addressing Lafferty, "is in poor health to-day. I found the fact definitely annoying when I called upon her. I questioned her as to the way she has recently been spending her evenings. She told me. She was wise. If she hadn't, I should have found a means of making her. You have the satisfaction, you scar-faced hound, of knowing that your conversation has made Rosina ill. What a tribute to your powers of attraction." Tafari laughed lightly at his own gibe. It seemed that the fullness of his rage had passed. He changed the subject. "How's the 'Duke' these days, Lafferty? Temper and health both satisfactory—eh."

"As far as I know," said Lafferty sourly. "At least, *he* hasn't become a victim of my conversation. He's evidently a robuster specimen than your Rosina."

Tafari repeated his laugh. "Not bad for you, Lafferty. You're positively improving. There are times when you have gleams of intelligence. . . . Your periodical visits to Headquarters in company with the 'Duke' serve no doubt to sharpen your wits. For one thing, they're more frequent than of old." He watched Lafferty keenly to see how he would receive this last thrust. On the whole, Lafferty took it very well.

"Jealous?" he inquired with curt pointedness.

Tafari shook his head. Then he took his monocle from his eye and slowly polished it on a silk handkerchief. "There may come a time," he said softly, "one never knows—when I shall be well paid to hold my tongue. Or paid better, perhaps, to do a spot of talking. Either prospect pleases. No man may foretell his future, luckily for him, but I'll venture to assert that excitement looms ahead for each and all of us. Well, Lafferty—under which king? Made your decision?"

Lafferty gave no sign. Tafari struck deeper.

"You didn't know, Lafferty, that I met you that night in October . . . when you were carrying it back . . . did you? The first time you used it, I mean. And I've never breathed a word of that to a living soul. No . . . not to a soul, Lafferty. Not even to a policeman. Say what you like, Lafferty, I've been most considerate towards you. Few people would have treated you as I have done."

Lafferty turned and stared at him. It seemed that Tafari, by a quick turn of the wrist, had exposed and touched the secret nerve of his soul.

"Carrying *what* back, Tafari?" he cried with shrill emphasis but unsteady voice.

"The ladder, Lafferty," replied Tafari, "the ladder of death . . . how many times have you used it since . . . I wonder? Once . . . twice?"

Lafferty's eyes held both amazement and fear as he turned from Tafari, the tormentor, and strode away. The latter, watching, saw Buckinger meet him outside L'Estrange's tent and immediately engage him in animated conversation. A few minutes later, Lafferty and Buckinger passed through the tent flap and were lost to view. Tafari made a quick movement of his shoulder and turned on his heel. "Conference," he said firmly, and then went on to quote Bacon, "and 'Conference maketh a ready man.' Ah, well—readiness is no man's monopoly."

Chapter XVII
THE FOURTH DEATH

STEPHEN Fletcher sat in the library at "The Cranes," East Hannington. He was listening keenly. Suddenly he went to the door of the room and called peremptorily to his man.

"Herapath! Herapath! There's somebody outside! I'm certain of it. I heard the wheels of a car. See who it is. It can't be the Guv'nor. He'd have let us know if he were returning to-night. It's a perfectly foul night."

He was right in this last statement at all events. Herapath knew the truth of it as he made his way to the front door. Rain was falling in merciless torrents, and the wind was savage in its lashing fury. Herapath slowly opened the big front door, put his shoulder to its edge to combat the force of the wind and peered out into the blackness of the night. Slowly his eyes took in the lines of the whole picture. Two men stood on the porch. Their coats were buttoned tight to chin and their hats brought down hard to head and ear.

"Is that you, Herapath?" cried the man who was obviously the younger, "is Mr. Stephen in? I'm Peter Brailsford. You know me, don't you?"

"Oh, come on in, sir," cried Herapath with undisguised relief, "come right in, sir, do. As it happens, Mr. Stephen's in the library. Good gracious, sir, but what a terrible night to be sure. It's not fit for a dog to be out. I reckon you need good food and warm shelter."

Peter turned impulsively to the man who stood with him. "Come in, Guv'nor," he cried. "We're lucky. Stephen's in—thank the Lord. We can get busy at once." His voice held the high-pitched note of excitement.

Sir John Brailsford followed his son across the threshold. Stephen Fletcher stood at the library door and greeted them.

"Welcome," he said with silky sympathy, "dear orphans of the storm. Why choose a night like this for visiting the sick and needy? Has the week no other evenings?"

Peter disregarded Fletcher's satire and came to the point immediately. "You must pardon us, Stephen," he said, rather emotionally, "for bursting in on you so unceremoniously as this. You can bet there's a good reason for our so doing. First of all, let me introduce my father—Sir John Brailsford. Dad—this is Stephen Fletcher, son of Colonel Fletcher—you've heard me speak of him tons of times."

"Pleased to meet you, Fletcher," said Sir John.

"Thank you," returned Stephen drily and without enthusiasm.

"Now, there's no time to lose," cried Peter, "and I must skip for the time being all kinds of things, which, in the ordinary way, I should touch on. Why we're here and for what we've come. But what I must say is this! Three hundred yards up the road there's been an accident. But for the Guv'nor's sharp eyes there would probably have been another. My God . . . it was so close . . . that when I think of it now the thought gives me the cold shivers. I was warned by him just in time and, as a result, was able to pull up. There's an overturned car and a dead girl lying in the roadway. The girl's past everything, let me tell you. I was at her side just long enough to be sure of that. Anyhow, I took the Guv'nor's advice, put the body under the shelter of the hedge and came straight on here. Dad thinks the best thing to do . . . the only thing in the circumstances . . . is to 'phone for the police and a doctor. He won't be able to do anything—that's a certainty—but I suppose he ought to be up there as soon as possible. It's usual, isn't it?"

Stephen's face was white and bloodless. It was as though the blood had been drained from it by the most sudden of operations. "Did you say a girl, Peter?" . . . he muttered almost inaudibly . . . "did you see her face? Who she was?"

Peter Brailsford stared at him in amazement. "Why—what's troubling you, Stephen? Of course we saw her face. But I can't tell you who she is. Identify her—I mean. It's nobody we know. It would have been a marvellous coincidence if it had been—surely. There are thousands of girls in the world whom I don't know, you see."

He stopped suddenly. Light had broken in upon him. "Oh—I see. Of course. What a dunderhead I was. But that hadn't occurred to me. No, Stephen—don't worry. It's all right. It's not Margaret. But hadn't you better get on the 'phone at once?"

Stephen Fletcher nodded mechanically and went into the hall. Sir John nodded significantly to Peter.

"You gave him a shock, Peter, my lad. Took it badly. You were over-impetuous. You ought to have remembered his little spot of trouble and been more tactful than you were. After all— we rather resemble the thunderbolt, you know."

They could hear Stephen's voice in the hall. He was speaking on the telephone. The voice was querulous now—and high-pitched. "Yes, yes," they heard him say, "so I understand— dead." An interval of silence followed. Fletcher, evidently, was being questioned. Then they heard his reply. "Sir John Brailsford is here now. Yes, yes, I know. He and his son have both seen the dead girl. They were motoring to my place and almost ran right into the overturned car. Sir John thought it best to leave things more or less as they were, seeing that no real good can be done. All right, then. You'll come here first? Of course not. I don't mind in the least. Very good. As you say—it's a priceless night. But that's just how things happen. Pure coincidence." Minutes passed. Stephen, recovered a little, lounged back to his visitors. "I've just 'phoned through to Altminster. The Inspector's coming over at once, with the Divisional Surgeon—if he can get him soon enough. If not, the medical bloke will follow later." He paused abruptly to put a question. "I say, Peter—does anything strike you about this?"

Peter glanced at his father before replying. The latter nodded as though he were giving his son permission to speak freely. Peter thereupon answered Fletcher's question.

"Of course it does! And I know what you mean, too. The Guv'nor and I thought the same thing simultaneously. How could we avoid the thought? That's why he counselled leaving the girl's body out there."

Sir John assented. "I didn't like the look of it at all, Fletcher. Taking everything into consideration—that is. These 'car' cases look to me very fishy. This is the fourth of its kind, is it not?"

Stephen nodded gloomily. "The fourth, Sir John. More than that even."

"How do you mean?" Sir John was manifestly puzzled by Stephen's last sentence. His self-assured, significantly-reserved manner lost a little of its ordinary poise.

Stephen supplied details. "Consider the localities, Sir John. They're the sign-posts of evidence as far as I'm personally concerned. Sign-posts, with indicating fingers, from which, try as I may, I find myself unable to get away." He took a cigarette from his case and absent-mindedly returned the case to his pocket.

"Localities?" Sir John repeated Fletcher's word. "I'm afraid that I don't perhaps—that I'm not quite so conversant—"

Stephen interrupted him with an impatient movement. "This is the second case of the four to happen *in this district*. There was a girl killed at East Hannington before. Found dead beside an overturned car. Her name was Vera Sinclair. She lived near here. That's the special point that I'm making." Stephen lapsed again into the groove of his gloom.

Sir John eyed him shrewdly. "H'm! I will confess that that point *had* eluded me. Curious!" He fingered the ridge of his jaw contemplatively. "Very curious." He came again to Stephen Fletcher. "What's your real point, Fletcher? The point behind all that you've been saying? You've made me wonder. Are you by any chance coming into line with an opinion that I heard expressed before? I wonder."

Stephen sprang to his feet. His cheeks were flushed and his hands clenched. "My point, Sir John? Why—this. That there's a homicidal maniac at large somewhere. And in this particular district, most probably. And I'm not going to rest till I've laid him by the heels."

Peter came to him excitedly. "And count me with you, Stephen. All the way and then some. But first of all, my dear chap—don't forget something else. We have a duty that comes before all this. We must find Margaret."

Before Stephen could find words of reply he heard Herapath's footsteps outside the library door. "Come in," cried Stephen. The door opened and two men entered at Herapath's behest. The first of these was tall and clean-shaven and carried a bowler hat in his hand. The second was short, stout and also clean-shaven. Blue eyes with an inclination to twinkle were the most prominent feature of his face. The tall man glanced towards Stephen.

"Good evening, Inspector."

"Good evening, Mr. Fletcher. This gentleman is Doctor Cherry."

Stephen bowed and made the necessary introductions. Then he turned to Inspector Power. "Shall we go along at once, Inspector?"

Power nodded and Stephen went to find more suitable clothes with which to face the elements. A few minutes later Peter's car left the grounds of "The Cranes" and made slick speed along the wet and heavy road. Nobody of those who rode in Peter Brailsford's car spoke a word. Until Inspector Power uttered a sharp exclamation.

"Hold on, sir. Here we are. Bring your car to the side."

The men descended. The scene was as the Brailsfords had described it to Stephen Fletcher. The Inspector attended to the overturned car. He and Peter moved it to the side—clear of the mainway. Doctor Cherry turned his coat-collar up for protection and went to the body of the girl. It lay where Peter had said—under the hedge. The doctor was short and sharp.

"Dead, right enough. Put her in your car, Mr. Brailsford, and take her up to the house. I can tell you more when I get her there. O.K., Power?"

"Suits me, Doctor," said Power. "I'll see to the car later on. It's well out of harm's way over there—especially on a night like this. A skid, I expect, on the crown of the wet road. Same as most of 'em."

Sir John made a sharp gesture of dissent but no remark left his lips. They came to Fletcher's house.

"Put the body on the settee in the dining-room," said Fletcher, directly Crench had opened the door to them.

The girl's body was laid where Stephen had indicated. Doctor Cherry busied himself with it. He rapped out scraps of information as they came to him out of his examination. "Age about twenty-eight I should say. Extensive injuries." His hands explored and sought evidences. "Shoulder-blades broken. Yes . . . and wrists. Yes . . . dislocation of the spinal column. Death almost instantaneous, I should think. Sad. Very sad. Ah, well . . . the toll of the road. Gets worse every year. Your turn now, Power."

Power was curt. Not by special intention. It was his way. "Nothing much on her. As a means of identification, I mean. Just the ordinary handbag with a few possessions in it. Nothing startling. We shall have to wait for news. It won't be long in coming, you bet."

Stephen's lips curled contemptuously at the matter-of-factness that showed in the man's tone. "Another accident you think, then, Inspector Power? A skid on a greasy road?"

The Inspector eyed Fletcher steadily. There was the shadow of disapproval in his hard grey eyes. "I am an Inspector of Police, Mr. Fletcher, and a plain straightforward man. Not an amateur Sherlock Holmes. I prefer the evidence of my eyes and the ordinary reasoning of my brain to any of your fantastic theories. Car accidents are as common in these days as tabby cats."

Sir John Brailsford looked antagonistic. Stephen nodded complacently at Power's words. He gave just the slightest indication of interest. Peter sensed atmosphere and addressed himself to Doctor Cherry.

"What do you think about it, Doctor?"

"I told you. That is to say as far as my job goes. I really don't see why I should trespass elsewhere. I leave that to others." Doctor Cherry was cheery and imperturbable. Stephen went across to the settee and looked closely at the girl's body. That he had something on his mind was obvious to all of them. Without saying a word he put his hand down and touched the dead girl's neck. A puzzled look came into and took possession of his eyes. "What are you going to do with her, Doctor?" he asked. "Will you take her along to the mortuary now or leave the body here?"

Cherry looked at Inspector Power. "We'll send down in the morning, if it's all the same to you, Mr. Fletcher. When I see to that car that's up the road there. It's well out of harm's way now. Mr. Brailsford here and I saw to that. Well, what do you say, Doctor? We can't do any more . . . here. Shall we get back and make our report?"

Stephen pressed the bell. "You must have something before you go, gentlemen. I had almost forgotten my duty as a host. This isn't warming or congenial work by any means. Glasses—Herapath—at once, please. And tell Crench to shut the doors of the garage. I fancy that they are open."

Herapath brought the glasses and Stephen poured out five stiff pegs of "Scotch." Doctor Cherry drained his with unconcealed relish. "That's saved my life, Mr. Fletcher. I shall recommend you for the Royal Humane Society's Medal. Men have got it for less, believe me."

Inspector Power returned to the earlier conversation. "I'd like to tell you something, Mr. Fletcher. With regard to your ideas about these car accidents. I could see the direction your mind was heading for. Hundreds of young girls disappear every year in this country. They walk out of their homes . . . and they're never seen again. They vanish . . . without any trace. Well . . . there you are . . . this is my point . . . all the dear old ladies sipping their cups of tea when they hear facts and figures like that . . . mumble in unison of the dreadful 'white-slave traffic' and regale one another with stories of drugs and dope. Now then, I'll tell you what *I* tell people when they bring those yarns to me. How about the two hundred and seventy-two elderly men who vanish annually? Does the white-slave traffic claim them? No, sir—I don't think."

Stephen made no answer, but a smile played round the corners of his mouth. Power took his hat from the corner of the table. He had no more to say.

"Fit, Inspector?" Doctor Cherry nodded to him.

The good-nights were said. Stephen escorted these men from Altminster to his front door. When he returned to his own friends he said something which surprised both Sir John and Peter. "Excuse me a minute, you chaps. But I've something important to do. I'm going to use the telephone again." They heard him go into the hall and ask for a number. They heard him speaking . . . vigorously and emphatically.

Chapter XVIII
MR. BATHURST INTERVENES

THE night was old and Anthony Bathurst drove hard. Sir Austin Kemble, the Commissioner of Police, had waved him a good-bye and had stood watching while the "Chrysler" had shot away. The boom of its exhaust grew fainter as it sped down a hill round the bend of the road and out of sight. Clear of the town, Anthony sought speed and yet more speed. The foulness of the night helped him, for few were abroad to check his way. At times he retarded to a seemingly decorous thirty miles an hour. He ran into places of dry weather. White roads coated with feathery dust came to meet him. The car took them all and bestrode them as Cassius spoke of Julius—like a colossus. Roads twisted and turned until the car came out on to the straight broad highway which runs its whole length to Altminster. Raining in torrents again now! Anthony accelerated to a cool fifty. The car came to the cross roads for East Hannington and Anthony turned it smoothly. His thumb found the button of the horn. The car went down a narrow winding road high-hedged and badly surfaced. Rain had undermined the sandy top and the holes met the car in reckless and prodigal profusion. "Made a mistake," said Mr. Bathurst to himself. "I should have done better to have taken the road that I took before. So does Time tyrannise over us all. All the same, 'The Cranes' can't be so far away." He drove on fiercely and relentlessly, and in four more minutes found himself outside the house which bore the name "The Cranes." It was a square house of red brick which, to appearances, dated back to Georgian days. Anthony swung the "Chrysler" through the gates and up the gravelled slope of the drive. The rain still beat hard against the screen. Then he heaved himself from the car and pressed a rather obtrusive bell on a big oaken door. The man-servant, Herapath, looked at Crench, lifted himself from a chair with an air of supreme resignation and opened the door to Anthony Bathurst.

"Mr. Stephen Fletcher?"

"Yes, sir. Come this way, sir. Mr. Stephen is expecting you, sir." Herapath had evidently been primed by instructions.

Anthony gratefully crossed the threshold. He seized the unforgiving minute to take stock of all that he could see. This home of the Fletchers . . . Colonel Aubrey Fletcher . . . Stephen Fletcher and Margaret Fletcher . . . must hold a fund of interest for him. In the first place, Vera Sinclair had been an East Hannington girl! The hall of "The Cranes" had been furnished with exemplary care and taste. Facing the front door, at some distance from it, was another door which stood ajar. Anthony, following Herapath discreetly, could see the figure of a man partly screened by this half-open door. From this attitude, it seemed to Anthony that the man was listening. Either to somebody in the room or to what was going on outside. Herapath escorted Mr. Bathurst to this same door. Stephen Fletcher stepped forward. He stopped abruptly as Anthony Bathurst came face to face with him.

"Well," said Mr. Bathurst, "so we meet again sooner than we had anticipated."

Fletcher gave him a half-smile. He jerked his head towards the wall. "Perhaps. In the dining-room. Want to see her at once?"

"Naturally," replied Anthony drily. "That's one of the things for which I've come. I haven't tarried, let me tell you, since I got your 'phone message. Who is it this time?"

Fletcher shook his head. "We don't know. No means of identity at the moment—or so the Inspector of Police said a couple of hours ago. Still—that's not so frightfully important, is it?"

"Ask yourself! It might be. It might not. Who can tell at this stage? Certainty as to identity would help rather than hinder."

Anthony came with Stephen Fletcher to the dead body of the girl. "Pretty sure of what you told me, Fletcher?"

"Dead certain, man. I looked for something and discovered something else. As one frequently does. Try her for yourself. Cherry—that's the doctor, evidently didn't realise the significance."

Anthony put his hand on the girl's face. On her neck. On her throat. Down to her breasts. "Cold," he said curtly. "Stone cold." He paused.

"Yes. Too cold."

"H'm! How long had she been lying in the rain and cold, do you think, before she was found? That's the vital point of it all, surely!"

"I've thought of that and only common sense can answer the question."

Anthony suddenly raised his head. There was inquiry in his eyes.

Fletcher understood and explained. "You can hear voices. Sir John Brailsford and Peter are in the library. It was they who found her. They were on their way here to see me. This was some hours ago—remember. And she *may* have been there on the road at least an hour or so before the Brailsfords came along. It's been a dreadful night and there must have been but little traffic along there—quite conceivably none at all. It's a deserted road at the best of times."

Anthony looked up at him quickly. "It's just possible. I grant you all that." Anthony put a question. "Do the Brailsfords know that you've sent for me?"

"Yes. I told them after I 'phoned to you. I could see no reason why I shouldn't. Does it matter?"

"Not a hoot. As it happens we've met before. Bring 'em in, will you, Fletcher. They might be able to help me."

Stephen nodded and slipped from the room. Anthony went on his knees quickly and examined the dead girl's wrists. But Fletcher was back almost immediately. He had brought Sir John and Peter with him. Anthony rose from the floor.

"Sir John Brailsford . . . Peter Brailsford. Anthony Bathurst."

Sir John stared incredulously, but Peter gave way to a whistle that in the circumstances sounded almost profane.

"Why, my dear sir," said Sir John . . . "surely we've met before! Now where did I . . . ?"

A triumphant Peter cut in impetuously. "I've got it! Lotherington! At Great Kirby. We met you in the . . ."

Anthony smiled and held out his hand to them. "Fletcher might have said 'Anthony Lotherington Bathurst' . . . but he didn't. Then you might have understood. When we met before . . . you must forgive me the slight deception. . . . I was travelling 'incog.' Now please tell me all you know of to-night's work."

Sir John accepted the invitation and gave a brief but concise account of what had occurred. How Peter had been driving through the blinding rain on the way to "The Cranes," and Sir John's eyes had picked out the obstruction just in time to avoid another disaster. How they had then come post-haste to Stephen Fletcher's and broached the news to him.

Anthony listened to Sir John with infinite patience. The three men who watched him were amazed to see Mr. Bathurst suddenly rub his hands.

"Injuries," he said trenchantly—"tell me all that the Doctor said."

Stephen Fletcher repeated what Doctor Cherry had told them. Anthony nodded understanding as each detail was reached and given to him. "Broken shoulder-blades. Yes. Injuries to the wrists. Yes. Spinal column dislocated. Yes. All in order and true to the pattern—as I'm beginning to see things."

Stephen bit his lip in thought. Then his lips parted. But Anthony's impetuosity checked what Fletcher had been about to say.

"Fletcher, you said that this girl carried nothing on her that would serve to identify her. What was this Inspector's name?"

"Power. He's in charge over at Altminster. He told me that he had found a handbag on her. An ordinary handbag, he said. Containing the usual things that a girl of this sort naturally carries."

Anthony's grey eyes gleamed as Stephen spoke. He struck. "Any money on the dead girl, Fletcher? Can you answer that?"

"Yes," said Stephen slowly. "There was some money. I saw Power look at it and then put it back in the handbag."

"This money was in coppers, of course," contributed Mr. Bathurst nonchalantly.

"No!" said Stephen with sharp insistence.

"No?" Anthony furrowed his brow.

"No," repeated Stephen Fletcher. "There were four one-pound notes, three ten-shilling currency notes, a half-crown, a florin, a shilling and a sixpence. Five pounds, sixteen shillings in all. I saw Power count it all back into the bag. As far as I could see there wasn't a single copper coin in the dead girl's possession. But you can confirm that by asking Power himself."

Anthony made no reply. His fingers went to his clean-shaven lip . . . a habit of his when puzzled. The long fingers caressed the lip . . . once . . . twice. Strange! Incredibly strange! Theories all toppling over now. The foundation-stone of his case pulled violently away and the whole edifice seemingly in jeopardy. Sir John Brailsford and Peter pressed forward towards him . . . sympathising instinctively and almost unconsciously with the problem that they could see was worrying him.

"Notes and silver—eh? Not a copper."

Fletcher nodded at Bathurst's words. Anthony paced the room. He repeated to himself deliberately, "Four pound notes, three ten-shilling notes, one half-crown, one two-shilling piece, one shilling and one sixpence. Eminently comprehensive I must admit. Sum total—five pounds and sixteen shillings." He went across quickly and looked at the dead girl's clothes. The three men's eyes followed him as he crossed to her. "Extraordinary," they heard him mutter. "Not in the right district and not carrying the right stuff. And spine dislocated. Yes. That's out of order, too. That is to say unsatisfactory on each of three counts." Sir John overheard the words and questioned him.

"What's troubling you? After all, there may be less than you supposed in that theory of yours?" Peter's face showed unmistakably that he was puzzled by his father's statement. "Why?" he inquired—"I don't know that I—"

Sir John showed impatience. "Lord, boy, use your wits. Mr. Bathurst has a theory about these overturned car deaths—don't you remember him telling us about it? This is the fourth case of the kind. But whereas the other three girls who were killed only carried copper coins, this last case seems to be very different. I'm beginning to remember the details now. That's Bathurst's particular problem at the present moment."

Sir John looked quickly from his son to Stephen Fletcher. Neither of them spoke. Each was intent on Anthony's inspection of the body. He looked at the soles of the shoes that the girl had been wearing. He examined the shoes themselves. He shook his head either at what he saw or at what he didn't see. He looked again at her hands. Then at the head, then back to the hands again. He busied himself there for a matter of minutes. "Come over here, gentlemen," he said suddenly. The three of them went to him in a unity of obedience. "Did this pair of gloves belong to the dead girl, do you know?" There was no answer to his question. He looked from one to the other of them. "Well, I'll put the question in another form. Was she wearing these gloves when she was picked up?"

"I can answer that," said Peter after a short interval of thought. "She had one glove on when I found her in the road . . . right hand, I fancy it was. And I noticed that the Inspector picked up the other glove by the side of the overturned car. Anyhow, what's your point?"

"I'll show you. Try that left-hand glove on the girl's hand. Go on—there's no catch in it."

Sir John Brailsford looked surprised but did as Mr. Bathurst instructed. He fitted the glove on to the dead girl's left hand. Stephen Fletcher and Peter watched the proceedings with curiosity. Sir John then turned to Anthony.

"Well?" he inquired, "What do I do next?"

"All in good time, sir. *Festina lente*—you know. Does anything strike you?"

Sir John looked at the dead hand and shook his head. "No, can't say that it does. Perhaps I'm unnaturally dull. Lighten my darkness."

Anthony smiled with good temper. "Well, let me put it like this? Does the glove fit, Sir John? That was the detail about which I harboured a doubt."

"I think so. It went on comparatively easily."

"Now try to fasten it, Sir John. It's one of those old-fashioned spring-fasteners, you'll find. The buttons press."

Sir John bent down and brought the two parts of the glove towards one another. But try as he would, he was unable to get them to meet. It was impossible for him to button the glove.

"Well?" queried Anthony. "How now?"

"The glove is too small," said Sir John. "At least a couple of sizes too small."

"Exactly," said Anthony. "And if you try it, you'll find the right-hand glove is much the same. If the girl were wearing it when she died, as Peter Brailsford says, I'll guarantee that it wasn't done up." Peter considered the statement that Anthony had made. "Now you mention it, I'm blessed if I don't think that you're right."

"Consider the discomfort at least," proceeded Anthony, "wearing gloves that didn't fasten properly to drive a car, especially on a night like this has been."

"By Jove, yes," agreed Sir John in admiration, "but I can't understand how you come to notice such a thing. Most extraordinary, I call it."

"I noticed it, Sir John, because in a way I was looking for something of the kind."

Sir John knitted his brows. "Looking for gloves of the wrong size? Come, Mr. Bathurst, much as I believe in your sincerity and respect your powers, I find that statement extremely difficult to believe." Anthony smiled at Sir John's forcefulness. "I didn't say that I actually sought for badly fitting gloves . . . or shoes . . . but I looked for something like that, something, let me say, of that nature . . . it might even have been a matter of a hair-slide or false teeth. Would you like me to *prove* my point?"

It was evident that Stephen Fletcher and Peter shared Sir John's mystification. Stephen translated it into words. "How do you mean, Bathurst? About *proving* anything?"

"Please don't think me didactic. I have no intention to be that, I assure you. But come close—will you—and look at this young lady's shoes."

Once again the three men silently obeyed him. Each looked at the shoes. Nobody spoke.

"Well?" inquired Anthony. "Does anything strike you with regard to this pair of brown shoes?"

Stephen at once essayed a contribution. "The heels are badly worn down."

"That's true. But I must submit, Fletcher, that there is nothing really *remarkable* in that fact." Sir John looked thoughtful. Peter shook his head and frankly admitted that he was nonplussed.

"Let me help you then by going one step further," observed Anthony. "Disregard the shoes themselves."

Sir John sought explanation. "Disregard—how do you mean—I don't understand you."

"Turn your observation from the shoes themselves. Consider the attachments."

Stephen's alert mind was the first that followed him. "You mean the laces, don't you, Bathurst?"

"Now you're getting warm as the children say in their games. Well, what about the laces? Can you see what I mean?"

The two Brailsfords, now acutely interested, bent down with Fletcher to look more carefully at the pair of brown laces. In a second, Stephen uttered a sharp exclamation.

"Yes . . . yes . . . I get your point, Bathurst. You mean the way in which these two laces have been tied."

Anthony smiled in approval. "Good man! That's exactly what I do mean. The lace of the left-hand shoe has been tied in an ordinary 'bow.' But if we look at the right-hand lace we see that it has been tied in a much more elaborate way. What I should describe, for want of a better description, as in a double-looped 'bow.' Look here!" Anthony put a finger on each of the laces. "The two methods are absolutely dissimilar."

Sir John nodded his head slowly at Anthony Bathurst's demonstration. "Now that's very true . . . and at the same time most interesting. And what, moreover, do you deduce from it, Mr. Bathurst?"

Anthony shook his head disclaimingly. "Now you ask me something that I can't so easily answer. There *might* be two explanations—equally feasible and logical."

"And what are they?"

"One, that the girl was in a hurry when she set out on her last journey . . . and was assisted in her dressing . . . or . . . that two people dressed her."

Stephen cut in quickly. "Or put her shoes on . . . as distinct from 'dressing' her."

"The gloves, Fletcher . . . don't forget the gloves. Shoes *and* gloves remember. Once again, the value of evidence increases on account of its accumulation."

"I'm sorry. Yes, I'd forgotten the gloves for the moment. Yes—I agree with you now."

"Which do you think the more likely of your possibilities, Bathurst?" The question came from Peter Brailsford.

"I have an open mind, Brailsford. I must have at this stage of events. Sooner or later, however, something will come to me and that something will give me a definite direction. But until that something comes, well—" Anthony shrugged his shoulders—"I prefer to keep, as I said, an open mind."

"The whole thing seems to me to be extraordinary. From beginning to end." Sir John spoke emphatically.

Anthony faced him. "And yet—if we could but see it—there must be a shining truth behind it all. A sound reason. Otherwise it wouldn't have occurred. We have to dig out the truth and the reason. That's our job."

Stephen assented. "Again I agree. What's your next step, Bathurst?"

"I'm going to have a few words with the Divisional-Surgeon at Altminster. And then I'll have a couple of glances inside the young lady's car. What's the doctor's name? Cherry?"

"Cherry," returned Stephen shortly.

"I like cherries," answered Mr. Bathurst whimsically—"they happen to be my favourite fruit. The Bigaroon is perfect. Just compare its luscious beauty with, say, that abomination, the banana. I'll interview the good doctor in the morning. You can put me up here, of course, Mr. Fletcher?"

"Delighted. I sent for you to come down here. So that, in the circumstances, giving you a bed is one of the least things that I can do for you. Sir John and Peter will also stay the night. I've already made arrangements for them. Peter has an important proposal to make to me in the morning about Margaret. He came really because he's worried concerning my sister. I'll see about your room at once if you'll excuse me." Stephen made his exit.

Sir John Brailsford and Peter at once plied Anthony with questions. He could see that he had created a profound impression upon both of them.

"Spare me, gentlemen," he answered at length, "give me time, give me breathing space, I implore you. When I feel that I can, I'll clear up all your difficulties and I hope all your doubts. But for the moment, I'm groping very much as you are doing. There are straws in the wind, certainly, and a tide in our affairs which we'll do our utmost to take at its flood. Beyond that—we have to watch and wait. Let's hope that that period of watching and waiting will not be too long or too wearying. That's all I can say."

Stephen Fletcher returned as Mr. Bathurst completed his sentence. "I've seen to everything for you. Your bed's ready when you are."

"Thanks, my dear chap. I appreciate your kindness immensely. If you fellows don't mind, then, I'll turn in. It's getting very late and I'm tired, and tomorrow looks like being one of the busiest." Anthony Bathurst walked to the door. Having reached it, he stopped for a moment before turning towards his three companions. "By the way, gentlemen," he announced quietly, "I fancy that I can clear up one of your difficulties immediately. It's a solution that should serve to help *me*, *you*, and also the good Inspector Power from Altminster." They stared at him wonderingly. Stephen Fletcher at that moment felt Anthony's attraction. "I allude," Mr. Bathurst continued, "to the question of identifying the dead girl. I don't know her surname—but her Christian name happens to be 'Rosina,' late of 'L'Estrange's

Travelling Showground.' You've heard of the concern, no doubt. It tours the country—you know the idea—'heigho—come to the fair.' You've seen the girl once before, Peter." Anthony closed the door behind him.

Chapter XIX
DR. CHERRY THINKS TWICE

Inspector Power whispered important words into the ear of Doctor Cherry. The latter's good-tempered face fell from grace at their reception.

"What!" he exclaimed with definite asperity, "why on earth should I? What's the big idea?"

"I can't tell you that, Doctor. I can only inform you of what I know. There's one thing—you won't have far to go. The body's in the mortuary."

"Charming prospect," snapped the Doctor, "you've no idea how thrilled I am."

"I think I should have a chat with him—if I were you," urged Power persuasively—"you know what Sir Austin Kemble's like when the maggot bites him. It would be as well to be on the safe side, I think, Doctor. After all, we don't quite know what the man wants and I don't want to qualify for any unnecessary trouble. Especially at this stage of my career."

"Why the hell can't he say what he wants? Does he think that I've got nothing to do except run about to suit him? It would do some of these people good to have a spot of healthy work to do as a Divisional-Surgeon. A damned dog's life! Where is the fellow now?"

"The 'phone message from Mr. Fletcher's said that he'd be at the mortuary waiting for you."

"Blasted considerate of him—I'm sure. I've a good mind to tell him to go to the devil. It's a solemn fact, Power, I have."

Power attempted to supply oil for the troubled waters. "Shall we walk across, Doctor? To the mortuary, I mean, not to our mutual friend. He might take the hindmost. Safety first,

Doctor—that appeals to me as a rule and I find this occasion no exception."

Still grumbling audibly, Doctor Cherry followed the Inspector out of the police headquarters at Altminster. When they came to the door of the unpretentious building that housed the dead body they found two men waiting for them. One of them—Stephen Fletcher—came forward to greet them.

"Good morning, gentlemen," he said, "many thanks for coming along to see us. Oh . . . I forgot . . . this is Anthony Bathurst . . . I've brought him along to see you. Sir John Brailsford and his son have returned to town. Bathurst, this is Doctor Cherry . . . Inspector Power. Now you all know each other."

The blue eyes of Doctor Cherry and the grey eyes of Anthony Bathurst met and challenged each other. Then Anthony impulsively thrust out his hand. "I am delighted to meet you, Doctor, and I must add my most grateful thanks to Mr. Fletcher's. It is extremely good of you to spare us some of your valuable time. And you, too, Inspector Power. I appreciate your kindness immensely." He gave his hand in turn to the Inspector.

"H'm," said Doctor Cherry, stroking his chin. "So much for the preliminaries. I suggest that we waste no more time over them. Now, Mr. Bathurst, getting right down to business—I'm a blunt man who usually knows his own mind—what's your programme?"

Anthony smiled. He detected the aroma of antagonism. Cherry's tone was not uncongenial but there was something about the set of his jaw that served as a warning to Anthony to tread warily.

"I want your advice, Doctor Cherry. Rather badly, I'm afraid. The advice that you will give me out of your special knowledge."

"I?" Cherry stared.

"You—Doctor. For the time being, at least, consider me as wax in your hands. But if you'll come in here with me—I'll explain my needs to you more fully."

Doctor Cherry nodded assent and the four men passed through into the mortuary. Anthony at once ranged himself at the doctor's side.

"If we dig deeply enough into the natural world, Doctor, so as to expose its foundation, and to reach what may be termed 'unknown' ground beneath, that ground we discover will be necessarily of a nature different from that of the superstructure. Consider Newton and the principles that we associate with his name. He perceived that the very 'first cause' was certainly not mechanical. In that case then, electrons, wave-groups and quanta of action are equally certainly not mechanical. In time physicists will possibly formulate a new atomic model. But when intelligible mechanism *does* fail, we shall be left face to face with the greatest mystery of all—stark reality. Let me show you something." He moved the sheet which covered the dead girl whom he had named "Rosina." "I have an astonishingly weird theory about this case, Doctor Cherry. That's why I've sought your valuable help. Is it possible that this lady was . . . shall we say . . . poisoned . . . that will do as well as anything else . . . *before* the car turned over?"

Cherry stared at him.

"Of course . . . it's possible. Everything's possible. Anything's possible. But why on earth suggest such a thing? Are you plumb crazy?"

Anthony shook his head slowly as though the Doctor had failed to understand him.

"I'll tell you why, Doctor Cherry. Because I don't think that this young woman *was* killed in a motoring accident. I think that she was in all probability dead *before she entered the car*. Your greater knowledge may *prove* that fact for me."

"You flatter me," said Doctor Cherry. "Quite candidly I regard your theory as richly humorous. If there's anything in—"

Anthony interrupted him a trifle coldly. "Show me that I'm wrong then, Doctor, and I'll beg a hair of you in memory and bequeath it as a rich legacy unto my heirs."

Cherry saw Power's eyes fixed on him. He remembered their conversation before they had met Bathurst. Anthony, seeing that Cherry made no reply, followed up instantly.

"Come now, Doctor, I'm not asking anything outrageously absurd. I'd lay a thousand to one that when you were called to the body you never considered such a contingency. Who shall blame you? Take the question of the bruises, for instance, and the condition of extravasation generally. I'll guarantee that—"

Doctor Cherry wrinkled his forehead and went to the body. "Have it your own way. Mother's words come home to me. Always the perfect little gentleman. I'll do a pukka P.M. for you. Then we shan't be risking anything. I'll report results later. Satisfied?"

"Thank you, Doctor," said Anthony, "and when I say thank you—I mean it. Care to come for a stroll with me, Fletcher? Doctor Cherry will, no doubt, be some time."

Stephen and Anthony sat in "The Cranes." The hour was dinner. Herapath had done his best to be the complete butler. Since they had left the Divisional-Surgeon to his gruesome task, Anthony had deliberately avoided all conversation that might in any way touch upon the case. Also he had made no reference to Margaret. The dinner to which Stephen Fletcher had invited him had been in every respect excellent. The food was splendidly cooked and the service in the hands of Crench and Herapath. The sherry and the claret had been wines of distinctive merit. Stephen, however, had been a long way from his usual sparkling self. Much of his sparkle, of late, had indeed departed from him. Anthony had been forced to break most of the eggs for the omelette of conversation. When Herapath brought port upon a silver tray Stephen became more talkative. At length he led the way into the lounge. Anthony chose a comfortable arm-chair. Herapath came again ... with tiny cups ... coffee pot and spirit-lamp. "Black ... sir ... or white?" he said to Anthony.

"Black . . . please." Anthony found cigarettes. Stephen smoked too. The air grew heavy with smoke. The bell rang. Stephen gestured to the servant. Herapath put down his apparatus and walked to the door with a serene solemnity. Doctor Cherry followed him back into the room. Stephen and Anthony rose almost simultaneously to greet the doctor.

Cherry wasted neither words nor time. "Bathurst—you owe me an apology. There's not a trace of poison."

There was silence. Anthony stared. Cherry smiled and went on. "But—don't worry—it's an *entente cordiale*—I owe you one, too. That woman down there in the mortuary at Altminster *was* dead before she entered the car. The superficial injuries that I found on the body were all inflicted *after* death."

Anthony was quiet in the moment of his semi-triumph. Eventually he found words. "How did she die, Doctor? I confess that *I'm* rather puzzled now."

Cherry enjoyed his little success. "She died, my dear fellow, from a rupture of the heart. Or, in other words, from natural causes. How does that suit your book—eh?"

Stephen Fletcher drank black coffee.

Chapter XX
"THE CALF" AGAIN

Inspector Andrew MacMorran of New Scotland Yard frowned at the telephone which rang insistently at his elbow. He picked up the receiver with a look of beatific resignation. "Hallo . . . hallo," he said sorrowfully. But a moment or so later his face completely changed. "Oh . . . good morning to you, sir . . . no, no, no, you know perfectly well, Mr. Bathurst, that I'm nothing less than delighted. Although I'll not be denyin' that I wasn't too pleased when I heard the 'phone ring . . . but hearin' your voice at the other end has made all the difference. Well—what's the latest spot of bother?" MacMorran drew a scribbling-pad towards him and listened carefully as Anthony replied. He punctuated Mr. Bathurst's reply with a series of nods and remarks. "Yes . . . yes . . . Sir Austin Kemble has let on to me once or twice about it. When the news came through from East Hannington concerning this last girl, Rosina Kirk, he got quite excited, I can tell you. Almost approached garrulousness. I took it from what he told me that you'd sort of prepared him for something of the kind." Anthony gave him more information. MacMorran's face then registered signs of surprise at what he heard. As Mr. Bathurst's information developed in detail so Inspector MacMorran's surprise increased also. At length his amazement manifested itself in actual words. "Well, I'm jiggered—you don't mean it? If that's so—and I suppose there's no doubt about it from what you tell me—it's a bewildering business altogether. You say that she had Treasury notes—pound and ten shillings—and four silver coins? From half a crown downwards? It's a tremendous pity she couldn't have put up a threepenny piece—to be sure. Surely the harvest festivals haven't taken them all. Well, Mr. Bathurst—I'll say this—it fairly beats me."

"There's one thing for which we may be thankful," Anthony gave it to him unemotionally, "the newspapers haven't given a lot of tongue . . . yet. Especially what we may call 'the more staid' of them. So far there have been no journalistic thunder-claps and even moderate 'yelpings' have been few and far between. No challenges have as yet been flung at the 'Yard' adjuring the great, wise, and eminent to 'do something'—variously defined. An innocent-sounding little paragraph in a comparatively obscure 'local' paper from 'our own correspondent' has been the most eloquent that I have yet seen. But I didn't 'phone you to talk aimlessly 'round the affair.' I expect, MacMorran, that you're as well aware of that fact as I am myself. Now, listen, I want the ownership of a certain car traced . . . as quickly as you know how . . . particulars as follows . . . just jot them down, will you."

MacMorran took his pencil and used the pad that he had in front of him.

"Morris Oxford Tourer, 1929. Excellent condition. Shows signs of fairly recent general overhauling—five good tyres, one below standard. Re-bored, hood almost new and engine in good condition. Number plate bearing registration AXM 222."

"I'll repeat all those over to you, Mr. Bathurst, check up, will you please . . . that's right then. The registration number is probably false . . . if I'm any judge. Still, I'll do all I can and as quickly as possible. You know that you can rely on me."

The Press advertised the matter generously, members of the B.B.C. staff added it to their announcements of fat-stock prices, their mispronunciation of the names of placed horses and "probable Shahs in Ahland" and several subordinate emissaries of the

"Yard" found it for the next day or so a trivial round and common task, which furnished a good deal more than they needed to ask. In two days' time this combination of MacMorran's celerity of organisation and Anthony Bathurst's resourceful initiative was rewarded. A thin-featured man, undersized, and with a white twisted face who turned and twirled a greasy cloth cap in his hand, arrived at the "Yard" early in the morning and applied rather tentatively to see Inspector MacMorran . . . "about the motor-car advertisement" was his method of describing the reason that lay behind his personal call. Much flattered at the attention given to him he was immediately shown up into MacMorran's presence. Definite instructions had been given by the Inspector himself to this effect. MacMorran quickly sized up his visitor. He saw that he belonged to that category of men who obtain their livelihood by precarious jobs usually designated as "odd." By reason of his many years' experience, MacMorran was well able to deal with individuals of this type. He rang for his shorthand-typist and at the same time gestured his visitor to a chair. The undersized man found one near to him and seated himself upon the edge thereof.

"You've come about the 'Morris Oxford Tourer' advertisement, I understand?" The man nodded. "First of all, then—your name and address, please."

The man shifted uneasily in his chair. MacMorran was kindness itself, and hastened to reassure him.

"Merely a matter of form, that's all. You've nothing whatever to worry about."

"Albert Grayston, 17 Hagleby Place, Pimlico."

"Occupation?"

"Car washer—employed at a garage in Coverdale Street."

"Thank you. Name of employer?"

"Victor Coleman."

"Thank you—I know the firm—now go ahead with what you have to tell me."

Grayston shifted his cap to his left hand and rubbed the end of his nose with the tip of his forefinger. "I haven't what you'd call a rare lot to tell you, Inspector. But what I have got to say is to the point, I think. Which is worth a good deal, ain't it, Guv'nor?"

MacMorran nodded. He felt only too pleased to confirm what Grayston had just stated. "If it's true and reliable—certainly. If not, I don't know that it matters. Still—let's hear what it is that you have to tell me. Come on, now."

"I've seen your car—this Morris Oxford Tourer you're inquirin' about—many and many a time. That's the extent of my information. Nothing sensational about it. Just plain unvarnished truth."

"Good. The truth is what we want. Now where have you seen it?"

"Where do you think, Guv'nor? Have a guess." Grayston cocked a shrewd head at the Inspector.

"In and around London—I suppose you'll tell me." Grayston's eyes held the light of triumph. "Better than that. Much better than that. An exact place. Where I used to set my eyes on it most nights, let me tell you. And without going to any trouble either. At the rear of a night-club place called 'The Purple Calf.' It's in Coverdale Street—this club—not a stone's throw from where my job of work is."

MacMorran now knew for a sheer certainty that he looked on the fair image of truth. He knew the interest that this night club of "The Purple Calf" already possessed for Anthony Bathurst. But all the same—true to habit—he tested the strength of his visitor's information.

"Sure of this, Grayston?"

Grayston grimaced the absolute invulnerability of his statement. "Beyond the shadow of a doubt, Guv'nor." He proceeded to tick off on the tips of his fingers the various points of his assurance. "Morris Oxford Tourer. Registration number AXM 222. Been recently overhauled. Hood as good as new. Lor' bless you, sir, I know the old 'bus well. Seen it no end of times in the yard at the back of the 'Calf,' in Coverdale Street. I wish I 'ad a quid for every time and no error. Save me working till next Christmas. You can take what I say as Gospel, Guv'nor."

MacMorran nodded to his stenographer and, at the same time, noted the terms of Grayston's answer on the pad in front of him. "No idea of the owner, I suppose?"

"Ah—that's where I can't help you, Guv'nor. Sorry—I wish I could. Shouldn't take you long, though, to find that out. I guess you don't want me to tell you how to run your own business. Well—how do I go now? Will you want me for anything else, Guv'nor?"

"No, I think not." MacMorran looked over the notes that he had made. "Just one minute, though, before you do go, Grayston. You say that you have seen this car in the yard at the back of 'The Purple Calf' *many times*. What period of time would that cover?"

Grayston leant back in his chair and thought over the Inspector's question. "Since when I first saw the car, do you mean?"

"This is what I mean. From the first time that you saw it—to the last time that you remember seeing it—how long would that be?"

Grayston wrinkled his brows and measured time. "Let me see now. I started at Coleman's about the last week in February. Say, six months, Guv'nor—and you won't be very far out."

"Thank you. Six months. I'll make a special note of that. I have your address. If we want you again I'll let you know. And many thanks for the information that you've brought me." MacMorran escorted his visitor to the door and watched Grayston shuffle down the corridor. Returning, the Inspector went to the telephone and put through an inter-departmental call. "Inspector MacMorran speaking. Is that you, Norris? Any news yet in regard to that special investigation?"

"No—Inspector. Nothing's come through so far. Nothing has been sent along from any of the Licensing Authorities. I told you that I didn't expect there would be. It's a false registration—there isn't a doubt of it."

"O.K. then. We'll leave it at that for the time being. Now listen. Make arrangements to meet me outside 'The Purple Calf' in Coverdale Street at eight o'clock to-night. I'll pick you up a hundred yards or so from the main entrance. Plain clothes. Mr. Bathurst may be with us. But I can't say definitely about that till

I've had a further word with him. Anyhow, don't be surprised at anything. There's a lot about this 'Purple Calf' show that needs investigating. What's that you say? Mr. Bathurst's usually right?" MacMorran smiled expansively. "You're tellin' me, Norris."

Chapter XXI
THE MAN AT THE INQUEST

ANTHONY Bathurst and Inspector MacMorran met Norris at the appointed time and place. As unobtrusively as possible, they entered the precincts of "The Purple Calf." Bathurst and MacMorran had conferred on the matter and had decided to make a formal inquiry and no more. Also, it may be observed, Mr. Bathurst was garbed very differently on this occasion when compared with the dress of his previous visits. MacMorran, directly he found himself inside, beckoned to the *maître d'hôtel*. The evening was young and there were comparatively few people clustered in the foyer. Pierre, the *maître d'hôtel*, came forward to the Inspector's gesture rather unwillingly.

"What is it that you require?" he asked. His tone bordered on the truculent.

"Who's in charge of this place?" demanded MacMorran curtly.

"Why do you wish to know? Is it that you have—?"

"Now you can cut the sulky stuff as soon as you like. Then we shall understand each other better. There's my card. Take a good look at it so as to satisfy yourself. Inspector Andrew MacMorran of Scotland Yard. Take me to the manager. If you can't do that bring the manager here. Which will suit me even better. Now run along, there's a good fellow—I should hate to be kept waiting."

Pierre half hesitated. He was already finding the interview distasteful. He gave Anthony the impression that he was uncertain as to which of the Inspector's suggestions he was inclined to adopt. Eventually he shrugged his shoulders and said—"If you stay here I will see if I can bring the manager to you. But he is busy, let me tell you, and if I cannot—"

"If he's busy—he's lucky these days. I know a lot of people who'd like to be. What's his name?"

"His name is Palestri. But he will no doubt talk to you himself."

"I won't contradict you there," said MacMorran. "Now make it snappy and produce this Mr. Palestri."

Pierre grimaced, made the best of a bad job, and departed on his errand. "Let's sit here," suggested Anthony, indicating a table conveniently unoccupied, "we shall attract less attention if we sit here and make ourselves moderately comfortable. Too much publicity is not desired."

MacMorran and Norris joined him at the table. They had scarcely taken their respective seats when there appeared Pierre piloting an articulate and frowning Palestri. The frown was an unpleasant, forbidding frown. MacMorran rose and opened the ball.

"Ah—Mr. Palestri, I believe. It is good of you to have come so quickly. Especially as I understand that you are snowed under with work. But your *maître d'hôtel*, here, has told you no doubt who I am."

Palestri, who needed no opportunity for self-justification, was in at once. "Yes. And what is it, may I ask? And what is it that you want here? When I see you, I see trouble. That is all you people ever bring with you. We are not here—breakers of the law. We are dutiful citizens who abide by the law—always. We do not sell the drink after the proper hours. We do not play the cards for money. We do not allow anybody to—"

MacMorran raised a hand in protest. "Now, now, now," he expostulated with a grim authority, "don't blether till you're hurt. And calm yourself down. In your present condition, you're not safe. You talk too much by a long chalk. Sit down here." He indicated a vacant chair next to Norris. "And you can dismiss your satellite. I don't think that I shall want him any more. Also, he doesn't please me. Got that?" Palestri nodded sulkily and waved to the *maître d'hôtel* to return to his ordinary duties. MacMorran waited for Pierre to place himself beyond earshot.

"Now," said the Inspector, "we'll get to business. The upshot of my business is just this. I'm endeavouring to trace a car."

"There are no car-thieves here—so you can—"

"Now, sonny, you leave the talking to me. Conversation's a dual art, I'd have you know, besides being a very much neglected one and in this instance I'm the talker and you're the listener. Silence for you will be golden. As I said a moment ago—I'm trying to trace a car. I'll describe the car to you. It's a Morris Oxford tourer and the registration number is AXM 222. Know anything about it?"

Palestri became vehement. "No. A thousand times no, Who am I, do you think? Do I look after such things as cars? I tell you, Inspector MacMorran, that it takes me all my time to—"

"That's all right." MacMorran again cut him short. "Now let's understand one another. If you can't help us yourself you must have somebody on your staff here who can. Who looks after your cars?"

"No cars are allowed to park here. You should know that. The police—"

"An admirable body of men—so don't criticise them. I shall have to sell you a ticket for their sports. Now about the cars that are sometimes in your yard at the back of this place—as both you and I know very well—who looks after them?"

Palestri sulked. "There are very few."

"One's enough for my purpose—thank you. Now then—who looks after them?"

Palestri's reply came slowly. "A boy—named Augustus."

"Send for him, then, Mr. Palestri. At once." Palestri was about to demur but a look in the Inspector's eyes convinced him that this was no time for profitable argument. He signalled therefore to an industrious waiter who hovered in the distance. The man bustled up to Palestri's side.

"Get the boy," snapped Palestri, "the boy they call Augustus. And waste no time."

The waiter clicked heels. "Very good, sir. I will attend to it at once."

A short stocky boy with unruly hair appeared, a little scared-looking, after an interval of a few minutes.

"You had better ask him what you want to know," declared Palestri to the Inspector. Then he turned aggressively to the boy. "Answer the questions, Augustus, that this gentleman is going to ask you. It is all right. It is only about a car."

Anthony was quick to note the words that Palestri used. He felt certain in his own mind that Palestri was attempting to assure the boy who had been summoned that the inquiry was on different lines from those which the staff of "The Purple Calf" might reasonably have anticipated. If it were so, it suited Mr. Bathurst's book with admirable and commendable exactitude. Augustus nodded understanding at Palestri's statement.

"I'm an Inspector from Scotland Yard," said MacMorran. "I want certain information about a car. A Morris Oxford Tourer. Registration number AXM 222."

Augustus opened his mouth as though about to embark upon an explanation. Then he suddenly shut it again.

"Know anything about it?" MacMorran pressed him instantly.

Augustus nodded affirmatively. "Yes, sir."

"What do you know of it?"

"It's . . . it's . . . been stolen."

"Stolen? What do you mean? Where from?" Augustus jerked his head backwards. His hair fell round his ears and the movement made him look more unintelligent than ever. "From the yard at the back."

"How do you know?"

"How do I know . . . why . . . of course I know." MacMorran's eyes glinted. "How do you know for certain that it's been stolen? Mightn't it be in use? As you're so sure of the theft . . . answer these two questions. Who's the owner of the car? And has he reported the loss?"

Augustus nodded several times in succession. His certainty now approximated mental violence. "Yes, sir. He has. Or at least

THE CASE OF THE PURPLE CALF

he's told me about it. *That is why* I told you the car had been stolen. See? That's how I came to know. Three nights ago it must have happened. It's Mr. Dexter's car. Mr. Dexter's a gentleman who comes here a lot. Plays up in the—"

Palestri's cough effectively drowned whatever else the boy had intended to say.

"Orchestra?—were you going to say?" MacMorran's tone sounded peculiarly guileless as he turned towards Palestri, but Anthony caught the glance that came to him from the corner of the Inspector's eye.

"Yes, sir," said Augustus with imperturbable effrontery, "in the orchestra, sir."

"Dexter of all people," thought Mr. Bathurst—"again the plot thickens. Clare Kent's brother-in-law. Or in other words—Dexter now becomes sinister."

"L'Estrange's Travelling Showground" and "The Purple Calf" once again rioted in combination through his brain. Suddenly, as he was dwelling on these things, he became aware of a man wandering on the edge of their own group round the table. Anthony Bathurst recognised him at once and trusted that the recognition was not mutual. It was the big square-shouldered man who had annoyed him on the occasion when he had gone to the gaming room in the company of Margaret Fletcher. Anthony put his hand up carelessly and caressed his face. He was not desperately anxious to be recognised. He was somewhat relieved to see that the man appeared to be paying far more attention to Inspector MacMorran than to himself. Anthony watched the watcher. His eyes followed him round the circle that he covered. They caught the side of the man's face. Instantaneously Anthony found it familiar. Where had he seen it before? And recently at that? Like whom was it? The answer to his questions was speedy in its coming. The face at which he found himself looking was strikingly like the face of the dead girl, Rosina Kirk, whom he had seen lying on the settee in Stephen Fletcher's home at East Hannington. But MacMorran, unaware of the attention that he had attracted, was following up his line of inquiry.

"How did this Mr. Dexter come to tell you that his car had been stolen? Why did he choose you for his confidences? Eh, Augustus?"

"He told me to-night, sir."

"That's when he told you—not the reason why he told you."

"Well, sir, I go off duty at midnight. Mr. Dexter often leaves here much later than that. You see—he plays—I mean the orchestra plays very late."

MacMorran grinned at the boy's readiness of mind. "Exactly. I understand. Go on."

"You see, sir, the night when Mr. Dexter missed his car he must have come down to get it pretty late. Well after midnight it must have been. And I'd come off duty and gone home, you see. So that he wasn't able to call me and tell me at the time. Do you see, sir? When he came in to-night . . . I hadn't seen him in between as it happens . . . he came and told me how he'd lost his car. It had been stolen from our yard, he says. That's all I know about it, sir."

MacMorran looked significantly at Anthony Bathurst. The latter gave the Inspector the semblance of a nod. MacMorran returned to his interrogation of Augustus. "You haven't answered one of the questions that I asked you. Did this man Dexter say whether he'd reported the loss to the police?"

"No, sir."

"He hasn't reported it do you mean?"

"No, sir. I mean that he didn't tell me whether he had. The point wasn't mentioned." Augustus cast a side-glance at the knot of men seated round him.

MacMorran turned in his chair to Palestri. "Has the matter of this stolen car been reported to you?"

Palestri spread out his hands with an expression of severely injured innocence. "Why, no! How could it have been? Should I not have told you if it had?" His face changed suddenly to an air of crafty insolence. "But why not ask my patron, Mr. Dexter himself, all these questions? That seems to me the reasonable thing to do. Then surely you might receive much more satisfactory answers."

MacMorran eyed him sternly. "Don't you worry yourself about that. Rest assured that I shall. When I get the first favourable opportunity."

"But it is here, Inspector," Palestri spoke excitedly. "Both the opportunity, as you call it, *and* Mr. Dexter. Look for yourself." Palestri pointed vigorously over the Inspector's shoulder. Anthony's eyes followed the direction of Palestri's pointing finger. The manager's words were true enough. There approaching the group of them was the man whom he had heard giving evidence at the inquest on Clare Kent in the mission-hall at Great Kirby. MacMorran rose to greet him.

"Good evening, sir," he said. "You'll excuse me, but I hear that you've lost your car."

"You're late by about seventy-two hours," returned Dexter with cool nonchalance. "But why do you mention the fact? Have you got it back for me? Or do you know where it is? In the circumstances, either contingency will suit me very well."

"Just a minute. I am Inspector MacMorran of Scotland Yard. I can inform you that your car was found overturned two nights ago on a road approaching the village of East Hannington."

Dexter paled at the words. Anthony was watching him closely. "East Hannington? How the devil did it get there?"

"Also—I may as well finish my story—the dead body of a girl was found in the road beside the car. The girl's name was Rosina Kirk."

Anthony tried to catch the face of the big man who he was certain had been eavesdropping a few moments before, but the fellow was too far away for Mr. Bathurst to form any distinct impression.

Dexter's discomfiture was now complete. "A girl? Another girl? The fourth?" The three questions left his lips in quick succession and spontaneity. Nobody spoke in answer to him. He continued to stare at MacMorran. "Who was she, did you say?"

"Her name was Rosina Kirk. She was employed in a sort of travelling fair. Run by a man known as L'Estrange." MacMorran thought that Dexter flinched at the name.

"In my car," they heard him mutter to himself. "The brutes. The bloody-minded brutes." Then he came eagerly again to the Inspector. "How did she die—this last one? Tell me that. Was her spine dislocated and her shoulder-blades broken, or was she cut by splintered glass? Like the girl at East—" He paused with the abruptness of shock. "East Hannington," he said to himself softly. "East Hannington—the same place again." Then he turned fiercely to Inspector MacMorran and repeated his previous question with another added to it. "Tell me—how did she die? And what was the exact sum in copper coins that she carried with her to her death?" He seemed to have no eyes for anybody but the Inspector.

MacMorran chose the words of his reply carefully and deliberately. "Medical opinion tells us that the girl died from a ruptured heart, Mr. Dexter. That is to say, from natural causes. I fancy that you have allowed your imagination to run away with you somewhat in more than one direction. Because her money possessions amounted to the sum of five pounds sixteen shillings. In currency notes and silver. As for coppers—it's rather remarkable—considering what you said—that she didn't happen to have a single copper coin with her. What have ye got to say to that?"

MacMorran's brogue was peeping out.

Dexter's jaw dropped as though he had received the greatest surprise of his life. His eyes flickered strangely. Anthony still watched him closely. Suddenly he turned to Palestri. "Bring me a double whisky and soda, Palestri," he said sharply. "Mix me a stiff one, and book it to my account."

Palestri beckoned to a waiter and relayed the request. Anthony leant forward and touched MacMorran lightly on the arm. He spoke to the Inspector quietly. MacMorran listened attentively and nodded. The waiter brought Dexter's drink. The Inspector spoke to Norris. The latter attached himself to Palestri and persuasively led him away talking violently. Anthony left the chair in which he had been seated and went to the chair that was immediately on Dexter's right.

"Good evening, Mr. Dexter," he said placidly. "May I nourish the hope that you remember me?"

At Anthony's words Dexter checked his glass almost to his lips. A look of amazement spread across his face as enlightenment came to him. "Bathurst," he said incredulously, "again! In the name of all that's wonderful. I met you at Great Kirby . . . at the inquest on poor old Clare. What on earth are you doing here?"

But Anthony answered him with another question. "Do you remember my words at Great Kirby? When I told you that the verdict on your sister-in-law didn't satisfy me?"

Dexter nodded. "Yes. Very well. I don't think that I'm ever likely to forget them. You promised to keep me posted, too. You told me that you'd let me know directly you discovered anything. Well—tell me. Have you?"

Anthony's reply to this string of questions was uncompromising. "It seems to me that the boot is on the other foot. That's obvious. Or you wouldn't have spoken as you did a moment ago. Consider what *you* said. Four deaths! Four overturned cars! Copper coins! Shoulder-blades! Splintered glass! Your reasoning reminds me so unmistakably of my own. What have *you* discovered, Mr. Dexter? I could bear to hear every word of it." Anthony's grey eyes were eager. Dexter drank and replaced his glass on the table. He glanced questioningly in the direction of MacMorran. Anthony hastened to ease the situation. "You can speak freely, Mr. Dexter. You can regard the Inspector and me as two hearts that beat as one."

Dexter half-shook his head. "I can't take you into my confidence," he said, "for the simple reason that I have no confidences to impart. The destitute man has no power to be generous. The spirit may be intensely willing, but the pocket far too weak. That's how I'm placed as regards to what you asked me, Bathurst. I'm sorry."

"I find that a little difficult to—"

Dexter raised his hand. "Hold hard for a minute. Can it never have occurred to you that you yourself planted my feet on the road? Your attitude at Great Kirby just after the death of Clare? The various questions that you put to me? After you left me, when I had to catch my train, I did a job of hard intensive thinking. Kept at it for days . . . and nights . . . worse luck. One night I had a brain-wave. Something came to me out of the blue. I remembered the death of Lord Sturt's daughter. In somewhat similar circumstances to Clare. I tried to piece things together. I ordered all the newspapers which had accounts of Phyllis Welby's death. I read the reports greedily. Then I decided to search the files for further significances. You know the idea. Like the 'Brides in the Bath' business—that chap George Joseph Smith with the hypnotic eyes. Well, you can guess what I found. In time I came across the Vera Sinclair case at East Hannington last April. I should have been a dull-brained fool if I hadn't seized on the striking similarities. I kept thinking of you. Of your questions. Of what you had asked me in relation to Clare's private life." Dexter paused. "It didn't take me long, let me tell you, Bathurst, to become highly interested in 'The Purple Calf.'"

"Keep your voice down, man," interposed MacMorran sternly, "I don't like this place a little bit."

Promptly at MacMorran's intervention, Dexter lowered the tone of his voice. "But I don't know, when all's said and done and despite all my activities, that I have discovered anything or accomplished very much. If you say that I'm holding a watching brief, you'll have said just about all that there is to say." Anthony looked at him intently. The man's face was frank and open and his manner sincere. Anthony decided, however, to try him with two questions.

"Tell me this, please. In your investigations, Mr. Dexter, during the exercise of what you have just described as 'your watching brief,' have you in any way happened upon the name 'L'Estrange'?" Dexter knitted his brows in consideration and then shook his head. "No. I can't say that I have. You mentioned the name a few minutes ago, didn't you? But what's the point of your asking?"

Anthony proceeded calmly along the lines of his inquiry. "You have never encountered the title 'L'Estrange's Travelling Showground,' then? In any connection whatever?"

"Never, Bathurst. Never heard of the affair. What is it?"

"A travelling fair, Dexter. It travels the country. Roundabouts, chair-o-planes and a variety of sideshows. And it interests me exceedingly. To tell the truth, I am a trifle disappointed at your complete ignorance of it. Had you recognised the name I should have felt of a certainty that my own theory had been strengthened by confirmation from you."

MacMorran intervened. He spoke in low tones to Dexter. "You're certain that you've never heard that name 'L'Estrange' mentioned within the four walls of this place where we are now—'The Purple Calf'?"

"Never, Inspector. I'm absolutely certain on the point."

MacMorran accepted the statement without comment and nodded to Anthony to continue from where he had started.

"Now I want to ask you something else, Mr. Dexter. Now how shall I put it?" Anthony paused. The pause was a comparatively long pause. He seemed to be considering something that was situated a great distance away. At length Mr. Bathurst found the words which he wanted. "I don't know *quite* why I ask you this question, Mr. Dexter. But I feel in honour bound to exploit every avenue that may even present to me just the fair promise of success." He paused again. Dexter's brooding eyes never left Anthony Bathurst's face. "Do you remember," asked Anthony, "mentioning to me in that hotel at Great Kirby the name of an actor—Harding Argyle?"

Dexter started slightly. "Oh—very well. The incident is comparatively fresh in my mind. As one of the two men whom I had heard Clare mention when she had been discussing her life. Harding Argyle—and the other was . . . Buckinger. I remember the two names as well as though our conversation had occurred yesterday."

Anthony leant forward and spoke with a deliberate weighing of words. "Have you seen or . . . heard from . . . that man Harding Argyle . . . since you mentioned his name to me?"

Again Dexter's answer was negative. "Neither. What gives you the idea that such happenings were likely . . . or even possible? He was a friend of Clare's—not of mine." Anthony shrugged his shoulders.

"I don't know why I asked you. I simply felt that the question should be put. That was all." He rose and changed the subject. "You haven't the least notion who stole your car, I suppose, Mr. Dexter?"

"Not the foggiest. When I came down for it the other night . . . I was on the point of going home . . . it had gone. Enquiries of the usual kind brought me nothing that could be regarded as satisfactory. The news of it that you and the Inspector gave me was the first that I have received."

"Thank you. You are insured against its loss, of course?"

"Oh—yes. I've nothing to worry about in that direction."

Anthony turned to MacMorran. "In the circumstances, I don't think we need stay or detain Mr. Dexter any longer. Fit?"

The Inspector followed Mr. Bathurst out of "The Purple Calf" into the comparative darkness of Coverdale Street. Anthony was unusually silent. A quarter of an hour after he had returned to his flat his telephone bell rang. Mr. Bathurst stretched an arm across and answered the ring. The caller was Sir Austin Kemble. The Commissioner dealt in cynicism. "That you, Bathurst? Sir Austin speaking. Ah . . . good . . . what I want to say is that I consider you owe me a new hat. You know the size, I fancy. Don't pretend that you don't remember, either."

Anthony smiled and sought enlightenment. The Commissioner was eager to supply the factor. "The fourth girl . . . my dear boy . . . this fourth girl of the death procession . . . Rosina Kirk . . . did *not* die in the same way as Vera Sinclair. You bet me a new hat . . . you know—"

Anthony's voice in reply was stern and grave. "Neither did she die from spinal dislocation, sir. Please don't overlook that."

The Commissioner expostulated down the telephone "That maybe . . . that's all very well. . . but I want to know this. Where does Rosina Kirk fit in?"

"I don't think, sir—at the moment—that she *does* fit in."

"What . . . what on earth . . . why man, she was an employee of 'L'Estrange'—your own *bête noire* . . . surely you—"

Mr. Bathurst broke in on the Commissioner's astonishment. "That, Sir Austin, for all we know, may be the explanation."

Sir Austin returned to the subject of his hat. . . . .

Chapter XXII
MR. BATHURST ATTACKS

A FULL week passed after the events related in the previous chapter without any untoward happening. No word came to "The Cranes," East Hannington, Essex, from the daughter of the house, Margaret Fletcher. Stephen, her half-brother, urged at last into semi-action by the more impetuous Peter Brailsford, took the case of his missing relative to Scotland Yard, where he was fortunate enough to obtain an interview with Sir Austin Kemble, the Commissioner of Police himself. Sir Austin listened interestedly to his narrative and immediately put the matter into the able hands of Inspector Andrew MacMorran. Curiously enough, the Inspector had no later than that very afternoon, completed a report upon a certain aspect of criminology which had been specially requisitioned by, and prepared for, Anthony Bathurst. Having read this report of MacMorran's carefully from end to end, Mr. Bathurst saw things much more clearly in at least one respect, than he had done when he had first looked into the case. For one thing, he was able to place definitely Buckinger. "Very satisfactory," had murmured Anthony to himself, when he had reached the final paragraph of MacMorran's report. Immediately following, he took pen and paper and wrote letters to Stanley Langford, Peter Brailsford and Stephen Fletcher himself. "I *must* have help," he advised himself seriously, "if it were ever an impossibility to carry a job through single-handed this is one here. MacMorran, or any of his men, simply must *not* appear—even in the background. It would be risking too much at this stage. Also, I have two ends of a pipe to watch . . . and I can only watch one of them myself." Brailsford and Fletcher were asked to concentrate on "The Purple Calf" end. But young Langford received certain mysterious instructions with regard to "L'Estrange's Travelling Showground." He was asked certain strange questions in relation to such an article as a ladder. A telegram which Anthony sent in the hope of reaching Harding Argyle, miscarried, as the actor had suddenly left the cast of "The Moss-Gatherers," through indisposition, and was "resting." For three days subsequent to the activities that have been noted, nothing of any consequence occurred. At the end of this second interval of stillness, Peter Brailsford 'phoned Anthony from "The Purple Calf" to say that things there were almost ominously quiet. "It seems to me," he said on the 'phone, "that it may well be the calm before the storm." His father had left for one of his periodical cruises to Trinidad and as a consequence he, Peter, was going to do but little flying for a week or so. But young Langford's letter contained more than one statement of extreme importance. For the reader's benefit it is reproduced here in full.

"Bishop's Avebury,
"Near Lubbock.
"Wednesday Evening.

"DEAR MR. BATHURST,

"In accordance with the instructions that you gave me I am forwarding my first report so that you may get it tomorrow. I will try to give it to you as you asked me. Under the headings, too, that you suggested to me. *(a)* L'Estrange himself. Not with the show, but according to the rumours that are buzzing round, expected before the end of the week. *(b)* Lafferty—very quiet and keeps himself very much to himself. If I'm any judge he is showing signs of worry. Some days he scarcely shows himself at all. *(c)* Buckinger—hardly ever shows himself. Possibly lying low on purpose. Has a special tent or booth and stays in it nearly all the time. *(d)* Rame Tafari. Also very quiet—in a different way from Lafferty, for example—but a tough customer from every point of view. Shouldn't like to fall foul of him or make him my enemy. Resembles his own alligators—cold, cruel and cunning. *(e)* I have seen the woman that you mentioned. They call her Molly. Big enough to be a man. She is constantly grumbling about having too much work to do. I shall watch carefully tomorrow for what you tell me. You can rely on me *all the way through*. I remember Vera *and I won't let her out of my sight. (f)* I have seen the *ladder*. Only once though. *You are quite right.* It is used in connection with the big swing-boat. I think that it's the tallest ladder that I've ever seen. It's a creamy-white in colour and if you look at it in the dark it gives the appearance of 'shining'—something like a glow-worm does. I had to crawl along the grass the other evening when I had a chance of seeing something and was afraid to get too near to them for I was running a big risk of being discovered. From what I was able to see from where I was lying, this white ladder is hinged in perhaps three places and the whole contrivance may be folded up and laid across one of the wagons for convenience of transport. With it are a long rope and a pulley-block. If I can find out any more about this ladder, I will let you know it in my next report. *(g and last)* I have seen nothing at all suspicious in either Tafari's tent of alligators, or in the waxworks' outfit. Though, of course, it would be a comparatively easy matter to hide anything in this waxworks' show. It would be difficult, indeed, to think of a more suitable place. But I have *seen* no other contrivance that I could reasonably describe as 'unusual.' But there is just this that I think you should know. You told me to use my wits and I've honestly tried to do my very best. I say to myself all the time, 'It's for you, Vera!' and that little thought screws up both my intelligence and my courage, and makes me brave when I feel 'anything but.' The night before last I heard Tafari say to Lafferty, 'don't forget, my young friend, that I also caught a glimpse of your comforter when it was being moved.' Then he laughed and went on to say, 'The hand that rocks the cradle doesn't *always* rule the world.' I don't know whether there's the slightest point or importance about this remark, but I thought that I would tell you about it directly I had the opportunity. More later—I remain,

"Your obedient servant,

"STANLEY LANGFORD."

"P.S—I hope you are quite well."

Anthony's grey eyes held the light of excitement as he read the young fellow's letter. His mind pivoted rapidly on salient points. The white ladder. The tallest that Langford had ever seen. With hinges. A long rope and a pulley block. A "comforter." "The hand that rocks the cradle rules the world." The shafts of light were beginning to break through the mists of doubt at last. But what was this "comforter"? And *where* was it? Would Langford's hint concerning the "waxworks" hold water? He had truly said that they would make an easy and attractive hiding-place. The idea was certainly a feather in the lad's cap. He himself hadn't considered them in this special light. If so . . . as the theory took hold, Mr. Bathurst thrust his hands into his pockets and commenced to pace the room. Was he himself taking too big a risk? There was but little doubt that the crucial test was near at hand from the standpoint of *time*. He debated the problem with himself over and over again. Suddenly he tossed his head and simultaneously came to his decision. He must at all costs, catch the arch-villain red-handed. *In flagrante delicto!* That must be the end towards which he had to work. Otherwise the lean-jawed fish might well wriggle from the net that he was spreading for it. If all his cards were played according to the instructions that he had issued to his auxiliaries the time of anxious waiting should not be over-long. He looked at his pocket diary and made a rapid mental calculation. Perhaps . . . if the situation could be sufficiently forced . . . the crisis would be there by the end of the week. MacMorran himself was in instant readiness. Although the Inspector would work in the background. A word would be enough to set the entire Bathurst machinery moving with all its customary smoothness and efficiency. When the crucial time did arrive that word would be spoken without the slightest delay. His thoughts rioted again. The white ladder. The long rope. The pulley-block. The hand that rocks the cradle . . . perhaps, when another report from Langford came, it would contain fuller detail and help him still further. Mr. Bathurst took pen and paper. After a duration of carefully calculated thought he wrote the following letter:

"My Dear Auxiliary,

"I have decided to abandon my original idea of holding no communication with you at your end, but on the other hand to write to you with the intention of strengthening the chain of our case as far as its weakest links go. I have reached this decision after considerable exercise of thought. The news that I have had of L'Estrange's general outfit will, I have no doubt, prove eminently helpful to me. It has confirmed and strengthened many of my previous theories. I am excessively curious concerning his white ladder, his long rope and his pulley-block. It is the knowledge *and the intense fear* of these three things that have been the primary cause of my writing to you now. To give you advice and additional instructions which you must be most careful to obey implicitly . . . *to the uttermost letter*. Although the help I promised will be close at hand, failure to carry this out might well bring disaster and if that were to happen it would be impossible for me to forgive myself ever for having asked you to expose yourself to such a fearful danger. So caution—*please*—for both our sakes. Now listen carefully. Should you be asked—*refuse in any circumstances to climb a ladder. Any* ladder. Even though the invitation may seem innocently fair and completely guileless. It will come to you in some way, I feel confident, as soon as you show your hand in the manner that we previously arranged. *Understand—refuse it.* Make any excuse that you like—that occurs to you on the spur of the moment. You have no interest, for example, in aviation. Immediately you are able—after the ladder suggestion has been made to you and you have refused it—communicate with me by means of the channel of which you know. I shall act *instantaneously* so have no fear for the consequences. Be *brave*—if only for the sake and the memory of the girl whose death we—you and I—are endeavouring to avenge. The girl whom you loved. My plans are almost complete now in every detail and, as far as I can see at the moment, sound and sane whichever way one chooses to look at them. Any alteration that I may be forced to make will be an alteration *for the better*. Finally, don't forget the words—'the hand that rocks the cradle'—and their customary context.

Personally, any meaning to these words other than the ordinary, is obscure, but perhaps if *you* concentrate on the consideration of them, something may emerge from the clouds of vagueness, and what is now hidden and obscure to me may become clear and comprehensible to you. You might even be assisted towards a better understanding by reason of your present conditions and circumstances. You have the terrific advantage, you see, of being absolutely on the spot. Anyhow—heads up and shoulders squared and God bless you for your wonderful pluck. I remain, Your sincere friend and companion in adventure,

"Anthony L. Bathurst."

Mr. Bathurst folded the sheet of note-paper, took an envelope and then paused, pen poised in hand. He caressed his chin thoughtfully. Then he took a smaller envelope from his table which he addressed. This he placed inside the large one. "Safer, this method, I think—on the whole," he said to himself. He addressed the covering envelope. "Yes . . . this way will be the better, without a doubt." He checked the address, mentally. "Mr. Stanley Langford, c/o General Post Office, Bishop's Avebury, Near Lubbock—*Poste Restante*." Anthony looked at the clock on his mantelpiece and walked to the door. As he turned, he heard the telephone bell ring sharply and insistently. With a curious expression on his face, Anthony picked up the receiver. The voice at the other end was the voice of Stephen Fletcher . . . one of his lieutenants at "The Purple Calf" end of the affair.

Chapter XXIII
COUNTER ATTACK

"I'm speaking from 'The Purple Calf.' And I'm afraid that I've bad news, Bathurst. News so bad that I thought the best thing that I could possibly do was to let you know at once." There was no mistaking the agitation in Stephen Fletcher's speech. Anthony's reception was curt to the point of severity. He realised at that moment, more acutely than ever before, how the man had changed since the evening he had first seen him. "What's happened?"

Fletcher was equally terse. He too, recognised immediately how Bathurst felt in the matter and embraced the same direct mood almost instinctively. "Brailsford's been got at."

"Peter Brailsford, do you mean?"

"Yes, of course. His father's on the high seas. Peter, as you know, was working this end with me. The idea was yours—wasn't it? Well—they're nobbled him somehow to-night."

"Details, please, Fletcher."

"He was to have met me here to-night. I made the usual—"

"One minute, Fletcher, please. Are you actually speaking from *inside* 'The Purple Calf' at the present moment?"

"I am. I'm using the telephone kiosk that's opposite Rudolf's special bar."

"Is the coast absolutely clear or are you risking anything?"

"Don't worry about anything of that sort. My eyes are open for all that, you bet. Besides—the box is supposed to be sound-proof."

"That's all right, then. Go ahead."

"I had arranged to meet Peter this evening at the corner of Coverdale Street. Outside the big garage. The appointment was for half-past eight—sharp. It's been our usual place for meeting since we came into this watching job for you. Well—I waited a solid quarter of an hour. Then thinking perhaps that we had missed each other in some way, I decided to come on here to the 'Calf.' Peter wasn't here. He hasn't been here all this evening. I put discreet inquiries round in various quarters. Not a soul had seen him. I came to a quick decision. I 'phoned to his father's place in Lancaster Gate. Bathurst—it was as well that I did."

"Why? What did they tell you there?"

"This! Peter had set out for 'The Purple Calf' at eight o'clock precisely. In his car, mind you. Now this is important. He was driving the Lagonda 'tourer'—the new car. He's only had it about a fortnight. He told his man that he was meeting me at the corner of Coverdale Street and coming on to the 'Calf.' Well, I made no bones about anything and told them that I had been waiting for him for some time and that he hadn't shown up here.

Then I got one of the shocks of my life. It appears from what his man told me that one of the maids who had been out had come into the house again. With a *story*, mind you, Bathurst. This is it. She had seen the young master—meaning Peter, of course—standing by the kerb in Bellenden Street, just where it converges on Morstan Street—'talking to two men.' The door of the car was open. Two 'strange men' was this girl's description of them. One was a dwarf about four feet in height and the other was a dark foreign-looking man who wore a monocle. She said that the young master seemed to be arguing with these men ... almost protesting against some policy which they evidently were desirous of forcing upon him. When she passed them, she says, the three of them were still arguing and she heard Peter say—'It's like your damned sauce to stop me.' Then she saw the dark bloke hold Peter by the wrist. Well, Bathurst, the long and short of it is that Peter Brailsford hasn't turned up here. I don't desire to be an alarmist but there isn't the slightest doubt in my mind that he's been nobbled in some way. What do you think of things yourself?"

Anthony, deliberately challenged as he had been, felt disinclined to commit himself. For one thing, the data were too scanty. It was clear that Stephen Fletcher firmly believed in the truth of the suggestion that he had put forward. The facts as related by him were certainly disquieting, not to say alarming. But there *might* well be an explanation which wasn't obvious at the moment, and that explanation possibly a comparatively simple one. He decided to steer a middle course.

"I'm afraid that it's on the cards you may be right, Fletcher. But we'll hope against hope that you're not and that there may be an ordinarily simple explanation of Brailsford's failure to keep his appointment with you. After all, there's no necessity to scream before we know that the house is on fire. Perhaps, if we—"

"Oh, for God's sake, don't take it so coolly, Bathurst. There's Margaret's case, too, remember. It isn't only the one case now. How do we know that—"

Anthony checked him abruptly. "I can't see why we should connect your sister's flight with this failure on Peter Brailsford's part to keep an ordinary social appointment. Why do you do it so certainly? She wrote to you when she went away and generally speaking made a clean breast of things. Told you quite frankly that things weren't straight with her—that she was involved in a spot of bother and was taking a way out. This affair of Brailsford belongs, it seems to me, to an entirely different category. That's how I'm looking at things."

Fletcher frowned. "I suppose you think that I'm too fussy— eh? Is that the idea? Making mountains out of molehills? Should have known better than to worry you?"

Anthony hastened to reassure him. "Not a bit, my dear fellow. Don't run away with that idea. I appreciate both your kindness and the thoughtfulness that prompted it. Also I can well understand your anxiety. All I say is—in effect—why connect Peter with Margaret? You have acted exactly as you should have done—as I wanted you to. Very many thanks. If any news of Brailsford should come through, please let me know at once. In the meantime I'll get on to MacMorran at the Yard and pass your news on to him. The machinery that he can use at a minute's notice will be of value. Good-bye."

Stephen Fletcher replaced the receiver and thoughtfully stepped out of the telephone-box. As he did so, he noticed Palestri waiting anxiously for him outside. Stephen encouraged himself with the thought of what he had told Bathurst—that the box was sound-proof. Palestri approached him with an eager persuasiveness. It appeared that he came forward with a complaint that in some way concerned Mr. Fletcher. Stephen listened. His listening was more aggressive than patient. Palestri punctuated his complaint with sundry nods and gesticulations. Eventually Fletcher seemed to consent to the suggestions that Palestri was putting to him and he accompanied the manager of "The Purple Calf" along the apartment until they came to a green baize door, high up in front of which a red bulb of light glowed. Palestri stood on one side and ushered Stephen Fletcher across the threshold. An acute observer might have been forgiven for thinking that the latter was distinctly angry.

Anthony, as soon as Fletcher had rung off, 'phoned MacMorran as he had promised that he would. The Inspector received the message with his habitual caution and flung a question back at Anthony almost immediately.

"Ah well—is that so—and what's your own opinion of it, Mr. Bathurst?"

"Well, there isn't the slightest doubt that the people we're after are becoming alive to the fact of our close pursuit. All recent happenings point to that state of affairs. This last piece of business with regard to Brailsford may well be yet another indication of their new activity. They are making every effort to thwart us and will leave no stone unturned, my dear Andrew, to do the job properly. I think that we may bank safely on that. The one chance that we shall have of getting them will come when they make their inevitable mistake. In the circumstances, therefore, and knowing what we do know, I suggest that you put one of your best men on to the Brailsford job. We shouldn't neglect it—either of us. Something may turn up out of it. You never know."

"All right, then. I'll do as you suggest. Directly we pick anything up, should we have any luck, I'll communicate with you. That stolen car business, Dexter's car, remains as big a mystery as ever. Whoever stole it from the back of 'The Purple Calf' did a slick piece of work. There are no two minds about the truth of that, Mr. Bathurst. Chatterton's been at work on it this week. He's not brilliant, I know. But he's safe and sure. Norris was put on to that other job you wanted done. The two things taken together were too much for him. What did you think of Norris's stuff?"

Mr. Bathurst expressed his opinion and then asked the Inspector a question. MacMorran made haste to reassure him. "Oh—have no fear with regard to that, Mr. Bathurst. As soon as you give the word, I'll be ready to move. Exactly as we arranged."

"Good. Now listen to this." Anthony took from his pocket the letter which he had recently received from young Langford. He read certain parts of it to the Inspector. MacMorran greeted them with sundry exclamations. The mention of the white ladder, the hinges on it, the long rope and the pulley-block and the curious sentence of the rocking cradle interested him immensely. He whistled softly as Anthony came to the end of his reading. Then it was his turn to put a question. "And if you can see daylight through all that Mr. Bathurst—you're a better man than I am, Gunga Din."

Anthony laughed. "I have strong hopes, my dear MacMorran. You will find, I'm pretty certain, that the solution will turn on a little matter not unconnected with military discipline. And also, if I have collected all my facts correctly, that our killer is one of the most cunning criminals with whom you and I have ever had to deal. And we've met a few in our time. Good-bye, MacMorran."

Chapter XXIV
L'ESTRANGE DIRECTS OPERATIONS

"L'Estrange's Travelling Showground" was once again moving serpentine across country. It was, on this occasion, *en route* for Leicester by Luton, Bedford and Kettering. It passed through Kinsbourn Green, on through the town of straw-plaiting itself, up Barton Hill through Barton-le-Cley, that village famous for the Barton "pippins" of the sixteenth century, on again through Silsoe, Clophill and Haynes West End. Down the hill it came to Wilshamsted and three miles onward to Elstow—the Helenstow of the Domesday. L'Estrange, the "Duke," who had rejoined the show that bore his name sent orders down the line of the procession. A stoppage was to be made a quarter of a mile this side of the town of Bedford, so it travelled past the beautifully-wooded village green, past the cottage of John Bunyan "the inspired tinker," and past the barn, the original guest-house of the now disestablished Abbey, which has seen the successive stages of Court House, Moot Hall, Market House, school and granary. Then, within a field on the banks of a tributary of the Ouse, the cavalcade halted. Sharp words of command issued from the "Duke" and within an amazingly short time the various tents were pitched and pegged. Again the lad Lafferty was used as the "Duke's" emissary. He called on Buckinger, Rame Tafari and on the new girl who had taken the place of the ill-fated Rosina Kirk. It may be interesting to note the respective happenings that followed upon Lafferty's summoning. Buckinger trembled and hastily crushed in his hands the flimsy piece of paper upon which he had been scribbling. Rame Tafari removed his monocle, nonchalantly polished it and contented himself with an exercise in eloquent sarcasm. Then he looked straight at Lafferty and swore . . . softly. But there was a silky menace about the softness that Lafferty thought rather . . . terrible and terrifying. When Lafferty came to the tent of Rosina Kirk's successor, he almost collided with the woman known as "Big Molly" on the point of coming out. The latter cuffed him soundly for his clumsiness and with his hand to his ears, Lafferty entered the tent. His half-opened mouth dropped still further as he beheld the beauty of the girl who stood and faced him.

"Well," said Margaret Fletcher, "and what do you want in here? Tell me quickly and then clear out. Because I'm busy."

The eyes almost fell from Lafferty's head as he watched her and the ugly powdered scars across his cheek seemed to stand out with a greater distinctness.

"The 'Duke' wants you," he said in his hoarse whisper. "The 'Duke,'" he repeated as though he were fearful that the girl might fail to understand the reference, "the Boss of the outfit. In the centre tent. I've had orders to come and tell you. At once . . . if you don't mind, please, miss." Lafferty hesitated to leave without impressing upon her the importance of her instant obedience.

Margaret Fletcher whitened, for it was clear to her that a crucial time was near at hand. She had known for some time now that it was certain to come, but like all certainties of which there is ample anticipation, it shocked her, nevertheless, at the actual moment of its arrival.

"Very well," she answered Lafferty courageously, "if you show me the way, I'll come with you now."

Lafferty nodded awkwardly and then sought refuge in an attempted interchange of confidence. "Bucky's taken his tools with him, miss," he announced with an air. "Guess the 'Duke' will want to see more of his cleverness. There ain't one as clever as our Bucky in the whole of England. Or abroad either—come to that. I heard a young lady—like you something, she was—say that 'Bucky' was the eighth wonder of the world. It's his touch that counts, you know—it's so light and . . . delicate. None of the others on the job can turn the work out like Bucky does."

Margaret made no reply to this laudation of Buckinger's prowess, but followed her pilot through the line of tents across the grass. When they reached L'Estrange's tent, pitched in the heart of the gathering, Lafferty pulled aside the canvas of the opening for the girl to pass through. Margaret Fletcher saw to her surprise that his hand was trembling as it clutched at the flap of the tent. With an odd air of courtesy, Lafferty stood aside for her to enter. This done he slipped silently into the tent behind her.

L'Estrange's eyes caught the girl's immediately and held them. The man was wearing a dark red uniform with gilt buttons. But she screwed up her courage to face him unflinchingly. He motioned to her imperiously. "Sit there." He gestured towards a long wooden form that faced the table at which he sat. Margaret seated herself. She listened with interest to the talk that was passing between the men. L'Estrange for once was finding praise for Buckinger, and praise from L'Estrange on an occasion when he held court was praise indeed. Buckinger was holding a thin sheet of paper in front of the man to whom he referred as the "Duke."

"That's damned good, Bucky," L'Estrange chuckled. "Better than good. I'd give it 'excellent,' only in that case you'd get more conceited than ever, you misshapen hound. All the same, the design's good and the lines are as perfect as anybody could ever hope to get 'em. Come and look here, Tafari! Look at the work of a better man than you'll ever be, and only half a man at that." He held up the paper for Rame Tafari's inspection. Tafari stuck out an aggressive head and looked at the work of Buckinger. For a time he made no audible comment. "Well," cried L'Estrange, with a note of challenge in his voice, "have you lost your tongue, or don't you call that a swell piece of work, Mr. Critical?"

"Not bad," returned Tafari suavely—"but every man to his trade. My trade's not the same as Buckinger's. And yours isn't the same as mine. Though perhaps if we went into things more closely, Lafferty's might be . . . the same as yours, I mean." Tafari's face grew hard and lean as he looked at the "Duke."

L'Estrange put down the paper very deliberately and glared at Tafari. "Meaning by that?" he asked softly.

Tafari showed teeth and shrugged shoulders. "Thought you'd sit up and take notice. Cryptic, wasn't it?"

"Too damned cryptic for my liking, Tafari. I fear that I shall be compelled to introduce you to a little . . . discipline. I assure you that I regret the necessity exceedingly, but if this goes on much longer it will be most plainly indicated."

Margaret saw the veins swell in Tafari's forehead. It was plain to her that the man was straining to hold himself in check. He put his two hands on the table in front of the man who had threatened him and spoke slowly and with studied care.

"Look here, 'Duke,'" he declared, "let me pass on some advice—don't worry such a lot about me. I appreciate your sympathy, but I don't calculate that the time's far away when all the worrying you'll do will be with regard to yourself. Do you get me? You'll be all for preservin' that precious skin of yours and it'll take you all your time to do it—believe me, 'Duke.'"

Buckinger chattered meaningless words, while Lafferty, almost spellbound at Tafari's temerity, crept forward towards L'Estrange's table. Margaret watched the four of them, oddly fascinated. It needed little to tell her that the tiniest spark now would be enough to cause a tremendous explosion. Even the callous L'Estrange seemed impressed by his henchman's words. He leant across the table towards Tafari on propped elbows.

"What do you know?" he demanded with quiet directness. "Out with it."

"I know this. That you're not quite so clever as you imagine, 'Duke.' Here's something that'll make you think twice about things. There's been a man trailin' this outfit for days. Best part of the time since you've been back. Soon after Rosina so surprisingly sought fresh fields and pastures new." He turned and spat on the grass. "Trailin' Rame Tafari, if you please. I like these super-optimists. They please me and they appeal to me ... to my extraordinary sense of 'justice.'"

L'Estrange was silent. Tafari paused for a moment before continuing.

"But I doubt, 'Duke,' whether they would appeal *quite* so forcibly to *you*. They can't appeal to your sense of justice. You haven't any."

L'Estrange rose and faced him across the table. "Come to the point, Tafari, or it'll be the worse for you. Who is this man? Do you mean that we are being spied on—watched? By the police? Is that the point?"

"My acquaintance with the police ... of this country ... is strictly limited. I am not so cosmopolitan as you, for example. I tell you, my dear 'Duke,' simply what I know. And I know just a little more. I'll describe this man to you. That is, of course, if you would care for me to do so." Tafari's face held a mocking smile.

"Do so," returned L'Estrange curtly. "Nothing would please me better."

Tafari selected suitable adjectives. "Tall. Exceptionally tall. And fair. A young man in the early twenties—I should say—without a doubt. I put my field-glasses on to him one afternoon when he was hanging round one of the farther tents ... about two hundred yards away from me ... to see if I could get a line on him. He's a stranger to me. I can tell you that, 'Duke'."

L'Estrange resumed his seat and scratched his cheek. "It didn't occur to your great mind, of course, to bring him in and to find out what his game was?"

Tafari replied sharply. "What good would that have done? If he's hand in glove with the police, as I suspect he is ... oh, yes, I share your apprehension, 'Duke,' it would have brought a hornets' nest about our ears in no time. Do you want that? Tact and discretion have always been my long suit, 'Duke.' You know the truth of that as well as I do."

"You don't know," growled L'Estrange in dissension—"that's only good as far as it goes—which isn't very far in this case. At any time, knowledge is better than being in the dark. Especially situated as I am . . . as *we* are, Tafari." He swung round suddenly in his chair and addressed the other man. "Have you seen any sign of this fellow of Tafari's, Buckinger?"

Buckinger shook his head. He was as nervous as a kitten under L'Estrange's scrutiny. Tafari's many hints and warnings had gradually brought him to a state that bordered on terror. "No—'Duke'. I haven't as much as set eyes on the man. I was never one to go looking for trouble. Perhaps Lieutenant Tafari is mistaken in what he has told you. Let's hope that it is so." Buckinger moved his head again and tried to look wise.

For a few moments there was silence. L'Estrange stayed at the table, lost in thought. Then he beckoned to the girl who sat and watched—Margaret Fletcher.

"Come here, you," he called stridently.

Margaret checked her impulse to scream and obeyed him. As she stood in front of his table she knew that her moment had come.

"I'm told that, taking you all round, you've been satisfactory . . . so far. According to Buckinger's records, you've already been instrumental in clearing over four hundred. Now that's not too bad. That's when you swell young society dames come in useful. You aren't exactly worth your weight in gold, as they say, but you can handle things much more easily than the common herd, I'll grant you that. I'm no Socialist. I know full well what democracy's worth when it comes to the acid test. Put a beggar on horseback . . . you know the rest as well as I do. I always insist, when I'm tackled on the point, that Democracy's the worst autocracy of all. What do you say yourself—eh, young lady?" His long fingers pulled at his beard. At that moment, she noticed with an odd fascination the heavy signet ring which L'Estrange wore on the little finger of his left hand. Then she realised that she had been asked a question by the man and she pulled herself together in order that she might answer it intelligently.

"I don't suppose, 'Duke,' that you called me in here for the purpose of discussing politics with me. I can't think that you would ever intentionally waste time like that. What is it that you require of me?"

The man eyed her curiously. "So *you* call me 'Duke'—eh? Why?"

She smiled and shrugged her shoulders at him. "The others here all call you that. Why should I, therefore, set out to be different?"

The answer seemed to please him, for a shrewdly calculating smile showed in his eyes. "Hear that, Lafferty?" he cried with a note of approval. "And you, Tafari? There's a motto for each of you in that. What's sauce for the gander is sauce for the goose. I commend it to *you*, Tafari, with an especial pleasure. Because you take a delight in being different. Being, I suppose, a naturally contrary swine always suckled from the wrong breast."

Tafari replied softly. "Have a care, L'Estrange. Even *you* might one day go too far. You were praising the value of knowledge just now. May I point out that it can be 'two-edged'? That it sometimes cuts two ways?"

"You're telling me." L'Estrange delivered himself of the last sentence in a contemptuous tone and then suddenly rose from his seat and pointed a finger at Margaret Fletcher. The girl quailed at the fierceness which she saw blazing in his face.

"You," he cried, "I want the truth from you. Here and now. I can see my way more clearly. If you lie to me things'll go hard with you. Who's this man that Tafari's seen trailing round? A friend of yours?"

Margaret's tongue was dry with fear. But she stood up pluckily to the implied accusation. "How should I know? A friend of mine . . . indeed! How absurd! I've not seen anybody. If I had I should have probably taken him to be one of the hands attached to your 'Showground.' I certainly haven't had time to meet and know them all—I can assure you."

L'Estrange strode forward and caught her by the shoulder with his right hand. "Don't lie to me, my girl. And I know that you're lying. Come clean and you've got a chance. Double-cross me and I'll break you—like that." He snapped finger and thumb together.

Margaret watched the action as a paralysed rabbit watches the snake that is about to strike and destroy it. She shook her head . . . foolishly, she felt. It seemed that she could find no words with which to answer him. All her stock of words and phrases seemed to have suddenly vanished. He shook her by the shoulder.

"Who is the man? Answer me—do you hear? Answer me . . . answer me."

Her breathing came convulsively now. But she still shook her head as the man attempted to break down her silence by sheer force. Lafferty made a step forward as though to interfere, but he caught the look in L'Estrange's eyes . . . and the look promptly checked him. The habits of years are desperately difficult to discard.

"Who's the man?" cried the "Duke" again.

Margaret set her lips tight. A little courage had come back to her and she was resolutely determined to yield not an inch of ground.. She argued to herself in this wise. Things had turned out differently from her intentions, but if she said nothing *now*, L'Estrange couldn't be absolutely *sure* of her treachery to the extent of definite proof. The one denial that she had already made to him was still in being because it hadn't been retracted.

"So you won't speak—eh?" said L'Estrange. He took his hand from the girl's shoulder. "That's your game, is it? Well—we'll see if we can find a way to make you. It's been successful in the past, believe me. More than once. With people just as obstinate and stubborn as you are. Tafari! Buckinger! Clear out, you two. And take your books with you. This interview, as far as you're concerned, is finished. Understand? I'll deal with the rest of it myself. Lafferty—you stay here with me . . . and with this young lady assistant of ours."

Tafari looked towards L'Estrange, shrugged his shoulders nonchalantly, and made his exit. Buckinger followed him. From his personal standpoint, the sooner he left the "Duke's" company the better and the more healthy for him. L'Estrange turned to Lafferty with a quick gesture. "I forgot. Go after Buckinger and get his key. You know which one I mean. Quick! If you can, ask him for it when he's not with Tafari—I don't trust that cunning devil. The less that he knows, the better. He's as slippery as one of his own alligators."

Lafferty nodded vacantly at the "Duke's" words and ran rapidly to execute the "Duke's" errand. Margaret pluckily faced her captor.

"What are you going to do with me?" she asked quietly. "Was this what you intended when I got your message for the first time at 'The Purple Calf?' Have things all gone according to plan? Is this all part of the same horrible trap?"

L'Estrange made no reply. Ignoring the girl entirely he waited patiently and silently like a carved statue for Lafferty's return. When the latter entered he handed his chief a key.

"Good," said L'Estrange, "and what did friend Bucky say when you asked him for it?"

"Nothing whatever. He looked a bit scared—that was all," returned Lafferty hoarsely.

L'Estrange laughed softly as he held the key in front of him. At that moment Margaret realised the amazing truth. The same amazing truth towards which Anthony Bathurst had been groping, but was now only just beginning to guess. She lost her discretion at the shock and thereby sealed her own fate.

"I know you," she cried wildly—"you're the man who—" She stopped in abrupt excitement. "And you are—"

L'Estrange put a rough hand over her mouth and dammed her further words. "Then you know too much, young lady," he declared between set teeth . . . "and little girls who know too much . . . will soon wish with all their hearts that they didn't. Lafferty, help me put her in a safe place. Just for a time . . . shall we say?" The words were ominous. Lafferty, somewhat reluctantly, went to assist the "Duke." Margaret felt the two men close on her. Resistance on her part was utterly useless and futile. They seized her by the arms. Thoughts of the past and the future raced perilously through her brain. They wouldn't have any mercy on her now . . . they would force her to do their will

... there was no doubting that ... and then ... but she wouldn't ... no, she wouldn't—she'd refuse at all costs ... whatever it was that they did to her ... whatever it was that L'Estrange had threatened. Then by a dispensation of Merciful Providence she fainted and slid from Lafferty's grasp to the grass.

L'Estrange turned and looked at her critically. "Good," he said, "I'll get her ready for to-night!"

Chapter XXV
"SPEED ECHOED THE WATCH"

It was at twenty minutes past six when Anthony received the telegram which was to set the machinery that he had prepared, working at full speed. His telephone at once put him into communication with MacMorran at the Yard. Anthony spoke at length. MacMorran took down the various facts as they were given to him. Anthony came to the conclusion of his message. "You and Norris will meet me, then, in half an hour's time say, at the Walbrook corner of the Mansion House. Look out for me. I hope to have Fletcher with me. I shall be driving the new Chrysler. Bring a revolver. Tell Norris to do the same—we're in, I fancy, for a ticklish night's work."

"There's little doubt of that," returned MacMorran as he replaced the receiver—"God grant that we don't arrive too late."

Anthony waited until the last possible second for Stephen Fletcher, but eventually gave it up as a bad job. Two minutes afterwards, the eight-cylindered "Chrysler" purred its way to the appointed rendezvous. Inspector MacMorran and Norris were waiting. They were in the car like a flash.

"Where's Fletcher?" asked MacMorran as he took his seat.

"Don't know," replied Anthony curtly. "Wish I did. Wish I knew lots of things. Damned dark already, isn't it?"

"It is," returned MacMorran. "Which way are you going?"

"On the North Road, Barnet, St. Albans, Harpenden, Luton and Elstow. It's not too far. About fifty-two from here. I intend to reach our destination by a quarter to nine. So sit tight, friend Andrew."

"Do you know exactly where they are?"

"Within a little. Past Lubbock and Bishop's Avebury. Somewhere between Elstow and Bedford. Pretty well to the latter, I should say. I know the 'Duke's' habits you see."

For a time Anthony drove in silence . . . through Barnet and past Ridge Hill.

"The right-hand fork in St. Albans," said MacMorran.

Anthony nodded. They crossed Harpenden Common and in ten minutes crossed the Bedfordshire boundary. "The county of our dreams, MacMorran," murmured Anthony. "It's been a stern chase since the Welby girl died in Loxeter, but we're nearing the end, thank God."

MacMorran grunted his agreement.

"Descending into Luton now," commented Anthony as the powerful car swept on. "Twenty miles to go—not much more. We're doing pretty well—all things considered."

The car flashed through Luton and was soon climbing Barton Hill. It hurtled down the long magnificently-graded descent. The pace increased. Norris found a handkerchief and mopped fresh beads of sweat from his freckled brow. This "Chrysler" had a swift and smooth majesty of its own and he found it most difficult to believe that the speedometer needle's indication of "55" was an indication foundationed upon truth. Norris glanced at his inspector. The sole satisfaction that he obtained from the exercise was the drooping of MacMorran's eyelid. The "Chrysler" swept on unchallenged and unchecked. They passed the *Flying Horse Inn* between Clophill and Haynes West End.

"About six miles from Elstow, now," remarked Anthony. "And when we're through Elstow, MacMorran, keep your eyes skinned. Because it might be anywhere from there onward. I don't know anything for certain beyond that. But when the time comes, I'll slacken pace a bit."

MacMorran responded to the call. "That's all right, sir. Rely on me. Norris can take one side of the road. I'll watch out on the other. Between us we'll cover the lot. Go ahead."

Anthony gradually diminished the speed of the car to forty-five. "Somehow I don't fancy that the 'Showground' will be in full swing this evening. That is, from information received. I think that they'll be 'pitching' seriously at the week-end. That's why the outfit won't be so easy to pick up. If they were 'showing' tonight, you'd see the glare in the sky some distance away. Still, there's no reason why we should worry. We'll pick out the tents all right." The car flashed through the village of Wilshamsted and then onward through Elstow itself. "We shall cross the Ouse in a few moments, MacMorran," said Mr. Bathurst. "I don't think that our destination can be very far away now. I'm going to crawl the rest of the way."

The words had scarcely left his lips when MacMorran leant forward and uttered a sharp exclamation. "There are tents about two hundred yards ahead. My eyes just caught the shape of one of them. I'm sure that I'm right. Do you see where I mean, Norris? Over there to the left."

Norris peered ahead. "Yes," he said at length.

"You're right, Inspector. There are tents in those fields over there."

Anthony immediately drove the car on to the grass at the side of the road. "Then this is as far as we're going, Inspector," he said curtly. "That is to say, by car. The rest of the way—we will walk." He went to the hedgerow and looked over. "Yes," he said again, "we'll cut across this way and approach them from the side. Quietly, MacMorran. We're not coming down like a wolf on the fold. I'd very much like to arrive unheralded, unhonoured and unsung." He turned noiselessly to the Inspector and Norris. "Revolvers all right? It's as well to be on the safe side."

The two men nodded their satisfaction and they crept forward through the darkness towards the tents of L'Estrange . . . Tafari . . . and Buckinger. When they reached the hedge border of the first field that they had traversed Anthony halted them with a swift movement of his arm.

"Stay a second here," he whispered. "Wait until I return."

They watched him crawl away under the dark shadow of the hedge . . . until he was out of sight. Norris made as though to speak, but MacMorran put his finger to his lips. Suddenly they heard the hoot of an owl. Once . . . twice . . . three times. Then all was silent again. MacMorran looked at Norris. Norris looked at the Inspector and shivered. "Too eerie for me," he whispered behind his hand. Before MacMorran could reply to him, the tall figure of Anthony Bathurst stood at their side again.

"I'm worried," he said softly. "I'm afraid that something's gone wrong. You heard my signal, didn't you?" The two men nodded. "I had arranged for a reply. But none has so far come. If there's no sign during the next five minutes, we must go forward at once and stop at nothing. My plans may have miscarried, Andrew! I'm worried." He looked at the luminous dial of his wrist-watch. "I'm going to risk five minutes. Not a second longer." His eyes watched the movement of the seconds' hand. "One minute," he whispered, MacMorran and Norris waited. The latter's heart was hammering at his ribs. The silence was uncanny. Amazing—considering that the tents of L'Estrange with their human freight were but a short distance away. "Two minutes," whispered Anthony. Another silence interval. "Three minutes." MacMorran's hand went to his revolver. Norris noticed the movement and found himself doing the same thing. "Four minutes," said Anthony softly. The consecutive seconds started on the circular span of their last lap. Anthony watched the hand intently . . . five . . . ten . . . fifteen . . . twenty . . . twenty-five . . . and MacMorran clutched him by the arm.

"Look," he whispered and pointed to a clump of swaying bushes. "Somebody's coming," went on the Inspector . . . "and towards us. What do we . . . ?" Anthony's eyes followed the direction of the Inspector's pointing finger.

"Pray God it's our man, MacMorran. I shall be able to tell you for certain in about ten seconds' time. If it isn't—"

The three men waited and watched. Then Anthony's voice came in undisguised relief. "It's all right, MacMorran. It's Langford. Thank God for that."

A minute later, Stanley Langford came into the midst of them and caught Anthony Bathurst by the hand. "Thank Heaven you've come, Mr. Bathurst. I couldn't answer your call.

I was too near to Tafari's tent. I had to be. It would have been far too dangerous to answer you because I could hear him moving about inside. But you haven't a second to lose, Mr. Bathurst. Come quickly—please. I will take you the shortest way."

"Where is she?" demanded Anthony curtly.

"In the waxworks' tent. She's been there for some hours," replied Langford. "I think they're going to kill her to-night." He spoke simply, but MacMorran knew of an instant that the lad spoke stark truth and that questions put to him would be but the waste of precious time. Anthony began to run with great noiseless strides. Langford ran with him. MacMorran and Norris followed them but a pace behind.

"What does it all mean?" asked MacMorran as he ran.

"Strappado," replied Mr. Bathurst over his shoulder, "and something more dreadful still—at which at the moment I can only guess." And so they ran until Stanley Langford checked them.

Chapter XXVI
THE CREAM-COLOURED LADDER

"If we go any farther along this way," he said gravely, "we must pass between the tents. It can't be avoided. We shall have to pass Tafari's tent, Buckinger's tent and also that of L'Estrange himself. It will be dangerous."

"What do you propose, then?" asked Anthony.

"That we make straight for the place where the waxworks are. We can cut round this way along this side. You see, they don't open to the public until to-morrow, but everything has been got ready. But the girl is in there now."

"Right," returned Anthony. "We must be where she is. Anything else is too risky. That goes without saying. Come on, MacMorran."

They started to run again. The night was very dark now—illumined by but few stars. Langford whispered explanations as he led the way.

"The waxworks' tent is the last one. The tents on this side of the show have been pitched in the form of a crescent."

Suddenly Anthony caught the lad by the arm. "Quick! Down on the grass. Look! You others, too."

Like lightning the four men hurled themselves flat on the green strip of grass that they were crossing. MacMorran and his henchman, Norris, wriggled up, so that the four of them lay abreast in a row. Anthony drew his revolver. MacMorran and Norris followed suit. It was a strange sight that met their eyes. Exactly opposite to the tent that housed the waxen effigies there had been erected the big wooden stand from which on the morning of the morrow would swing a capacious boat. A naphtha flare lit up the scene. Anthony gave his companions a quick sign and the four of them crept inch by inch along the grass until they came to the side of the canvas booth of the waxworks. In this position they could hear what was going on within the tent and see the work that was being done outside. Against the topmost beam of the wooden framework of the swinging-boat had been placed a cream-coloured ladder. Mr. Bathurst made a rapid calculation which gave him the idea that the top of the framework of the stand must be quite forty feet in height. Two figures came from the tent. He recognised them as L'Estrange and Lafferty. L'Estrange carried a rope, that had been passed through a pulley-block. When they came to the foot of the ladder, L'Estrange passed the rope to Lafferty, who climbed the rungs of the ladder with the rope over his right arm. When he reached the beam at the top of the framework, he attached the pulley-block to it. Then he descended the ladder and joined L'Estrange again.

"What the dickens does it all mean?" whispered Inspector MacMorran.

"It's the 'strappado,'" returned Anthony tensely, "originally practised in the State of Denmark. My informant is Jo'n Olaffson, an Icelander of the time of the Danish King Christian IV. Watch for developments. Thank God the devils can't act quickly. They're forced to take their time at this game."

They saw L'Estrange and Lafferty return to the tent. There was some scuffling inside and the two men appeared again. In their arms they carried the apparently fainting figure of a girl. Anthony's hand raised a revolver. But Langford was quick to restrain him.

"No, sir, no! That's not the young lady. Can't you see what it is? It's one of the wax figures from the show."

Anthony nodded. "Of course. Or more probably a specially made doll. I must be losing my nerve." He turned to MacMorran. "I fancy it's a dress rehearsal," he whispered. "Watch it carefully. You'll find it interesting."

Lafferty and L'Estrange laid the figure on the grass at the foot of the long ladder and returned once again to the booth. They went inside. Voices were raised although nearly all the words that were spoken were indistinguishable. Anthony heard a man say, "Now, my girl, I've something to say to you." Then he looked at his three companions with amazement depicted on his face. For he had not only heard a voice that was intensely familiar to him . . . but also another voice . . . the voice of Stephen Fletcher—of East Hannington, Margaret's half-brother. Then there came a muffled scream . . . and an almost uncanny silence.

Chapter XXVII
MILITARY DISCIPLINE

L'Estrange and Lafferty emerged from the tent again. Lafferty, with his head sunk on his chest, walked to the foot of the ladder and picked up the prone figure. Then he ascended the ladder rung by rung with the figure bundled over his right shoulder, as a fireman holds the burden that he has saved from the flames.

"That is how they combine business with pleasure, MacMorran," said Anthony. "They advertise their waxworks for the people of the country-side to see and at odd times rid themselves of people who have over-stayed their welcome. Watch to see what he does. You needn't worry. It's all right up to the moment. The girl's in the tent. Trussed up like a chicken, in all probability."

Lafferty climbed the ladder as far as the beam. Here he stood on a convenient rung and made the end of the rope fast to the hands of the dummy figure that he had carried with him. It was at this moment that the naphtha flared up fiercely and Mr. Bathurst observed that the dummy's hands were tied together behind its back. The figure thus fastened to the rope through the pulley-block was propped upright against the ladder. Lafferty then carefully descended to the ground.

"Now watch," said Anthony softly, "and you'll see how Phyllis Welby went to her death."

When Lafferty had reached the ground, L'Estrange walked to the foot of the ladder and snatched the entire contrivance from its position against the high beam. MacMorran saw the figure that had been at the top lowered with one terrific jerk almost to the level of the ground. But not quite! In that frightful jerk the hands bound together behind the back were twisted above the figure's head and the whole body seemed to squirm and twist in counterfeit agony.

"That jerk, MacMorran," commented Anthony, "either dislocates or completely breaks the human shoulder-blade. Now do you get the idea?"

MacMorran passed his hands across his eyes as though to shut out the dreadful sight. L'Estrange looked at Lafferty significantly and nodded. They walked to the tent-opening again. As they went through, L'Estrange spoke again. "On second thoughts, we'll put the girl in the 'comforter.' Then we can use the ladder again afterwards."

"You mean for the—"

"I do. Best make a clean sweep. Much safer, my lad—believe me."

MacMorran looked askance at Anthony. There was anxiety clearly shown in his eyes. "You heard?" he whispered.

"Yes. We shall have to make our move at once. I'm in the dark as to what this 'comforter' really is. We'll work round quietly to the front of the booth. There are four of us and three are armed.

It will be as easy as taking money from a blind man. Tell Norris what I say. When I make a start you and he come with me. Quite quietly. I don't want to rouse any of the other members of the show. It's a good rule to let sleeping dogs lie. You keep to the rear, Langford. You aren't armed as we are. All fit?"

MacMorran passed the whisper on to Norris and the general movement started, Anthony leading. A couple of dozen stealthy steps brought them to the opening. Their footsteps on the green carpet of grass were noiseless. Anthony wasted no time. He stood in the opening flanked on either side by Inspector MacMorran and Norris.

"Put up your hands, L'Estrange," he said quietly "resistance is useless. And you, too, Lafferty. You are covered by three revolvers. Miss Fletcher, sit quite still. Don't move a muscle. Please. That's right. Now: come out of that chair at once, please. Just step forward. Ah—would you?"

L'Estrange had whipped his right hand to his pocket and drawn a gun. But Anthony had been too quick for him. He fired at L'Estrange's wrist and as the bullet struck him the man dropped his revolver on to the grass with a cry of pain. Lafferty stood helplessly by a strange chair out of which Margaret Fletcher slid unsteadily to fall on her knees at her brother's side.

"Langford," said Anthony Bathurst, "kindly untie Mr. Stephen Fletcher, will you? He's probably feeling extremely uncomfortable. Thank you. Now you, Inspector—take your men, will you. You know the charge."

MacMorran slipped the handcuffs on L'Estrange and Lafferty. "I charge you with the wilful murders of Phyllis Welby . . . Vera Sinclair and Clare Kent at Loxeter . . . East Hannington—" MacMorran recited the grim formula. Neither of the arrested men spoke. The silence of each was sullen. "Take them along, Norris," concluded the Inspector, "the same way that we came. I've made arrangements with the Bedford Police. They're calling for a gentleman by the name of Buckinger in the morning . . . I won't wake him up now . . . there's a warrant for him on another charge. We'll run these two fellows along in a few moments. Here's my revolver, Langford. You go along as well. Mr. Bathurst and I have one or two matters to clear up."

Norris forgot himself for a moment and pressed a revolver in the small of L'Estrange's back. "Come along, you—" he said . . . "march."

Stephen and Margaret Fletcher, hitherto silent watchers of the dramatic scene, came forward and took Anthony Bathurst by the hands.

"My dear people," he said with a shake of the head, "I owe just as much to you. Indeed, if it hadn't been for . . ."

Then the strain proved too much for Margaret and she burst into tears.

"Let me call your attention first of all," remarked Anthony, "to a somewhat remarkable chair. Don't on any account sit in it . . . until we have wrested from it the secret of its mechanism. Which I rather fancy is connected with its 'rockers.' That's why L'Estrange referred to it as a 'comforter.' Anyhow, let's have a closer look at it." The chair certainly resembled a rocking-chair. "The rocking-chair," proceeded Anthony, "is probably indigenous to America. Dated 1774, I believe. The idea of placing rockers on cradles was well known to the American colonists. This chair here has an easy backward tilt. I'll show you." His eyes went to the back of the booth where the collection of wax figures was stacked upon a raised wooden platform. "Bring me that long piece of wood, Fletcher, will you, please?" Stephen brought it to him. "And stand well away from the chair. Now watch." Anthony leant forward and prodded the arms of the rocking-chair with the length of the wood. Naturally, the chair began to rock backwards and forwards. Beyond the rocking movement nothing happened. Anthony looked puzzled. He thrust at the chair on the front of the arms . . . again and again. The chair tilted and rocked. Mr. Bathurst frowned his perplexity. Then an idea came to him. Reaching farther forward from a position at the side he pressed with his wooden weapon on each arm of the chair simultaneously. Suddenly and without the slightest warning there shot out from the back of the chair where ordinarily the sitter's head would rest, and with an almost ferocious velocity, a row of three curved knives. The people watching Anthony's experiment, cried out in amazement.

"There's the secret," he said quietly, "of how Vera Sinclair died. You will remember that her head was nearly severed from her body. This chair and the strappado apparatus should add more distinction to the 'Black' Museum. You must see that they go along, MacMorran. Of their kind they're unique, I should say. I'll leave you to make the necessary arrangements. Well—shall we be getting along?"

After MacMorran had seen to the housing of his two prisoners in the town of Bedford, Anthony and he, together with Margaret and Stephen Fletcher, sought the hospitality of an hotel. Eventually they found one close to the swan-dwelt Ouse. Anthony followed MacMorran upstairs to his room. Mr. Bathurst lingered before leaving him. "By the way, MacMorran," he said, "there's something I should have told you. I kept it from you . . . for the time being . . . because of the Fletchers. It will, I'm afraid, come as rather a shock to them . . . and possibly as a surprise to you. Though it's on the cards that Margaret may have stumbled on the truth." MacMorran stared. Upon the brink of what revelation was he standing now? Anthony put his hand on the Inspector's shoulder. "My point is this, Inspector. When you charge your two men officially . . . don't charge them in the names of L'Estrange and Lafferty. Call them both Brailsford . . . will you?" Before MacMorran could find words to reply, Anthony Bathurst had disappeared quietly into his bedroom.

Chapter XXVIII
THE FRAGMENTS ARE GATHERED

Sir Austin Kemble, Mr. Anthony Bathurst, and Inspector MacMorran sat in the lounge at "The Cranes," East Hannington. The host and hostess, Stephen and Margaret Fletcher, administered to the comfort of their guests. Margaret, having filled various glasses, came and seated herself next to Anthony Bathurst. The Commissioner frowned in mock disapproval.

"Much as *I* appreciate *your* appreciation of the gifts which the Gods seem to send you, my dear Bathurst, I think that you might improve the shining hours in another direction. That is, of course, with Miss Fletcher's charming permission."

Anthony smiled. Margaret added her smile to his. "Oh, Sir Austin, don't give me the impression that I count as much as all that. Mr. Bathurst can do entirely as he pleases."

Sir Austin grinned facetiously. "He always does, Miss Fletcher. It's a habit of the bird."

"What is it you want, sir?" asked Anthony, "the whole story?"

"I do. We all do, I think. Join the flats for us and then we shall all know where we are."

Anthony carefully lit a cigarette. The others waited for him to speak. "First of all," he said, "I will deal with the activities of the man whom we knew as L'Estrange. Afterwards, I'll try to show you how I was lucky enough to piece together the pattern of the puzzle. From the town of Loxeter to the last scene in the tent of the waxworks in the field between Elstow and Bedford. Inquiries that have been made since the arrest, prove conclusively that the murderer in chief had no right to the title by which we ordinarily knew him. An ancestor of his of the same name had gone to the West Indies early in the seventeenth century, but the title which was legitimately his died with him. Our man simply appropriated it and used it to further his own ends. It gave him a *locus standi* and was an asset in every way—socially and commercially. He left the West Indies and came to this country with his only living relative, his son, in an absolutely impecunious condition. But he brought with him a second asset besides his pseudo-title. The asset to which, or rather to whom, I refer, was in the person of one Matthew Buckinger. No doubt a descendant of the famous dwarf of the same name." Anthony turned to Stephen Fletcher. "Have you any idea, Fletcher, of the particular nature of Buckinger's personal value?"

"No, I haven't. To tell the truth, it's one of the points that has worried me."

"Well, the truth of Buckinger, when you hear it, may surprise you. He was skilled in the use of the pen. He forged the finest Treasury note that the Bank of England authorities have ever seen. It took one of their greatest experts twenty-two minutes to detect the first trifling discrepancy between Buckinger's note and the genuine currency article. Buckinger's skill gave L'Estrange—we'll continue to call him that for convenience—the germ of a big idea . . . 'snide.' To Buckinger's beautifully turned-out notes, he added counterfeit coining on a large scale. The press—which is a remarkable affair—ask MacMorran to tell you all about it—was installed in a place which he ran ostensibly as a night-club—you all know it—'The Purple Calf.' But as is the case with all 'dud' money, when it's worked on a big scale, the main trouble is the question of disposal. MacMorran will tell you that too if you care to ask him." The Inspector nodded confirmation of Anthony's statement. "This disposal must, to be profitable and effective, be 'general.' That is to say it must be spread over as big a geographical circle and area as possible. To confine operations to one or two districts is fatal. The vicinity gets flooded with 'dud' stuff and gradually the police are able to centralise the trouble and concentrate thoroughly on its detection and ultimate extinction. Now Buckinger, in his early days, had been attached to a travelling show and what he told L'Estrange about it fired that gentleman's imagination. A travelling show suited his book from more than one point of view. For one thing, its 'locale' was constantly changing. All parts of Britain were visited regularly and if the amount of counterfeit coin passed by L'Estrange's show, in *change*, to its patrons could be calculated, the result in figures would be staggering. That was where his silver stuff went. The notes of course, were mostly circulated amongst the *habitués* of 'The Purple Calf' . . . it formed a much better *métier* from that standpoint than the 'Showground.' There you have the general position, you see. Forged notes and counterfeit coin, half-crowns, florins and shillings . . . and I suspect even sixpences . . . 'The Purple Calf' and the 'Travelling Showground.' The younger man had an aviation certificate and the 'plane which he flew enabled the 'Duke' to make his periodical appearances and reappearances at his two headquarters of financial interest."

Sir Austin interposed a remark. "They flew from Lancaster Gate to the show . . . and . . . er . . . back again . . . when they wanted to—eh?"

"Exactly, Sir Austin. And to the 'Calf.' That was the regular programme . . . the big black beard and complete change of costume served to fit up L'Estrange. 'Lafferty' wore the scarred cheek and assumed that strangely hoarse voice . . . and vacant mentality. . . besides who knew them for what they really were, amongst the entourage of L'Estrange? That brings us more or less to the adoption of Phyllis Welby and the new turn that her advent gave to the alert mind of John L'Estrange."

Stephen Fletcher covered his eyes with his hand. Anthony proceeded. "I will explain first how he got his claws into her . . . Lord Sturt's daughter. Miss Welby was excessively 'modern' . . . and her search for the latest methods of modernity took her to 'The Purple Calf' . . . to its two chief attractions . . . the dance floor and the gaming tables. I suspect that she lost heavily. We shall never know the absolute truth. All the same, I'm pretty sure of my ground. L'Estrange, knowing this . . . watched her . . . and when the time was fully ripe went to her with an offer. She became his first 'society' medium for the disposal of Buckinger's notes. She had the *entrée* almost everywhere . . . and few would suspect in this connection the well-known daughter of Lord Sturt. She used the night-club and she travelled the country extensively . . . the notes were conveyed to her by L'Estrange, by Buckinger and on one occasion, I fancy, by Rame Tafari. Then something happened . . . what it was I can only conjecture . . . but she evidently 'knew too much' and as a result of this happening and her acquired knowledge the genial 'Sir John' or L'Estrange decided to remove her. Now 'murder' to him wasn't murder if he could bring it about in such a way that there would be no suspicion of foul play and that all the circumstances would point unmistakably to accidental death. He knew something of the old punishment called 'strappado' and with his charming son decided to experiment upon the unhappy girl whom he had enticed into his employ. The first thing that he had to do was to get her down to the 'Showground.'" Anthony addressed Stephen—"Oh—Fletcher—perhaps you can confirm this? Miss Welby was intensely interested in aviation, was she not?" Stephen nodded corroboration. "Tremendously, but she had never done any actually. She intended to take it up seriously. Wanted to get her pilot's certificate. And Peter had a 'plane."

"Yes. That's how they lured her to Loxeter, I imagine. Probably to go up in his machine. When she got down there, with the knowledge that there *had* been the previous misunderstanding at which I hinted and in the strange conditions and bizarre surroundings, she passed through a period of agonising fear. . . . I saw her . . . but I suppose her natural courage and keen desire triumphed over her apprehensions . . . and she eventually placed herself in the hands of these scoundrels . . . and went as a 'lamb to the slaughter.'"

A sob shook Stephen Fletcher's frame. Anthony waited a second or so and then continued.

"I'm inclined to think that they induced her to climb the ladder with her hands tied . . . under the pretext that they must test her nerve and body-balance for heights . . . 'before she could be trusted to fly.' Then . . . when it was all over . . . she was put back in her car . . . and the 'accident' staged."

Margaret took advantage of the interval of silence that followed this last statement to replenish Anthony Bathurst's glass. Sir Austin Kemble proffered his for a similar attention.

"The rest should be fairly clear," said Anthony. "Vera Sinclair was then taken on. I think that I can tell you how that happened to come about. In all probability, that is, Peter Brailsford visited your district with you, Fletcher, and somehow made the acquaintance of this local girl. They were looking round for somebody to work fresh ground for them and Vera Sinclair filled the bill—she was extremely intelligent . . . and the splendid salary they offered her . . . compared with what she had been getting . . . tempted her. Then, I think, L'Estrange came to the decision that he wouldn't keep any of these auxiliaries *too long*. It held a definite atmosphere of danger and dead girls tell no tales. As it had panned out the Welby murder had been child's play. So would the Sinclair murder be! But far from the fool that most murderers are—he remembered Smith of the 'Brides in the Bath' ill-fame and how the *coincidence* of the deaths brought him to the gallows one glorious August morning—and our man cleverly decided *to vary the method of murder*. Again—avoiding all suspicion and again in circumstances pointing most obviously to an accidental death. And in this particular direction our merchant of murder had a second string to his bow. Not for him were the red risks of shooting, knifing or poisoning. Besides death on the ladder there was also, at L'Estrange's, death in the chair! This second mechanism of death he had brought with him from the West Indies. You have seen it . . . you know how it works, simultaneous pressure on a certain part of the arms works a spring and from the back of the chair there is released a row of murderous blades . . . you, Miss Fletcher have been seated in it. I have made a sketch of it. Points A, B and C secreted the knives. Look for yourselves."

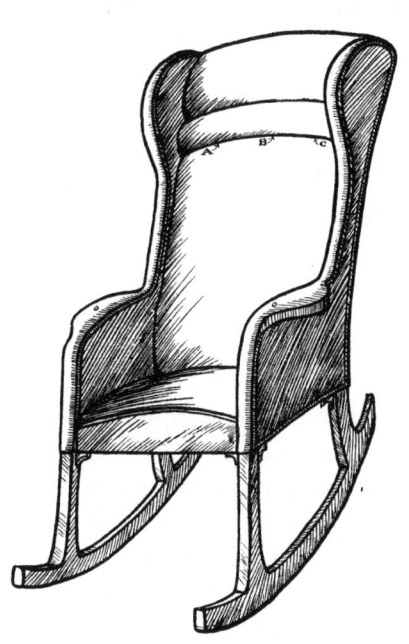

Margaret shivered. Anthony went on quickly. "It had, for our man L'Estrange, an especial recommendation. It killed in such a manner that . . . once again . . . the person whom it killed could be made to appear the unfortunate victim of yet another motoring accident. Neck and throat sliced by broken glass. And who worries about the toll of the road? A death this way is simply a matter of 'more or less' and passes in most instances almost unnoticed. L'Estrange, comparatively speaking, was on velvet. When the time came, the girl was invited to his tent . . . and once again the rest was easy. Then arrived Clare Kent, as a frequent visitor to 'The Purple Calf,' and she brought with her yet another avenue of usefulness . . . when she was in work she was an actress on the road—'playing' town after town. When she had served her turn . . . and acquired an embarrassment of knowledge, the method of murder was varied and 'strappado' was used again. How she was lured up the ladder will never be known, probably, but don't forget . . . she suspected nothing and I should say proved an easy prey for them. There you have the story of the three murders, gentlemen." He took another cigarette from the case which Stephen Fletcher held out to him. "What else do you want of me?" He smiled whimsically.

"In my case," replied MacMorran, "another stage in my professional education. That is to say, your deductive reasoning . . . step by step. For you saw things that I'm ready and willing to confess—I did *not*."

Anthony's answer came in all seriousness. "There are few bouquets attached to this case to which I can reasonably lay claim, MacMorran. The fruit almost fell from the branch into my lap. That was where L'Estrange was definitely unlucky. I was in Loxeter at the beginning of the affair . . . and saw Phyllis Welby in the 'Showground.' When the second and third murders came along, and I checked up on L'Estrange, and found him a common factor to all three deaths, the way was smoothed for me to a considerable extent. Dexter, Clare Kent's brother-in-law, put me on to 'The Purple Calf' and my visits there proved to me conclusively that there was a deep scheme at work, with the 'Calf' for its headquarters, that was of a criminal nature. The point was—what was it exactly?" Anthony paused and looked round the attentive circle. Nobody spoke. He continued.

"This was perhaps the most difficult stage of the problem. I asked myself a question. What was it, that had taken *(a)* a society girl, *(b)* a working-class girl, and *(c)* an actress, to a man like L'Estrange? The only answer which I could obtain that fitted the three indications was—that the connection in each case was obligatory—unavoidable. It had been made a virtue of necessity. He had a hold on each one of them . . . obviously the trouble, then, was financial. Each in her own way wanted money. By no means an unnatural desire, believe me. What, then, was his *quid pro quo*? How was he employing them? I cudgelled my brains considerably over this for some time. I tried more than one unprofitable avenue of investigation. Then I gradually began to see. From the data with which the three murders had furnished me. The three dead girls only carried copper coins. Why, oh why—oh why?" Anthony amplified his question. "Sir Austin and Inspector MacMorran know now—but do you happen to know, Fletcher?"

Stephen shook his head. "I haven't the slightest idea."

Anthony smiled rather eagerly and went on. "I argued to myself in this form. The importances were surely not what the girls had left to them . . . but what, probably, had been *taken away* . . . currency notes and silver were the normal and obvious answer to this. Which fact, of course, immediately suggested forged notes and counterfeit coin. Then I thought of Buckinger . . . and his uncanny skill with the pen—*vide* Clare Kent. Here was progress indeed. I requested Inspector MacMorran here to supply me with certain information with regard to this matter. He did so with his usual efficiency and thoroughness. The result was that I became aware that the authorities had known for some time that an extensive 'snide' scheme was undoubtedly being worked all over the country for the disposal of both forged notes and spurious silver. Up to the moment, the police had been completely baffled in their efforts to pin down the activity to any one particular centre. I felt . . . I *knew* . . . that a stroke of good fortune had put me on the track. But I made up my mind that I must get quite close to L'Estrange. That was imperative. I enlisted three real allies and a false one." Anthony turned gallantly to the daughter of the house. "Miss Fletcher here was the first of the realities. She had been Miss Welby's friend, you know, and her courage was superb. We staged a dissension for the benefit of the entourage of 'The Purple Calf,' she threw away a small fortune . . . which Sir Austin has promised to make good to her . . . that's quite all right, Sir Austin, you needn't apologise for anything. . . . H.Q. of 'L'Estrange' heard of her losses . . . she saw to that with my assistance . . . and then another girl entered L'Estrange's evil employ. You will forgive me, Fletcher, for the heart-rending letter that she sent you, because it was written at my request." Anthony looked whimsically at Stephen. The latter nodded. Anthony proceeded again. "My second ally was young Langford, the boy who had sweet-hearted with Vera Sinclair of East Hannington. He, too, was invaluable. He kept watch on L'Estrange for me at the fair-ground end and reported certain scraps of important information which he gathered that materially helped me to build up my final case. I knew and Miss Fletcher knew too, that the time was sure to come when her own life would be imperilled. . . . I warned her against being lured to do certain things and to communicate at once with Langford who, in turn, would communicate with me. My other *real* ally was Stephen here. The false ally was Peter Brailsford whom I deluded into the idea that he was working *with* me. You know what happened at the end."

"What gave you the idea of that 'strappado' business, Mr. Bathurst?"

The question came from MacMorran.

"The broken shoulder-blades. After a rare lot of hard thinking. I had read of the treatment somewhere historically, and although, of course, I wasn't absolutely sure of my ground, it struck me as a very likely possibility. When Langford partly confirmed my theory, by mentioning the hinged ladder, I felt that the possibility had become very much more akin to a probability. With regard to the death chair, the 'rocking comforter,'

I must confess that I was completely in the dark. I hardly knew what to expect."

"What made you first suspect the Brailsfords?" demanded Stephen with a sudden fierce eagerness.

Anthony paused and then when he spoke, gave his reply with an almost ominous quietness. "That's not too easy to answer. You referred to *first* suspicions. But let me call your attention to this most significant feature. L'Estrange and Lafferty were constantly away from the 'Showground.' That fact made me deduce 'the double life' idea. I remembered the case of the master . . . the immortal Holmes . . . handed down to history under the title of 'The Man with the Twisted Lip' . . . an English gentleman by name, Neville St. Clair . . . who made a splendid income as a tattered beggar in the City of London in the daytime. When L'Estrange and Lafferty were not at the 'Showground' they were at 'The Purple Calf' . . . that I felt was a certainty. Then another idea struck me, followed almost immediately by yet another. Sir John Brailsford often tripped off to the West Indies. Peter, his son, flew an aeroplane. Peter was an *habitué* of 'The Purple Calf.' He had no doubt, in the first place, taken a certain Mr. Stephen Fletcher there. He had walked round the 'Showground' with *me*. Possibilities, here, most certainly. Then, gentlemen and kindest of kind ladies, they delivered themselves into my hands! Utterly and completely! I had told them, in my assumed character of journalist at my first encounter with them at Great Kirby, of certain suspicions that I had formed concerning these 'deaths' in motor-cars. I even indulged in an exercise of vaticination. I told them of the tremendous significance that I attached to the copper coins. I made an especial point of it particularly to the elder man. I said that other deaths would follow . . . and more copper coins be found. Well—you know how Rosina Kirk was found. From the point of view of my pet theory—with *all the wrong coins in her possession*! But found—mark you—by the two men about whom I had begun to entertain grave doubts. Here, I said, is the fourth dimension, for which I have been waiting . . . but why the disturbance of conditions? From a close examination, however, of the dead girl's clothing, I found that here in the case of Miss Kirk was no similar murder." Anthony drank from his glass. "Her gloves had belonged to somebody else . . . they didn't fit her. Her two shoes had been put on and the laces tied by two different people. Doctor Cherry's p.m. confirmed my idea completely. Even *more* than I had anticipated. She had died a natural death at L'Estrange's and our two conspirators had 'used' the body cleverly to steal another car and stage another accident. . . which by reason of its 'differences' might serve to confuse me and ultimately divert me from my straight and original track. The coins that she carried were so full of colour and purpose! And I had told Sir John so much about those humble coins of copper. Yes . . . I harboured little doubt after that. I told the younger man how he could help me . . . he assented willingly . . . each was very confident of their joint security. Their disguises were excellent . . . the beard and the powdered scar and the altered clothes and voices. Besides, they had this immense advantage all the way through—who was there that had ever met them in their dual roles? Nobody! Who that went to the fair, paid a visit to the night-club in Coverdale Street? Nobody! The two clienteles were absolutely distinct. That's where they scored."

Stephen put another question. "Why was the son so worried about Margaret? I'll swear he sounded sincere when he came and spoke about her to me."

Anthony rubbed his cheek. "I can't answer for his emotions, false or otherwise. But don't forget this. They were all part of his game. He knew where she was . . . all the time. Consider, too, the bogus message that he had conveyed to you with regard to his own alleged 'capture.' You must draw your own conclusions from that, Fletcher. You knew him well, didn't you?"

Stephen clenched his fists at the reminiscence.

"There's still one thing that I don't understand," declared Sir Austin Kemble. "And that concerns you yourself, Fletcher. What were you doing in L'Estrange's tent . . . what induced you to take such a risk and to put yourself in his clutches? You might have upset Bathurst's plans entirely."

Margaret leant forward impulsively. "That was all my fault, Sir Austin. I suddenly grew afraid. I feared that Mr. Bathurst's plans might... after all... miscarry... and I felt that I *must* see Stephen again before... anything happened to me. I sent to him via Stephen Langford. I realise now how foolish it was of me. But, Sir Austin, please—do say that you understand." Margaret pleaded with both voice and eyes.

The Commissioner of Police began to pat her hand.

"My dear young lady..." he said....

Margaret looked up and glanced towards Anthony.

"I think," she remarked, "that I really owe an apology to Mr. Bathurst. For presuming to doubt him. I should have known for certain that he wouldn't let me down."

Anthony smiled. "You think not, Miss Fletcher?"

She nodded brightly. "Neither me... nor anybody, Mr. Bathurst. Ever! I'm sure of it."

Anthony rose. He looked humorously at Sir Austin.

"I don't know that everybody would agree with you, Miss Fletcher. For instance, Sir Austin here probably wouldn't. I fancy that he's still of the opinion that I owe him a new hat. In which opinion, let me tell you, he and I are doomed to differ."

Sir Austin began to pat Miss Fletcher's other hand. Even the word "hat" had failed to interest him.

"My dear young lady..." he commenced again.

FINIS

Manufactured by Amazon.ca
Bolton, ON